WINNING HER DUKE

Scots and Scoundrels, Book 1

Allison B. Hanson

ARE YOU SIGNED UP FOR DRAGONBLADE'S BLOG?

You'll get the latest news and information on exclusive giveaways, exclusive excerpts, coming releases, sales, free books, cover reveals and more.

Check out our complete list of authors, too!

No spam, no junk. That's a promise!

Sign Up Here

www.dragonbladepublishing.com

Dearest Reader;

Thank you for your support of a small press. At Dragonblade Publishing, we strive to bring you the highest quality Historical Romance from some of the best authors in the business. Without your support, there is no 'us', so we sincerely hope you adore these stories and find some new favorite authors along the way.

Happy Reading!

CEO, Dragonblade Publishing

CHAPTER ONE

April 1811

ANOTHER PAINFUL GROAN filled the carriage as Gia Landon squeezed her father's hand. Viscount Waverly had always been a strong man, facing an ague or a chill without complaint. It meant whatever ailed him now had to be substantially worse. Not that Gia knew specifically what was ailing him.

"Hold on, Papa. We'll be there soon," she encouraged as he moaned and pressed a hand to his stomach. "Please be all right," she whispered frantically.

Her father settled and patted her hand, "I'm sure I'll be fine, love."

"Doctor Flannery seemed to think it was quite serious. Why else would he have suggested we take you to London straightaway to see a surgeon?"

Her father offered a sound of dismissal. So like a man to think he was invulnerable to mortal illnesses.

"Country doctors don't know anything," he complained.

"Then perhaps we don't need to—" Her suggestion to return home to Elmhurst Manor was cut short by another loud moan. "Maybe we should stop somewhere—"

"Flannery said I needed to be taken to London."

"Yes," Gia said, refraining from pointing out that either the doctor was right that it was quite serious, or he was an inept country doctor who didn't know what he was talking about. Perhaps her father's mind had muddled from fever.

Except when she touched his forehead, his skin was dry and only slightly warm. Surely a good sign there was no infection. Not that she knew if there was cause to worry about infection.

In fact, she'd been sent from the room as Dr. Flannery examined her father and had not yet gotten the details of his ailment despite asking both men more than once.

The doctor hadn't been able to look her in the eye when he'd explained it was dire, and that her father was to be rushed to London from their home in Surrey immediately. She hadn't even taken the time to have her maid pack a bag.

Gia patted her father's arm.

"Try to get some rest. We'll be there soon."

He nodded and quieted as they sped along toward London.

London. The very thought nearly caused *her* to cry out in pain alongside her father.

Despite the fact Waverly Manor was only a day's ride to London, she had been there only once. During her come out at eighteen.

She found she was just as reluctant to return now as she'd been the last seven years. Each year her father had encouraged her to go to town and enjoy the Season, and every year she'd managed to resist. Instead, staying at home with her beloved horses.

Unfortunately, she had no choice now. Her father was the only family she had, and she would go anywhere and face anything to help him.

He was resting easy when they pulled up in front of an elegant townhouse.

"Is this the surgeon's home?" she shouted up to the coachman as a liveried footman came from the house to assist her from the carriage. The coachman, like the doctor, didn't meet her eyes as he simply murmured something about following orders.

"Please be careful with the viscount. You may want to retrieve a litter to carry him," Gia was saying to the footmen as her father stepped down from the carriage under his own power. "Father?" She turned a curious look on him.

He howled in pain and with his hand pressed to his stomach, he allowed the footmen to guide him into the house where the door stood open.

"Welcome to Tomison House. Please take him into the drawing room," the butler greeted them as if not noticing the wailing man who desperately needed medical attention.

"He needs to see the surgeon right away," Gia explained.

"The doctor has been called." The comment came from an elegant woman, maybe ten years older than Gia, as she descended the stairs. "How is he?"

"He appears to be in a great deal of pain, though at times, he seems to be improved. Apparently, it comes and goes."

The woman frowned. "Yes. I'm sure it does."

In the drawing room, her father made the introductions while reclined on a settee with a glass of brandy a servant had brought him. "Gia, this is Lady Tomison. Her late husband and I were good friends. Lydia, this is my daughter Gia. You might remember her from when we were in town years ago."

Gia curtsied to the woman whom she did not remember. She'd done her best to block out all memories of her time here.

"Of course. Please call me Lydia. I'm pleased you've come to stay."

Her father cleared his throat and Lydia let out a deep breath.

"That is, I wish it could be under better circumstances."

Gia didn't know the woman well enough to be certain, but Lydia looked rather annoyed with her father. Was she upset that he'd been brought to her home to be tended? Gia hardly had a chance to form the thought before an older gentleman with unruly, white hair and a leather bag was shown into the room.

Thank goodness, the doctor had arrived.

"Let's take a look." The man got right to business.

"We should have the ladies leave us," her father said.

"Papa, no. I want to—"

"Yes, yes. Off you go. I'll report back to you straightaway," the doctor said with a dismissive wave of his hand.

Gia squared her shoulders, prepared to argue when Lady Tomison intervened.

"Come. Let's leave them. I'm certain your father will be much improved very soon." Was the woman *glaring* at Gia's father?

Once they were in the hall, the woman transformed into the welcoming host one would expect when arriving for a visit rather than a dire medical emergency.

"I've put you in the garden room," she said as she ascended the stairs with a grace Gia had never accomplished. "Your father mentioned you enjoy painting, and that room has the best light."

"Thank you, but I'm sure we won't be staying long. Once my father is diagnosed, we will certainly return to Elmhurst. He will be more comfortable recovering at home in the country."

The woman said nothing, and Gia felt the need to continue her babbling.

"I don't even have a change of clothes, and I have horses to tend to." Though Owen, her stable master, and her small army of grooms would manage in her absence.

When they arrived in the Garden Room, Gia gasped. Not just because the room was beautiful with its floral wallpaper and a wide window that would bring in the light Lydia mentioned. But because on the bed sat a familiar portmanteau.

"I'll have Jessie see to putting away your things until your maid and trunks arrive."

"My maid and—"

"Please let me know if you need anything else. I'll have dinner served within the hour. I'm sure you and your father are famished from your travels."

Gia wanted to point out that her father couldn't possibly eat dinner in his condition, but Lydia was gone before Gia could argue or ask how her items came to be packed when they'd left in such a hurry.

Something wasn't adding up.

Jessie came in then and helped Gia get ready for dinner.

When Gia arrived in the dining room, her father was seated at the head of the table as a guest of his title was expected to. Lydia sat at the other end and another seat was placed beside her father, presumably for her.

"Father?" Gia rushed toward him as he stood, to help him if needed. But he was steady on his feet and wearing a different set of clothes she recognized as his own.

"I'm perfectly fine now. Not to worry. In fact, I believe I will benefit from this wonderful meal Lydia has summoned for us." Her father helped Gia take her seat before returning to his own, looking as healthy as ever.

He was an attractive man for his age. Perhaps a little thicker in the middle than when she was younger, but not to the point of being soft. His chestnut hair had grayed only at the temples. She knew the ladies back in Leigham fluttered around him like girls, and he did nothing to stay their attentions.

"I don't understand," Gia said while studying him. "You were ill and we raced to London…"

"And the good doctor gave me a tonic to restore my humors. All is well now." He patted her on the hand.

Lady Tomison made a noise but affected a perfectly innocent expression when Gia turned to look at the woman. Something was going on here, but there was only one thing that mattered now.

"We can return home."

He paused with a wine glass inches from his lips and offered a placating smile.

"We don't need to be hasty. Perhaps we should give it a few days to make sure the restorative continues working." He sent a sneaking glance to the other end of the table.

"Of course," Lady Tomison said dryly. "You are welcome to stay as long as you'd like. I am more than happy to offer my assistance to provide proper attire for your daughter. Ballgowns, perhaps, my lord?"

"Uh… well… yes. I suppose if we are to be in London for any length of time during the Season, it makes sense that we attend a few events." He waved his hand as if the events he'd spoken of were trivial.

Gia took in the exchange silently. As the seconds ticked away on the enameled clock sitting on the mantel, everything fell into place.

"Papa?" she said through clenched teeth.

"Oh, bother," her father winced, though not in pain this time since he'd apparently given up the charade.

"You lied to me. Tricked me into coming to London for the Season?"

Her father's face confirmed her suspicion, but he at least had the decency to answer her question.

"Yes, sweetheart. I did." He straightened his shoulders and offered a firm nod. "It's time you found a husband."

"A husband?" She'd thought her father had given up on this crusade years ago and had accepted she was content living at their estate, breeding and training horses. Her horses provided all the happiness she could ever want. And in the country, she was free to be herself. Without being reminded of her failure years ago when she'd attempted to follow the path of every other young lady and find a match.

"It is time. You cannot hide away in the country any longer," he said, pain and worry threaded through his voice. She wouldn't allow it to sway her anger.

"You shall pay dearly for your deceit," Gia nearly hissed her threat.

Lydia chuckled at the other end of the table.

"Oh, this will be great fun."

CHAPTER TWO

J EREMY HALE, DUKE of Roxburghe, leaned against a pillar in the Marksley ballroom and effected a look of disinterest that worked well to keep everyone at bay. If his look didn't adequately secure his privacy, he need only to greet the intruder with his thick brogue to make them scurry back to safety.

It had been an efficient and amusing strategy in the past.

By now, the only two people who might venture into his space and disrupt his peace were his best friends and unfortunately, they had yet to arrive.

As soon as they did, Hale would join them in the card room. Or perhaps they would leave the affair altogether in favor of some other entertainment.

Hale had worked hard over the years to build a notorious reputation as a rake in order to scare off innocent debutantes and their hopeful mamas. His size and general somber countenance had earned him an air of danger. While only the most desperate woman would brave enticing the Scottish barbarian, he was still a duke and therefore a candidate for a match.

The fact that not everything whispered about his reputation was true, didn't matter. The only thing that was of any significance in London was perception.

And he chose to be perceived as dangerous and unmarriageable. While the first was a stretch, the latter was highly probable.

Like many men of his age and title, Hale didn't want to marry. And like every other man with said affliction, he had good reason to feel that way.

Many of his cohorts chose to avoid the parson's trap because they preferred living the life of a scoundrel. Hale did not fall into this category. Nor did he fit in with the men who had loved and lost, loved and been betrayed, or loved and simply changed their minds.

Jeremy had never loved or been loved.

By anyone. Ever.

His mother and father had hated each other with a passion only rivaled by their individual hedonistic endeavors. Hale had met his father just twice before he'd died when Hale was just sixteen. Both times had been by accident when his father had planned house parties on the same country estate on which he currently resided.

Hale understood the confusion. After all, he was moved from estate to estate at random either because one of his parents needed the house and wanted him out of the way, or because they worried Hale would become too attached to the staff.

It was for that reason, Hale's tutors and governesses had been changed out repeatedly as well.

Somewhere in all the confusion of where Hale was living and with whom, it must have also escaped his parents' notice that their son had reached the age boys went off to school. Because of this, Hale did not start George Heriot's School in Edinburgh until he was four and ten.

But despite his late start, it had changed his life. He'd made his first friends and they remained his friends to that day. Even though they were excessively late to this bloody social event and would be one man short.

It still seemed odd, a year later, that Ethan was gone. On his deathbed, he'd called each of them into his room privately. Hale didn't know what the other men had discussed, but Ethan had forced a promise from Hale, that he find his passion.

Hale hadn't been sure what his passion was until a few

months ago when he purchased a racehorse with plans to train, race, and breed him.

He cleared his throat as the music began and the first group of dancers took the floor. He rather enjoyed dancing, but to ask any of the ladies in the room to dance would be perceived as interest and expectations would be inevitable. Followed by disappointment.

It was better to stay on the peripheral. The dangerous duke to be avoided.

The biggest fraud of all was that Hale wouldn't actually mind having a companion. To have someone to spend the rest of his life with sounded rather pleasant after a life alone. To have a constant friend who would never leave him would be the perfect cure to heal the boy in him who had never had anyone.

Unfortunately, finding a woman who was sincere, engaging, lovely, and ready to take on the role of duchess to a large Scot, whom he could also consider a friend, was a bit like finding a unicorn. A mythical thing that did not exist. *Ton* marriages were notorious for being insincere. Women, especially those seeking a match, were not to be trusted.

Young ladies of the *ton* were taught to twist themselves into reflections of the men they sought out. Learning what they genuinely thought about anything was much like speaking to oneself.

It was much safer to stay clear of such entanglements since it was utterly impossible to know who they really were. For they laughed at everything. Agreed with everything. Smiled at everything.

Except, he noticed as he stood up straight and gazed across the ballroom, for *her*.

The striking brunette opposite him did nothing to hide her disinterest in the event. He'd only just noticed her and already, she'd checked the clock twice and looked longingly toward the door four times. Anyone observing her would know her mind was set on escape.

He pressed his lips together to hide his smile. She was beautiful. Her emerald gown failed to hide her luscious curves. Her dark gaze fixed on him only briefly before moving on to the next person and the next.

He considered for a moment she must be looking for someone to break her free from the boredom of the event.

"Best of luck with that, lass," he muttered to himself, remembering he was still searching for his own friends. It was at that very moment that Lord Julian Huntly, Earl of Melville, came into view. Like Hale, he wore a tartan sash across his formal coat, fashioned with a brooch. While the Act against Highland dress was abolished in 1782, Hale and his friends chose not to scandalize the *ton* by showing their bare knees in a kilt. Rather preferring to scandalize them in other ways.

When Christopher Sinclair, Viscount Stormont, arrived a moment later from the opposite direction, the ball could now be considered perfectly disreputable. The savages had arrived.

They were also joined by Graham Dorsett, Marquess of Penbrook, who being of English blood and title should have lent an air of credibility to their group, but instead seemed to do the opposite.

After a hearty greeting, Julian proposed they head to the card room as expected.

Hale agreed with a nod then stayed his friends.

"Wait. Do either of you know that woman—" Pointing would have been rude, but Hale had planned to describe the color of her hair, gown, and proximity to the edge of the dance floor. But the woman had moved.

Hale searched for her by the door, assuming she'd managed to flee, but she wasn't there either.

"What woman?" Graham asked. "I'm sure I know her. I know them all."

Hale couldn't dispute his friend's reputation for enjoying the company of women.

"Never mind. It appears she's gone."

"Shall we?" Kit, as they liked to call Christopher, nodded toward the hall that would take them away from the manipulations of those in the room who strategized for that unholiest of unions.

A marriage of convenience.

Hale would never consider such a thing. He refused to marry someone he didn't care for. Especially for the sole sake of breeding an heir. He wouldn't be caught in the same situation as his parents, forced into an arrangement with a stranger.

He well knew who paid the highest price in that scenario.

He would be content for the time being to focus on the promise he'd made to his friend. He would focus on his passion for horses and stay clear of the trappings of the Season.

⟫⟪

"IT HARDLY MADE it worth the time it took to get ready for the ball," Lydia complained as the door to their carriage shut and they were off again for Tomison House.

"I promised I would attend the ball, and I attended. It is not my fault no one asked for an introduction or a dance in the entire hour we were there."

After her father's subterfuge to get her to London, he'd managed to trap her there as well by warning all the coachmen, if any took her back to Elmhurst without his permission, they would be let go without a reference.

After setting his rules in place, he'd conveniently had to leave town to attend to a matter at another estate. Gia was certain he was just avoiding her wrath by hiding until she'd calmed down and accepted her fate.

Never.

She would find a way to get out of the snare he'd set for her. Until then, she wouldn't feel guilty for leaving the ball before she'd danced or even met anyone.

"As if anyone could request an introduction when you practically glowered at everyone that looked in our general direction," Lydia mentioned.

"My father insisted I go to the ball. I went."

"I understand you do not wish to be here. However, I *do* enjoy the Season and would appreciate if you could see to stay for my benefit at least."

"Then perhaps you should have negotiated a longer stay." Despite her plan not to allow any guilt, Gia felt a twinge.

Lydia raised a brow, refraining from mentioning how tedious Gia had been.

Over the last week of fittings and shopping trips, Gia had to admit she liked Lydia immensely. She had a pleasingly dry wit Gia enjoyed. Especially when the countess turned it on her father. Lord Waverly wasn't always sharp enough to notice.

Gia had come to think of Lydia as an older sister of sorts. One that didn't hold too tightly to the rules of propriety.

Perhaps it was due to enjoying the freedoms of her widowhood for the past three years, or maybe it was that Lydia realized when it came to a woman of Gia's age there was little use in attempting to maintain the status of a debutante.

"Please don't punish me for the actions of your father. I didn't conspire to deceive you, I only found out about it by letter a few hours before you arrived."

"I will consider staying longer next time," Gia relented. The twinge of guilt had grown to a lump in her throat. "But you must refrain from any matchmaking plans you may have. I do not want a husband. Father cannot force one on me. I am content to stay at Elmhurst with my horses. I have friends in the village."

Not many, but there were a few women in Leigham that spoke to her when she visited.

"Why are you so sure you don't want to marry?"

"Men are deceitful. My father's scheme to bring me here did nothing but steady my resolve and prove me right."

"Not all men."

"You know of a man who would not lie to get what he wanted?"

Lydia frowned and offered no names.

"I'm sure it's not a life my father wished for me." Gia gazed out the window of the carriage at the inky blackness. "I don't mean to embarrass him. But I must be true to myself and what makes me happy."

"Your father is a dear friend, despite his lapse in judgement at times, but I do know he is not the least bit embarrassed of you. He only wishes for you to find happiness as he had with your mother."

"Happiness like you had with Lord Tomison?" Gia asked.

"My marriage was one of respect only." Lydia twined her fingers tightly in her lap.

"Not love."

"No. I fancied someone else, but he was… otherwise engaged."

Gia might have asked more about that, but it was clear from the woman's expression she would speak no more on the subject.

"Well, I don't fancy anyone, and I don't see a reason to get married simply for the sake of being called someone's wife. I shall attend events to satisfy my father, but I have no intention of marrying anyone. I'm simply biding my time until I can return home to the true loves of my life."

Three of which had just arrived that afternoon, escorted by Owen, her stable master and a man she thought of as a second father.

Unfortunately, she was forced to house her prized horses at Tattersall's since Lydia's stable was filled with her own horses, but at least Gia would have her four-legged friends nearby. And with close proximity to the park for riding.

"Did you not see anyone at the ball tonight you found intriguing?" Lydia asked, catching Gia off guard.

She hesitated too long and Lydia shifted closer, a smile growing on her lips.

"Who?"

Gia rolled her eyes, despite Lydia telling her many times already it was unladylike.

It was the word she'd used. *Intriguing.*

Had Lydia asked if Gia was interested in dancing with any of the men she'd seen at the ball, she could have instantly responded that she had not. But had she been intrigued?

There had been a man on the balcony taking in the crowd below as if he surveyed his kingdom. He should have appeared pretentious or snobbish, but he didn't hold himself as such.

He simply knew who he was. The tartan draped across his shoulder spoke to his desire to be true to himself despite what the *ton* thought.

How she'd known that from afar with her only experience with men coming from interactions with her grooms and stable boys, she wasn't sure, but yes, she'd found him intriguing.

His hair was blond, but that was too small a word for all the different hues of gold and bronze that reflected off the wavy locks in the candlelight.

"Who are you thinking of with that look upon your face?" Lydia asked.

"No one," Gia snapped quickly enough to bring a pout to Lydia's lips.

"No one, *yet,*" Lydia corrected. "The Season is still young, and we have plenty of time to find someone who intrigues you."

Gia looked out the window of the carriage into the night and wished she could go home to Elmhurst.

She hadn't wanted to tell Lydia but being at the ball this evening had been too much for her. It brought back memories of years ago when she'd attended her first ball. A young woman with hope and different plans for her future.

She'd remembered how lovely the room had been all lit up with glittering candlelight from the chandeliers. Everyone had dressed so lovely and smelled... well, overpowering. She'd choked on the cloud of heavy perfumes back then, just as she had tonight.

Her dance card had filled, and she'd made friends with the other debutantes coming out.

Everything she'd been told to expect had come to fruition.

But as quickly as she'd been spun up into the whirlwind of the Season, she'd been plunged back into the harshness of reality.

She didn't want to spend time in this town where people thought her less than them because of her mother's heritage. She didn't want to care about their opinions, but a thorn prick didn't hurt any less to a person who didn't favor roses.

Pain was pain, and this town had caused more than enough during her last visit. She would need to be careful not to let down her guard this time.

HALE FOUND HIMSELF still thinking of the dark-haired beauty the next morning as he set out on his daily ride. As was his usual route, he made his way past Tattersall's at the corner of Hyde Park. He enjoyed seeing the grooms exercising their boards and getting a peek of what would be coming up next on the auction block.

If he had not been born with a title, he would have been content to be a groom and spend his days working with horses.

He was about to turn for the park when a female caught his eye. Her dark mane flowed in the breeze, her rump full and strong. He stopped and she nodded at his mount. Godspell was known to attract the attention of the mares and this one was no different.

It was a sad state that he could identify perfection in a horse, but human women confounded him. He hated their trivial games and calculations to lure him to the altar.

Horses were easier. Honest.

"Is she for sale?" Hale asked the groom who was leading the

mare to the paddock. If she was, Hale would attend the auction and buy her immediately.

"No. At least not on the block. I reckon everything is for sale at the right price," the man said with a grin. True words.

Hale was fortunate that despite his father's lacking in many other areas, he was never a spendthrift. He'd managed or hired a manager that kept the estates flourishing and his coffers full.

"And who does this lovely lady belong to?" Hale inquired, knowing he could afford to make a tempting offer.

Checking the tag on the horse's bridle the groom read the name, "Giovanni Landon. At Tomison House on James Street."

Hale flipped the man a coin for sharing the information.

"Thank you. I shall pay him a visit." Hale didn't recognize the man by name, but for this prize piece of horseflesh, he'd be sure to make the man's acquaintance soon.

The mare would do well to help him fulfill his promise to Ethan to find his passion.

When his stallion nuzzled with the mare again as the groom pulled her away, Hale decided he would visit that very day.

CHAPTER THREE

G IA PUT THE finishing touches on a painting of Arabella and wiped her hands on a cloth as Lydia rushed into the room.

"Oh, dear. You're a mess," Lydia said, her hands going to her mouth in distress.

"Why, thank you for noticing." Gia rolled her eyes. "I'm only painting." She looked down at the old smock she wore over her dress that was wrinkled and spattered with paint, thinking it was quite obvious what she was doing. It was true she didn't look at all the thing, but again, she was only painting.

Had London become so ridiculous that ladies were expected to dress perfectly to paint?

"You've paint in your hair. That won't do at all," Lydia fretted. "You must hurry and dress."

"Whyever for?" She knew Lydia planned to drag her off to a dinner that evening, but there was plenty of time to get ready for that.

That is, if she couldn't find a way out of it.

"You have a caller. You must hurry. Bess, bring Jessie please. Help us right away," Lydia called for Gia's maid as well as her own who both looked as confused as Gia.

"A caller? How could I possibly have a caller when no one so much as spoke to me last night?"

Gia recalled the last time she'd come to London, hoping to find that special someone to spend her life with only to be faced with a room full of callers who assumed she would offer up favors in exchange for a few wilted blooms. Men were deceitful monsters, and she had no use for any of them.

Her older self became angry in defense of her younger self's naivety.

"It doesn't matter *why* he's here," Lydia went on. "Just that he's here."

"But who is here?"

"The Duke of Roxburghe."

"A duke…? A duke is here to see *me*?" Gia couldn't help but sound skeptical. "Is it possible he's heard the rumors from my come out and believes my heritage will pave the way for him to make a conquest? Because as hard as I'm trying, Lydia, if that is the case, I can't promise I won't plant him a facer."

"Young ladies don't go around hitting dukes."

"I'm no longer all that young, and dukes shouldn't do things to get themselves punched."

Lydia looked over her shoulder toward the door as if speculating their visitor's thoughts.

"We don't have time to puzzle out his intent now. The easiest way to know what he's about is to meet him and find out."

"And if his intent is dishonorable, I can punch him?" Gia confirmed.

"We'll see." Lydia was the one to roll her eyes this time, as if she hadn't told Gia how unladylike it was every day since Gia arrived. "Right now, you must get ready. Bess, put her in blue, she looks lovely in it. And Jessie, get the paint out of her hair. I'll go prepare the kitchens with instructions to bring tea."

Lydia scurried off as Bess and Jessie set to work on transforming Gia into a grand beauty in the shortest time possible. By the time Lydia returned, Gia was presentable and ready to meet the duke. Really? *A duke?*

She wasn't looking to land a husband at all, content to keep to her horses, but even she was impressed that she'd managed to earn the attentions of a duke. So long as his intentions were honorable. She didn't bother to get her hopes up on that possibility. Men feigned being honorable; few truly were.

She clenched her fingers into a fist. Donald, the stable boy, had taught her how to throw a punch and she was ready to defend her honor if called up to do so.

"Be sure to employ ladylike decorum during the visit. No eye-rolling, shrugging, or speaking of the stables," Lydia reminded her.

"Of course." She didn't want to ruin Lydia's excitement, but the closer Gia got to the drawing room where the duke waited, the more Gia was convinced it was some kind of mistake.

When they entered and Gia saw the surprise on the man's face, she was all the more certain the tall, blond Scot—the one who had intrigued her at the ball the night before—had not meant to call on her.

⁂

HALE LOUNGED ON the sturdiest-looking piece of furniture in the elegant drawing room where he was taken to wait for Giovanni Landon. He was surprised to be brought to a room like this instead of a study where men conducted business.

He turned when people entered the room, though neither of them were the person he'd come to see.

Two women bowed before him. Neither a debutante or a mama based on their ages but disconcerting all the same. He glanced at the door behind him that led out to the garden. It would make a suitable escape if necessary.

"Good day, Your Grace. It is so nice of you to visit us today," the older of the two women said. She looked rather familiar. He had probably met her in the past. Then he remembered the house he was in.

"Lady Tomison. It is nice to see you again." The woman smiled as if pleased he'd remembered her. He remembered her late husband who had been much older than his wife.

The countess looked the opposite of the other woman in every way. Tiny with pale skin, hair, and eyes, she seemed almost a ghost compared to the dark-haired, obsidian-eyed beauty he'd noticed the night before at the ball.

Though he kept his gaze on their faces, something about the younger woman made him feel like she would put him in his place if he were ill-mannered.

He had no idea why they were here in the drawing room. But if he were to be foisted into a frilly room like some awkward gentleman caller, at least it was with someone as lovely as her.

Still, he had no intention of being set upon by this woman or any other.

He turned to the younger woman who was clearly no simpering miss. In fact, she looked only slightly more interested now than she had at the ball last night.

When Lady Tomison offered to order tea, he worried she thought this was a social call.

"I believe we've met at other functions," Lady Tomison said.

"Aye. I knew your husband." Just from his club, but still it was an association and people clung to those in these situations. Heaven forbid, two people who never met simply start speaking to one another.

"Please allow me to introduce you to my dear friend, Miss Gia Landon. Should we sit?" She gestured to the room.

He waited for the ladies to settle next to each other across from the single chair he'd chosen. Miss Gia Landon tilted her head as if she were studying him. He assumed by her name she must be the daughter or sister to the man Hale had come to see about the horse.

"It is a lovely day, is it not, Your Grace?" Lady Tomison nudged Miss Gia as if prompting her to speak.

"Yes. The day is…" She quickly glanced toward the window and back to him. "Filled with daylight." She blinked slowly before going on. "As opposed to the night which has no daylight at all."

"Aye," he agreed. Clearing his throat, he sat closer to the edge of his seat, ready to put an end to this. For all of their sakes. "I'm afraid there's been some confusion."

He was certain he heard Miss Gia, murmur something that sounded like, "Oh, thank God."

"I've actually come today to speak to Giovanni Landon about a horse. Is he at home?"

Miss Gia's face lit up with a bright smile. He'd already thought her lovely, but when she smiled, she was breathtaking. For a moment he faltered, ready to take back his claim and instead visit with her, but then shook himself from such ridiculous notions. More talk of the weather and which parts of the day contained sunlight, left him with a feeling of dread in the pit of his stomach.

She moved to the edge of her seat mirroring him as her legs bounced in excitement.

"I am Giovanni—or rather Gia—it's a long story." She waved her hand dismissively. "Which horse did you wish to speak about? I have four in London."

It was as if he'd watched a butterfly emerge from its cocoon. Her face fairly lit up as she asked the question. Her body shifted from uncertain to proud.

"I saw a beautiful chestnut mare as I rode past Tattersall's earlier this morning. They said she belonged to... you?"

"Yes. That was Arabella. Isn't she beautiful?"

Beautiful? No. He'd thought so when he saw the horse in the paddock, but this lass? *She* was beautiful.

Arabella was merely a horse. Though instead of saying that he collected himself before answering.

"Quite lovely. I wanted to see if she was for sale. I would like to..." He couldn't say the word *breed* in front of proper ladies. "That is..."

"Oh! You're looking to breed her?" Gia blurted, making him smile and making Lady Tomison groan.

"Aye. She seemed to take a liking to my stallion, Godspell."

Gia's eyes went wide.

"Godspell? That would explain her interest then, but I would not recommend breeding the pair since they are brother and sister. Same sire and mare."

"Why would you think that?" His stallion had a verified record of lineage.

"Because I was present when each horse was born in my stables. I can assure you they are indeed siblings."

"I purchased my horse from a Lord Waverly through a Mr. Marley."

"Yes. Lord Waverly is my father. I employ Mr. Marley to ensure my horses do not end up with people who would mistreat them."

Mistreat a horse? There had to be a special place in Hell for such people.

She must have understood his concern for she frowned.

"Many people want horses of good breeding and training, though some do not deserve them."

He agreed, but he was still confused.

"I was told Dante is Godspell's sire." The stallion had won consistently last year and was expected to make a good showing this season as well. Hale hoped to have Godspell ready, but his stallion was having some challenges he hadn't yet worked out.

"Yes, Dante is the sire for both Godspell and Arabella."

"The racehorse that won at Ascot, Epsom and Brighton last year?" He was certain she was mistaken.

She laughed.

"Yes. Just as I trained him to do."

"Truly? *You* trained Dante?" He didn't mean to doubt her word, but she was a vision in her blue gown. He couldn't imagine her handling a large, cantankerous horse such as Godspell. Or a sleek racer like Dante.

"For obvious reasons, it is not information to be shared. My groom's name goes on all the documents for The Jockey Club. We wouldn't want them to get their breeches in a twist because a woman trained a racehorse."

Lady Tomison cleared her throat and Gia glanced over as if she'd forgotten the woman was still there.

"I imagine you are making that sound because I'm not to speak to the duke about other people's breeches?" Gia asked.

Lady Tomison simply let out a resigned breath and gave a small shake of her head.

"My apologies, Your Grace," Gia said seeming less than sorry for her wording.

"None needed. Please go on."

"I trained Dante as well as many others. I sold Godspell before his training was complete, however. I can't believe you purchased him. How is he?" she asked as one would ask after a real person. Though Hale did suppose he was guilty of treating his horses as people as well.

They were much easier to relate to. And his horses had been his only friends when he'd been a boy. They'd been the one thing his parents hadn't thought to take from him. And he'd formed a bond.

If it hadn't been for his horses, he would have been utterly alone.

Hale had become the duke only a few months before he turned seventeen and had vowed not to marry or have a child unless he was certain he could treat them in the way family should be treated.

Having no experience with such things, he didn't know what that meant, but he did know he'd never abandon his own children.

For now, what he knew was horses, so it was an easy thing to collect a number of them.

"Godspell is well," he answered. "I think he may be ready to race this season." He didn't get into the problem he'd been having with him.

"Excellent. Have you broken him of his desire to move to the outside? I was working with him on that when he was sold."

Hale found himself filled with excitement to discuss his horse. And not just what he knew of the stallion, but to learn what she knew as well. It seemed she cared for them as much as he.

"I'll check on the tea," Lady Tomison murmured before leaving the room. He hadn't even noticed if she'd left the door open as propriety demanded, he was too enthralled in conversation with the woman before him.

"He does still move out of the fray. He's getting better. I hope to have it corrected in time for the Epsom Derby. How were you breaking him of it if I may ask?"

"If I have a shy horse, I tend to put a heavier blinder on that side, so he doesn't notice the horses at his flank."

"Do they not sense the horses there anyway?"

"Yes." She nodded. "That's why I secure a thin blanket to that side, so they don't."

"Brilliant." He laughed. It seemed so simple.

"You might also try walking him in a tight group and working up to full run. I often think they feel less control at a gallop and are therefore more reserved."

"That does make sense." He was pleased to hear her speak of how the horses felt. He, too, took their feelings into account. Many people thought them to be just animals. But they had personalities and emotions. They surely expressed those emotions when he'd done something to displease them.

He'd been shot off a horse more than once.

"He is a wonderful horse with a kind heart. He won't want to step on another horse if it can be helped," she went on. "I'm sorry Arabella isn't suitable for breeding him."

"I bred him to my mare, Hera, soon after I purchased him last year. She will deliver in the next few weeks."

"How exciting," she said but he couldn't help but note the sadness in her dark eyes.

"If I may ask, why did you sell him? As I said, I purchased him from a broker and dinna know the reason he was being sold."

She let out a breath and shrugged. "I cannot keep them all."

"All? How many do you have?"

She tilted her head toward the ceiling in thought. "I have brought four to town and have…" She shifted on the chair as if uncomfortable and then mumbled something he couldn't make out.

"Pardon?"

"Thirty at home in Surrey."

"Thirty racehorses?"

"Not all are capable of racing. Some are great hunters. Some are excellent for new riders. I don't always know what they wish to be until they tell me."

Though her skin was not pale, he saw it grow darker with a blush.

"They tell you?" He couldn't help but ask.

"In their ways. Obviously not with actual words." She laughed though her eyes held worry. Had others misunderstood and thought her mad? Is that why he hadn't seen anyone ask her to dance last night? Not that he'd seen her long after the music had started.

To put her at ease he leaned closer and dropped his voice before saying, "I understand what you mean. Horses have always been my best friends."

Her smile was stunning and nearly had him leaning closer. Fortunately, he caught himself before he could do something so foolish.

"Would you like to see my other horses?"

She'd said she only brought four to town and he'd already seen Arabella. He would be pleased to see the other three.

"Of course." He stood when she did, expecting to be led out of the house to the mews. But instead, she held her hand out to stop him.

"Please excuse me a moment. I'll be right back."

A maid came in and set up their tea. He glanced around the very feminine room wondering where the countess had gone and why she had left him alone with her charge. Surely Lady

Tomison knew of his reputation as a rake.

Unless this was some kind of trap to make the girl a duchess.

Gia returned a moment later and took her seat, helping herself to a biscuit from the tea tray. He did the same, relaxing slightly when he saw she'd left the door wide open.

"It will just be a moment." She glanced toward the door expectantly. Then turned back to the tea. "Oh. I should pour."

He watched as she managed to pour them each a cup of tea, though it seemed it was the first time she'd ever done such a task. He smiled as she added nearly as much sugar as he had. It seemed they both preferred sweetness.

She glanced at the door again.

He wasn't certain what they were waiting for. Surely, she wasn't going to have the horses paraded through the drawing room. Though that would make the visit quite exciting.

He realized then he wasn't bored with the visit thus far. In fact, he was quite captivated by Miss Gia Landon.

Chapter Four

G IA COULDN'T BELIEVE her good luck. That the man who had purchased her beloved Godspell was sitting before her *and* was interested in talking with her about horses rather than the weather or whatever else proper ladies were expected to talk about.

She recognized him instantly as the man she'd found intriguing at the ball the night before. And took comfort in his low brogue, so much like Owen, her stable master.

The duke was even more intriguing up close, but she pushed that thought aside. He wasn't there to call on her. Well, not in the way Lydia had hoped at least.

Poor Lydia. Gia didn't have the heart to tell her father's friend she was destined to fail at finding Gia a husband.

Gia and the duke waited in comfortable silence for another minute until Bess rushed into the room carrying her paintings.

Gia had abandoned heavy canvases for stiff paper years ago for the sake of space, so her leather portfolio was stuffed with wavy pages. Each depicting one of her horses.

"Here we are. Let's put them on the table, shall we?" she said pointing to the table with the chessboard laid out. Gia and the duke quickly cleared the game out of the way so Bess could dispense with her load.

"Did you wish me to stay?" Bess asked, as her gray eyes darted between Gia and a man who was not a relative.

"No. We're fine. Thank you," Gia dismissed her maid.

The man had come to inquire about a horse. He wasn't there to see her specifically. He posed no threat.

Not that Gia hadn't noticed how handsome he was. His hair, the many shades of an oat field in the morning light. His eyes, she could see now that he was close, were dark blue.

She cleared her throat and set about sorting the pages as she removed them from the stack.

"Here we are. All of my horses in one place." She pointed to the bottom corner. "Along with their pertinent information." She'd included their names, dates of birth, sires, and mares along with siblings. In some cases, she added notes about their characteristics or temperament. She'd painted each horse's face as well as their body from the side to note their individual markings.

She flipped through the sheets until she found the one she was looking for and held it out.

"Godspell."

He smiled as he looked down at the page. "This is my boy. The artist captured him perfectly. See the way the star on his forehead is slightly to the right?"

"His back left sock comes up higher than the others," she pointed out.

"I don't think I've ever noticed that. What detail."

Gia shrugged. "I want to remember everything about them so I paint all the details I can."

His head snapped up. "*You* painted these?"

She nodded and shrugged. "There are many available hours in the country."

"I'm aware," he said quietly though he seemed unhappy about it. "These are lovely. You have quite a talent."

"Thank you. Though my father and Lady Tomison would much rather I focus my artistic designs on a nice landscape or vase of flowers. I find I much rather enjoy painting magnificent creatures."

His brows went up and his smile grew.

She pointed to the painting again.

"Here you see I have a note regarding the way he pulls out of a pack." She brushed her finger over the last note. "And the date he was sold."

"You miss him, even with thirty other horses vying for your attention?" he asked wistfully, as if he understood.

"Oh, yes. Each one of them touches my soul in their own way and I will never forget them."

Why had she said something so… personal? She couldn't tell him how much it pained her to have to sell Dante and Godspell to pay her father's debts and keep their estates flush. Her father had learned his lesson and given up aggressive investments after seeing how much it pained her, but she knew it was not easy to cover the expenses of thirty horses.

At least she still had Arabella. Unless the duke offered a prize sum for her and her father agreed.

While Gia called them her horses, the truth was, she was a woman and therefore didn't own anything. Despite all the work she put into them, they all belonged to her father and their fates were held in his hands.

Of course, since his trickery in getting her to London, he had kept his distance, spending time at his club to avoid her glares and his guilt. Surely, he wouldn't do anything to aggravate the current strain on their relationship.

"Thirty horses seems like a large undertaking."

"Actually, I also raise ponies and palfreys so gentle and sweet that lords will transport them as far as Lincolnshire for their wives and children. As well as work horses. Selling them covers the cost of upkeep on the racehorses, which are my passion."

"And the only horses you paint."

"Yes. There is something about watching a horse run at full speed that I find captivating."

"I know exactly what you mean."

A moment of deep understanding passed between them and she felt as if he were an old friend she hadn't seen in a long time.

She shook her head. She would be wise to remember men, even ones as attractive as the duke, were not to be trusted.

They went through her other paintings talking of each horse. In fact, she had lost all track of time until someone cleared their throat by the door.

"Lydia," Gia said in surprise.

"We should prepare for dinner."

"Already?" Gia turned toward the window to see the sun had left them at some point. "Oh."

The duke seemed startled as well. Clearly, he hadn't noticed they'd spent the entire day talking in the drawing room alone. Not only was their being alone improper, but the length of his visit was much too long. If anyone noticed, they would think he was courting her. Or worse.

"I'm afraid I must take my leave. I'm sorry for taking up so much of your time."

"Please don't apologize. I had a lovely time. Much preferred to talking of the weather or books. Not that I'm not interested in books. Except..." She tapped her chin. "While I'm in London, I'd love to get a copy of The General Stud Book."

His brows went up in surprise. Gia wasn't sure if it was because he knew of the book or was surprised to hear a woman utter the word "stud." He should have gotten used to her unladylike ways after spending the larger part of the afternoon with her.

As Lydia left again, Gia let out a deep breath.

"Poor Lydia."

"What is the matter?" he asked.

"She had been so excited for me to have a caller. I'm afraid I have disappointed her yet again."

"I might point out I *was* a caller," he said with what she knew was only mock offense.

"Yes, but she hopes to find me a husband." Gia barely refrained from huffing, but the eye-roll was inevitable.

"And you do not want a husband?" he asked. She couldn't

help but laugh at his reaction.

"I believe I've shocked you." She chuckled. "I am five and twenty, Your Grace, and of a scandalous birth as I'm sure you are aware. The only men who seek me out do not have marriage on their mind."

He winced.

"You have me at a loss. It's true, I dinna know your name before I arrived, but I've heard of no scandal attached to you."

"Perhaps I'm not as notorious as I thought." She shook her head. "My mother was an opera singer who married my father, the viscount, mere weeks after he saw her singing in London. As such, I am expected to be as hot-blooded and impulsive as my mother, you see. Filled with lustful, Italian desires."

She couldn't help but roll her eyes again. Proper or not, the idea of her being lustful was utterly ridiculous. She was as chaste as the next unmarried spinster and had no plans to change her status despite Lydia's attempts.

Other than a few bumbling kisses as a young woman, she hadn't even had the opportunity to entertain such thoughts.

"And are you?" he asked, his voice dropping low. "Filled with desires?"

For a moment she felt... something. An unknown warmth worked its way from her stomach past her spine and out to the tips of her fingers and toes. She'd never experienced such a thing and was glad when it was chased away by a shiver.

She worried this would be the moment he would transform from a friend to a deplorable rake. Would he suggest himself capable of seeing to her needs? Or perhaps he would say nothing and just thrust himself at her. When neither thing happened, she tilted her head and offered a dramatic sigh.

"I'm a spinster who spends her days with horses and paints. What do you think?"

"Hmm." His grin could only be described as wicked. "We shall see."

HALE CAUGHT HIMSELF smiling on three separate occasions as he made his way back to his home from Gia's house. Make that Lady Tomison's house, though he'd hardly seen the countess after the misunderstanding was revealed. It still baffled him how she willingly left her charge alone with a known rake.

Still, it had turned out for the best.

He couldn't remember a more enjoyable time spent with a woman. At least a fully clothed woman.

Perhaps it was because he'd seen more of her than he had ever noticed of other women. She'd opened up and abandoned her attempts to remain proper in exchange for laughter, shrugs, and eye-rolls.

He wondered at what she'd said about her mother. *Desires…*

And even more interesting was her use of the word *"passion,"* and how it so perfectly matched with his feelings.

He'd seen the hint of interest in her gaze, but her initial nervousness when she'd come into the room spoke loudly of her innocence.

Once he was sitting in his study with a brandy in hand, he realized he'd never gotten around to the business of asking her if her horse was for sale. Not that he would consider purchasing her now.

He'd seen the joy in Gia's eyes when she'd spoken of her Arabella and saw how much she regretted having to sell Dante and Godspell.

Despite what he wanted, he wouldn't allow her to be parted from her horse.

He'd only been home an hour when a message arrived from Gia.

Your Grace,

I will be riding in the park tomorrow morning at five. West of the Lancaster Gate.

If it is not too early, I would love to see Godspell.

Giovanni

Hale felt the oddest twinge of jealousy that she wished to see his horse, yet didn't mention any overwhelming desire to see him again. He laughed in the quiet of his study.

He couldn't remember the last time he'd seen five in the morning as the beginning of his day rather than the end. But rather than go out that evening with his friends, he stayed in and went to bed at a decent hour so he'd be ready to go riding with her.

He pretended his eagerness was to see her pleasure in being reunited with the horse she cared for. But he knew it went deeper than that. He simply wanted to be close to her again.

It was ridiculous, but it didn't keep him from having Godspell saddled in the early light of day to ride off to meet Gia in the most remote area of Hyde Park. He'd only been there one other time to witness a duel.

If it had been anyone else, he would have thought this an elaborate deception to trap him into marriage. But Gia had made her plans clear on any husband-hunting ventures.

He found her easily.

She'd brought Arabella who was cinched into a side saddle.

Gia was fitted beautifully in a dark blue riding habit with a jaunty cap on her head. But it was her wide smile that quickened his heart. The fact that the smile was for his mount rather than him only dulled his excitement slightly.

"You came," she said excitedly as he dismounted.

"I couldn't delay your reunion," he said as Godspell stood restless in what Hale could only describe as excitement.

Gia stepped forward. "Hello, sweet lad." Her soft words—though not for him—sent a thrill of warmth through his body. Had anyone ever spoken to him with such concern? He didn't think so.

Hale watched in surprise as Godspell dropped his head, placing his forehead reverently against Gia's chest. Hale hadn't thought her small until seeing his gargantuan stallion so close to her tiny frame. But now he noticed she must be a foot shorter than his six feet four inches. He refrained from gripping the horse's bridle, somehow knowing Godspell would never do anything to injure her.

Gia ran her hands over the horse's neck and again Hale flared with envy.

"So beautiful," she whispered and for a moment he wasn't sure if he'd heard her words or his thoughts.

"If it isn't too much to ask, would you mind if I took him for a ride?"

"Of course," Hale said before realizing what he'd even agreed to. Caught in the magic of her, he would have said yes to anything she'd asked for. But now that he'd agreed, he saw the ramifications of his promise.

Godspell was much too large for her. Not to mention he was strapped into a regular saddle.

He glanced over to the saddle on Arabella and considered how they might make it fit the larger horse. He didn't want to disappoint her.

But before he had the chance to make any suggestions, she had hurried back over to her groom.

"Help me out of this, Owen." She turned her back to the older man as she began pulling off the cap. "What is this?" She frowned at the cap.

"It's a hat," the groom answered what Hale had assumed was a rhetorical question.

"This bit of fluff and feathers would fly off in a matter of seconds."

"I dinna say it was an effective one." The groom laughed as he folded up the fabric at her waist to reveal large hooks.

Hale watched as the man released the heavy skirt from the waistband. Gia did the same in the front until the bottom part of her riding habit fell away and Gia stood before him in a short jacket and snug buckskin breeches. Her tall boots came to her knees in the same manner as his own.

She let her hair down from the bun and the heavy braid fell down her back.

He laughed at the transformation as she pulled her riding gloves back into place and strode over to his horse.

"I hope I didn't scandalize you too badly, Your Grace. I cannot ride in that contraption." Whether she referred to the saddle or the riding habit Hale wasn't sure. He thought maybe she meant all of it.

"Not at all. In fact, this somehow seems more fitting for you."

The groom had come to hold Godspell, leaving Hale to the duty of assisting Gia into the saddle. He hid the eagerness he felt for the opportunity to put his hands on her narrow waist. Or even to offer her a leg up with his hands.

However she wished to mount his horse; it would provide him with a chance to be closer to her. Or so he'd thought.

She whistled.

Three distinct notes and Hale gasped in surprise as his majestic stallion put out his front leg and lowered himself enough for Gia to reach the stirrup with her foot and effortlessly pull herself up into the saddle.

There was brief moment when her arse floated right before his face. He had only a second to take in the sultry curves and admire the way the supple leather cupped her glorious—

His thoughts were cut off by a gruff noise from the Scot who was now handing up the reins. The sound, something between a cough and a growl Hale was guilty of making, was a clear warning that the groom had seen what Hale had been focusing on.

Hale cleared his throat and moved his gaze up to Gia who looked like a goddess in the saddle. Of course, he still noticed the way her thighs gripped the animal and the way his saddle held her luscious arse like a lover, but it was something more than lust that had him smiling up at her.

She belonged there.

There was no question.

"I'm sorry. In my eagerness, I forgot to introduce you. Your grace, this is my stable master just come from Elmhurst, Owen McBride. Owen, this is the Duke of Roxburghe."

"Your Grace," the man, old enough to be her father, mumbled and gave a nod.

"Owen taught me to ride as well as everything I know about horses."

"Then I am grateful to you, good man," Hale said while patting Arabella.

Godspell stomped restlessly, clearly impatient to be on the move.

"I know, lad," Gia cooed. "You've probably not been run properly in some time. But you know you must be warmed up first. We don't want an injury."

As if the beast understood, he moved in a large circle. First a walk then an easy trot. Hale could feel the excitement coming from both horse and rider as they ramped up into a quicker pace with each lap.

Then, as if in some unspoken agreement, they came out of the circle and took off in a straight line across the open field.

"Good God," Hale said as his horse made work of the ground quicker than he'd ever seen. His moment of awe was soon overshadowed by concern. "She's going too fast. She could come unseated and—"

The groom made a similar sound as before though this one contained humor and nonchalance.

"I've been with the lass since her first ride at eleven years old. She's never once been unseated. She has a gift, that one. No horse would dare do anything to cause her harm. Even that giant beastie you have there."

"But he doesn't know the terrain."

"She knows it, and he trusts her."

In seconds, Gia and his horse were out of sight and he was left there to hope the crusty groom was right and she would come back to him.

He felt he might forever be adrift if she did not.

CHAPTER FIVE

THE WIND RUSHING past her ears, Godspell's hooves on the packed dirt, and her own laughter were the only sounds disrupting the warm morning air as Gia raced to the far end of the park.

She'd taken her horses to this discreet corner of Hyde Park every morning to run. But this… being able to run with Godspell again made it worth attending all the annoying London activities. How she wished they had more room so they could run longer.

Unfortunately, she reached the edge of the park too soon and had to turn him to race back to the man who now owned him.

She expected to feel a bit of jealousy toward the man who'd purchased her horse, but she was pleased Godspell was so well-loved by his new owner. It was the best she could have hoped for if she wasn't able to keep him herself.

The duke fairly beamed with happiness when she returned. She found he was more attractive when he smiled with abandon as he was now.

She didn't know him well, but she felt that he didn't smile like that often. Or smile in general all that much. Seeing it seemed like a rare encounter to be cherished. Like coming across a reclusive creature in its natural habitat.

She wondered if that's how he felt. A Scot in London.

When she stopped in front of him, she realized she must have been smiling as widely as he was. It was invigorating to be on the back of a horse. Though she couldn't account all of her current happiness to the horse.

She didn't need help dismounting but realized too late he'd intended to assist. What would it have felt like to have his hands on her waist? Or other places.

"He's a bit slower, but we can get him into shape before Epsom if you still plan to race him there." She only realized what she'd said and to whom when the duke's brows rose. "I'm sorry, Your Grace. Forgive me. Of course, you have his training well in hand. I didn't mean to presume—"

"No. Please. I would love it if you were available to help me ready him. Who better to get him into fighting form than the person he trusts more than anyone?"

"I'm certain he trusts you as well."

"Not like you."

"Perhaps. But he won't like me so much when I tell you to cut back on his oats. He's a little heavy. I'd like to lean him down before the race."

"As you wish," the duke agreed with a courtly bow. "Should we walk to cool him down?"

"Yes." Gia held Godspell's reins lightly. The horse didn't need to be led to walk next to her. In fact, holding the reins was unnecessary. She held them out to the duke who waved that she should keep hold of him.

They started along the same path she had just run and Owen followed with Arabella, thankfully keeping her in sight while staying at a distance.

She didn't need Owen's grumblings interrupting her conversation with the duke, and even more importantly, she didn't want to face Owen's teasing afterward.

"I have oats I can send for him," she said.

"I have oats. Aren't they all the same?"

"No. In the city they tend to soak them so they plump up and they can charge more for a sack. It can cause bloat."

Her face went hot when she realized she'd just spoken of

horse digestion with a duke. Lydia would faint if she'd heard her.

The word, "Bugger" escaped her lips making it even worse.

When she glanced over, he was watching with a grin. As if he knew she had forgotten herself.

She shook her head.

"You are wondering how you ended up in the company of the daughter of a viscount with the vocabulary of a stable hand."

"I am wondering how I was so lucky to meet you in the right circumstances to know this side of you. I think had we met in a ballroom I would have assumed you to be like any other woman and would never have known how intriguing you really are."

Intriguing. There was that word again, but this time he'd used it to describe her. Mainly her eccentricities.

"I'm not sure if that's true. Something about you seems to lure out my worst traits."

He laughed. "You're accusing me of causing your behavior?"

"It would sure make it easier to explain to Lady Tomison."

"The devil made you do it? And I'm to play the role of the devil?"

"Would you mind terribly?" she teased causing more laughter. Like his smiles, she wondered at how often the man laughed. He seemed almost surprised by the sound of it.

"One often sets aside propriety when in the company of a friend. Maybe that could be our excuse," he suggested.

"Might I consider you a friend, Your Grace?" She asked, hoping he would be pleased with only friendship. It was all she was willing to offer.

"I would like nothing more. But only if you'll call me Hale instead of *Your Grace*. It is what my friends call me."

"Very well." She glanced over and said, "Though not in front of Lydia." At the exact same time he said, "Perhaps not in front of Lady Tomison." Their easy understanding made them laugh.

For a moment she felt as if she could trust the duke. If he intended there to be more between them, he would be disappointed for this was all she would allow. And they were getting off to a fine start to their friendship indeed.

When they'd completed their stroll, she turned Godspell over to his owner and wished the duke—Hale—a pleasant day. She watched as he mounted and gave a wave as he rode away.

He cast a lovely view in his riding attire. The tight buckskins clinging to the curves of his muscular thighs and buttocks. She swallowed and turned back to her own horse where Owen was waiting with his brows raised.

"What?" she asked defensively. "I was just seeing him off, as is proper."

"You were definitely *seeing* him, but I wouldna say it was proper at all."

"He is a handsome man." That was a generic statement if she'd ever heard one. He was much more than handsome. He was smart and funny.

"I don't like him." Owen grumped as he shook out the skirt to her riding habit to help her hook it back into place.

"You don't like anyone."

"I like men who respect woman and don't ogle them as they mount a horse."

"The duke certainly wasn't ogling me." She rolled her eyes because it couldn't be helped and only Owen would see.

"I saw him do that very thing."

"I think you are mistaken. Why would a man be interested in a woman while she is wearing breeches?" As soon as the question was out, she considered seeing Hale in his tight-fitted breeches and thought she might know the answer.

"Men don't need much reason to appreciate a woman's backside, especially one that is at eye level and not covered by a loose gown. You take my meaning."

"I see." She fitted the silly scrap of a hat back on her head and got up in the uncomfortable contraption society called a saddle.

"Why are you smiling? I told you that so you'd be warned, not happy about it." Owen shook his head. "You should take care with men like him."

She frowned at the man who was like a second father, and in many ways knew her better than the man who sired her.

"Do you think there may ever be a man who shows interest in me that you might like?"

He took a second or two to consider her question before his face pulled up in a frown. "Nay. Never."

At least he was honest.

Upon returning back at Tomison House, Gia tended to Arabella herself as she liked to do, despite the chance at a lecture from Lydia on the things proper young ladies did not do.

Still excited by her ride and her time with Hale, she set up her paints in the morning room since everyone had finished their breakfast and the light was still coming in brightly through the large windows.

She painted Godspell, running in the park. The light had moved to the other side of the house, but she didn't bother to move. She was just putting on the finishing touches when the butler entered.

"A caller for you, Miss Gia."

"Is it Ha—His Grace?" she asked, her voice tinged with hope.

"Yes. I took him to the drawing room and offered refreshments, so you have time to change."

Gia looked down at the brown smock she wore for painting. Different colored speckles covered the front, but she didn't have the patience to go through the ministrations Lydia and the maids put her through the day before.

"I'll see him like this. He is a friend, not a suitor."

"Very well," Luther said with amusement. "If Lady Tomison takes issue, you'll be sure to tell her I suggested you change."

"Of course." She laughed and hurried to the drawing room carrying her latest painting to share with her friend.

HALE SETTLED IN to wait for Gia, remembering how long he'd waited the day before. He wasn't sure he should have come during visiting hours since he'd come the day before and had seen her in the park that morning, but he couldn't stay away.

He didn't have to wait very long at all. She rushed into the room wearing a hideous brown dress; her hair was pulled back in a braid as it had been that morning but like her dress there were splatters of paint here and there. Despite the state of her appearance, he'd never seen anyone more beautiful.

Perhaps it was the smile she graced him with when she entered as if he was the most important person in the world and she was as pleased to see him as he was to see her.

He held out his unconventional bouquet and watched her smile bloom into open laughter.

"A bouquet of carrots. How perfect for sharing with my friends in the stable."

"I thought they might be better received than roses."

"They are wonderful, and I don't have to worry about putting them in a vase." She took the carrots and put her nose to them like one would do to breathe in the scent of flowers. "Mmm… Lovely."

She sat across from where he'd been sitting and fluffed out her ratty gown as if she were wearing silk. "I hope you don't mind I didn't change for your visit. It would have taken so long, and I haven't the patience for all the primping now when I know I'll be faced with it again later tonight for the Redmond Ball."

"I don't mind at all. I am beginning to see that you will be a constant surprise."

She frowned slightly and he was quick to put her at ease.

"I rather like surprises," he added. He'd never been friends with a woman before, especially not one so lovely as Gia; he should be careful not to forget she was female before he found himself inadvertently compromising her and ending up dangling from the parson's noose.

But his inner warnings were forgotten when her eyes lit. He

felt like a king to have not only noticed her distress but to have acted appropriately to remedy the situation. He thought he knew his way around women, but Gia was not like usual women of the *ton*.

She was so much better.

"I made something for you. It is not a bouquet of carrots, and you will need to take care until it has fully dried, but..." she held out her offering with a shy smile.

He looked down at the wavy page and the painting of his horse running.

"It is lovely. You've captured him beautifully. The power and..." He struggled to find the word. He should have known Gia would supply it as if she shared his very thoughts.

"Delight."

"Aye. 'Tis that exactly."

"For not having many facial expressions, you can certainly tell what a horse is thinking and feeling if you pay attention and listen."

"Listen?"

"Not with your ears." She bit her bottom lip, and he knew she was nervous that she had shared something she regretted. "Forgive me. That is absurd."

"Not at all. You have a true gift to be able to hear the things they cannot say. They trust you because of that unspoken understanding. I saw the way Godspell walked next to you after your run. You could have dropped his reins and he would have continued to follow you. He wouldn't have left your side. As if compelled to stay with you."

Perhaps he understood because he also felt compelled to stay close to her.

"Take care with those kinds of words. I could be called out as a witch."

He leaned closer. "I will keep your secret."

"So, you are the devil, and I am a witch. We make a grand pair, do we not?"

"Especially when we combine our powers toward a common

goal."

"Like the Epsom Derby?" she suggested.

He could have come up with a few other ideas, but they wouldn't have been suitable for sharing in a proper drawing room with an innocent.

"Aye. Like that."

They went on with their visit as was becoming normal for them. Speaking of horses and planning for a horserace. But as they discussed training and diet, they were interrupted by someone entering the room and a loud gasp.

Lady Tomison stared at them with eyes wide.

"Gia, may I speak to you in the hall?"

"Run and save yourself," Gia whispered as she rose and followed the woman into the hall.

If Lady Tomison thought the hall provided any great privacy, she was wrong. Hale was able to hear their conversation clearly.

"What are you wearing to receive a duke?"

"He's not a duke. Or rather he is a duke, but he's not visiting in the capacity of a duke. He is only Hale."

Hale winced, knowing Lady Tomison would not appreciate Gia's use of his given name. Another loud gasp told him he'd been correct.

"And why are you carrying vegetables?"

"They were a gift from His Grace."

"Why...? What...?" The lady spluttered while Hale covered his mouth to hold in his mirth.

To spare Gia any further lecture, he rose and went to the hall.

"I thank you for your time and the painting, Miss Landon, but I must be on my way."

"Will we see you at the Redmond Ball this evening, Your Grace?" Lady Tomison asked.

He wanted to avoid the ball and any likelihood Lady Tomison would get the wrong idea regarding his visits to Gia, but he found himself answering, "I believe you shall."

At least he wouldn't risk being bored to his death with Gia in attendance.

CHAPTER SIX

"Looking for someone?" Kit interrupted Hale's third perusal of the ballroom since he'd arrived.

Not only was Hale attending his second ball in a week, but he had been eager to be here. After spending the morning and the afternoon with Gia talking about horses, he found he was excited to see her only a few hours after he'd last left her.

Not that he could share this information with Kit, Graham, or Julian. His friends would never let him live it down if they knew.

"Whoever would I be looking for at a ball?" Hale answered vaguely in a way that kept him from lying to his dearest friends.

"Don't think I dinna notice you haven't denied looking for someone. Who is she?" Julian began looking around the room as well, as if he could help without any direction as to who he was looking for.

"Whyever would you assume it was a she? Perhaps I have business to attend to with one of the gentlemen."

The only reply was a snort.

"Very well," Hale gave up. "Her name is Gia Landon. She has the most beautiful, well-formed, statuesque..." The three men leaned closer, identical smiles growing on their lips. Until Hale finished with, "...horse."

"Of course," Kit deflated while Hale chuckled at his friends' disappointment.

"Apologies. I couldn't resist." He slapped Graham on the

shoulder and froze when Gia entered the ballroom with Lady Tomison.

"Ow." Penbrook twisted out of Hale's grip. "What the devil—oh."

They all stood staring at the newest arrivals.

"I don't know about her horse, but she is lovely indeed. Perhaps you would introdu—"

"No," Hale cut Julian off as he left his friends standing there and went to approach Gia.

She curtsied when she saw him.

"Good evening, Your Grace. So wonderful to see you again," she said with a sincere smile. "I was afraid you might need to retire early after such an early start to your day."

Lady Tomison leaned in and whispered something to Gia. Hale only picked up part of it, but it was something about how speaking to a duke about his sleep schedule was inappropriate.

Gia frowned and gave a quick nod to her mentor. Something about the action irritated him. He understood what were and weren't appropriate topics for young ladies when conversing with men. But for whatever reason, he felt Gia should be immune to these silly restrictions. They didn't suit her. And, lord knew, no one expected a Scot to be held to such exacting standards.

Gia was a force. She was meant to be free and uninhibited by propriety. He didn't want society's inane rules to change her. She was quite perfect the way she was. *Who* she was.

A small frown had chased away her earlier smile and Hale felt he needed to do something to bring it back.

"Fortunately, I was able to take a nap before coming out this evening."

They both laughed at his joke, and he was glad to see her smile return. Lady Tomison offered a stiff smile as she glanced around. No doubt making sure no one was listening to their improper conversation.

"Lady Tomison." Hale bowed. "Thank you again for your hospitality today. I apologize if I overstayed my welcome. Again."

"Of course not. It was wonderful to have a visitor." She pressed her lips together as if she wanted to say something else but refrained.

Turning back to Gia, he glanced down to her wrist to see she had no dance card dangling there like the other ladies. He knew she hadn't danced the night he'd first seen her, but he wanted to talk with her further, and dancing was the easiest way to do so.

"Might you honor me with a dance, if you have one available?" he asked.

She failed to hide her surprise if she'd tried to hide it at all. Knowing Gia the little that he did, he didn't think she hid much.

"She would be delighted," Lady Tomison said. "I'll just get you a dance card, dear, since you must have missed them when we entered."

Lady Tomison scurried off to secure the needed card with a smug smile on her face.

"You dinna forget your card?" he said quietly.

She waved her hand dismissively.

"It seemed a waste of paper."

"Obviously not."

"You don't need to do this." Her smile was gone again. Her back stiff and chin up in a defiant way.

"I'm aware. In fact, I only *need* to do very few things. Eat. Sleep. Ride." They shared a knowing smile. "I enjoy conversing with you, and I'm afraid if we take up a drawing room here until dawn, Lady Tomison will surely lose her otherwise unyielding patience with me."

Gia laughed in earnest. Not a tittering, breathy exhale, but an actual laugh that brought the attention of a number of people standing nearby. Even he knew laughing was not done. Not that he agreed or understood why.

Lady Tomison returned and extended the dance card to him. Seeing the vast emptiness, he greedily inscibed his name in for two dances. The first dance of the evening and the supper dance.

He was about to take his leave of them when three large

shadows fell on Gia's surprised face.

"Bloody hell," he muttered to the men grinning at his flanks. Kit, Graham, and Julian wouldn't miss an opportunity to flirt with someone Hale was interested in, for no other reason than they were charming and disreputable flirts.

"Good evening," Lady Tomison and Gia said to the intruders.

"Hale, might you do the honors of introducing us to your lovely acquaintances?" Julian prompted.

"I would rather keep my acquaintances to myself, and not have them scared away by my beastly friends."

The men's smiles didn't falter in the least at his rudeness. They simply waited.

"Very well. If I must." He turned to the ladies and gave his most regretful look. "Please forgive me. I dinna know how horrid they were and now I'm rather stuck with them."

Gia covered her mouth in a poor attempt to hide her laughter while Lady Tomison waited patiently for their banter to lead to a proper introduction.

"Lord Melville, Lord Penbrook, and Lord Stormont," he gestured to each of the men as he spoke their titles. "May I introduce Lady Tomison and Miss Gia Landon."

Everyone bowed or curtseyed as expected and the introductions were over. He stared pointedly at his friends, silently telling them to go away. Of course, they didn't leave.

To his annoyance, Hale watched as all of his friends asked for dances and scribbled their names on Gia's card. After a few more pleasantries, he and his friends left the ladies alone.

No one said anything until they had moved out of hearing at the edge of the crowd. Then, as one, as if they'd practiced it, they turned toward him expectantly.

"What?" he said when ignoring them didn't work.

They simply waited, allowing him enough time to properly hang himself with whatever words spewed from his mouth next. It was a tactic he'd employed with them in the past to great success. He would need to be canny, so as not to get tangled.

"We share a fondness for horses. That is all," he explained simply. Hale wasn't sure why the truth seemed so difficult. And it was the truth. They shared a fondness for horses. *And, that was all.*

Why were ballrooms so bloody hot?

Gia was charming and lovely and talented. Not to mention funny and clever. And lovely. Damn, he'd already thought that. No reason to think it again. He shook his head. This could not happen.

Gia needed to remain a friend. No, better yet, an acquaintance and nothing more. He shouldn't have even come this evening. He was spending far too much time with her. People would think he was courting her.

He wasn't.

Except for a moment, he had difficulty remembering why he was so against such a thing.

He didn't want to marry. Yes, that was the reason.

But, no. He didn't want to marry for convenience. He didn't want to marry a stranger he had nothing in common with.

Despite only meeting her the day before, he didn't consider her a stranger.

Blast and damn. His reasons were slipping. But he didn't need to rely only on his own reasons.

Gia didn't want to marry either.

In fact, she seemed more than pleased to live out her days in the country with her horses. Away from the marriage mart, not to mention daily lectures from Lady Tomison.

"As I recall, sharing a fondness for something is what got Reggie leg-shackled," Julian so helpfully pointed out about someone from their club.

"That and his need for an heir," Kit added.

"I assure you that is not where this is headed," Hale said more vehemently than was necessary. "As you well know, I don't feel any such obligation to my title. I hardly knew my father and the two times we met, he didn't mention anything about procuring an heir. I rather felt he didn't care about it at all and wished he'd not been forced into the marriage with my mother. Perhaps he even wished he'd never had me."

Hale shook away the thought. It didn't matter and it wasn't relevant to their conversation.

"The point is, the best thing he could have done for me was not put the mantle of responsibility upon me on his deathbed. I am free to do as I choose."

"And in all of this talk about your freedom, do you find you want to choose her?" Kit asked.

"Of course not," he said. "As I told you, our meeting was simply a misunderstanding that resulted in a few hours distraction. Nothing more."

He wouldn't go into detail that it had been much more than a few hours. Admitting to two visits and an early morning ride would have them rolling about on the floor in hysterics.

"Don't forget, a dance," Julian said with a mocking grin. "No, make that, *two* dances." He held up two fingers.

"All right. Two dances. It was the least I could do after overstaying again today."

"Actually." Graham tilted his head and paused a moment as he tapped his index finger to his chin. "The *least* you could do was not attend the ball where you'd be forced into dancing with her."

Kit nodded in agreement, before adding his comments.

"But here you are, and I would even say, *eager* to get on with your dance with the lady."

"Two dances," Julian pointed out again, unhelpfully.

"I'm certainly not *eager*." Hale dismissed his lie with a wave of his hand.

"You've looked over at the orchestra three times as if they are not warming up their instruments quickly enough for you."

"Bollocks." His friends knew him too well. Why did he bother to have friends? All they served to do was harass him whenever possible.

When he'd showed up at Heriot's School alone, escorted

there by a footman rather than a loving parent, Julian and Kit—then awkward boys—had accepted him and offered their friendship. They'd, together, set themselves up in London so they wouldn't be the only Scots. Their constant friendship was a kindness he'd always felt he lacked the ability to repay. Until this moment when he thought he'd finally come to pay the price for their camaraderie.

Julian chuckled.

"You have only to tell us the truth to be excused from this torture."

"And thrust into a worse topic, I'm sure."

"We only want to prepare ourselves if you think to throw yourself into the parson's trap." Graham shook his head slowly.

"You know that is not going to happen."

"But if you were to find a woman whose company you actually enjoyed…" Julian suggested with a raised brow.

"So that I might entangle my heart just to have her seek out entertainments elsewhere? No, thank you," Hale said bitterly.

"Not all women are as disloyal as your mother," Julian answered.

"Watch yourself, Melville." Using the man's title was a warning in itself. They rarely used them, preferring to address one another as people rather than the titles they held.

Julian raised a hand in surrender.

"I haven't said anything you haven't said yourself."

"Surely, you understand why you are not permitted to disparage my mother regardless of my feelings for her."

He nodded. "Family is complicated."

Graham agreed with a grunt. Each of them had their own familial issues they only spoke of when the whisky was flowing.

Fortunately, Hale was granted escape when the bloody orchestra finally managed to begin the first strains of actual music.

"If you'll excuse me." He glared at his snickering friends and left to find his dance partner.

His irritation faded away when he saw her smile at him. He

held out his hand in invitation and she slipped her fingers across his palm.

Had he not known better, he'd have thought her a skilled seductress with such a movement. But they both wore gloves so it shouldn't have struck him that way.

He only registered the murmurs around them when they distracted Gia enough that she looked away from him. As they took their places, he was disturbed by the snippets of conversation going on around them.

"Of course, *she* would have attracted the attentions of a rake such as the Duke of Roxburghe."

"If she thinks he's of a mind to marry…"

"The two of them make quite a pair. Shameful."

"Scottish brute and the Italian harlot."

Hale placed his hand at her back and moved to start the dance. They were silent for a few turns and he realized they rarely shared a moment of silence during the hours they spent together. Speaking with her was as easy as breathing.

But now things were different. The world had intruded on their little bubble, and she would learn of his reputation.

Had he not wanted to embarrass her, he would have left the ball immediately. But he'd never do such a thing to Gia.

In the short time he'd come to know her, he realized he could never do anything to hurt her.

He cared for her too much.

CHAPTER SEVEN

GIA HATED THE silence between them even more than dancing. She wasn't certain of the proper way to handle the situation. She glanced over at Lydia who was too far away to help from where she stood smiling with an older gentleman.

Obviously, the venom being spewed about had not hit the countess on that corner of the dance floor. Gia was on her own.

The large ballroom suddenly felt too close. The light from the many chandeliers too bright. Everyone seemed to be looking at them. But worse than that was the silence that lingered between the duke and her.

She took a breath and went with her instincts. She had to do something. She couldn't stand for Hale to be upset because of her. Whether it was her fault or not.

Yet, if what was being said was correct, it didn't sound like he was completely innocent either.

"I'm not sure which one of us is destroying the others' pristine reputation," she said, hoping he wouldn't walk off the dance floor and leave her there to face everything alone. She didn't think he would. He had been nothing but kind to her, thus far.

Besides, he needed her to help him ready Godspell for the race. Certainly, that would be reason enough for him to stay. But they couldn't pretend people weren't speaking of them.

Hale stumbled a step but recovered quickly. Her boldness must have caught him by surprise.

He laughed and suddenly she realized she no longer cared at all about what the people around them were discussing, so long as this man laughed and smiled because of her.

"It is quite the conundrum," he said, appearing almost as relieved as she that the tense silence was over. "But I'm certain it is me who is at fault. I am known to be a rake. And, of course, just being a large Scot in this world of English dandies is a crime worthy of hanging. If you wish to end the dance, I will not push the matter. I should have warned you and considered how standing up with me would look."

"I will not allow a bunch of gossips to send us off the dance floor. Perhaps on its own, your reputation wouldn't have been noticed. You are a duke, after all, and a young one at that. You are above censure. However, when paired with the belief I was born a wanton seductress because of my mother, the old crones must be expecting us to copulate in the middle of the dance floor."

Lydia would fall over if she'd heard Gia say so many improper words. And all in the same sentence.

"I assure you, if you really were a wanton seductress, we wouldn't waste time dancing. I would already have you out in the gardens."

She blinked and his smile fell away as if he only then caught what he'd said in front of a lady.

"Forgive me. I forgot who I was speaking to."

She laughed. "I appreciate that you think of me as a friend instead of a lady."

"Aye." His eyes went wide. "That is, I do think of you as a friend, but you are also a lady. Obviously. You are both and that is what I forgot." Were his cheeks turning pink? It was difficult to see in the dim light at the edges of the dance floor, but she thought so.

What fun. Had she wanted to run away a moment ago? Now she didn't want to stop teasing him.

"Has anyone mentioned how much brighter the sun is in the

day than the night?" he asked tilting his head.

She slapped him lightly on the shoulder and smiled with just a hint of mischief.

"You seem flushed, Your Grace. Perhaps we should take some air. I wouldn't want you to overheat."

"Very well. You are a horrid dancer anyway." He offered a look of mock distaste which had her laughing again. She was no floating angel, but she managed proficiently. He was teasing her, and she enjoyed it more than she should.

"If I liked dancing, I might take offense, but I really don't," she said as he led her from the dance floor and out on the terrace. It was a cool April evening so there weren't many others outside, but they weren't alone either.

A few people glanced their way before leaning together to whisper. How ridiculous. They couldn't be more wrong about what was happening between her and Hale.

The duke was a flirt and nothing more. He didn't really have an interest in her beyond friendship and assistance with his horse.

He winced as he turned toward her.

"I feel as if I should warn my friends who risked their feet in a ruse to ask you nosey questions regarding our acquaintance." He tilted his head as if looking up at the dark sky. "On second thought, they deserve what they get."

They shared a laugh but when they fell silent, she considered his words.

"What would you have me tell them about our acquaintance?" Obviously, there wasn't anything scandalous to say, but perhaps he didn't want them to know of their friendship.

"I have already told them the truth. That I visited your home looking for a man, but realized I was looking for you instead and we became friends."

"That should be easy enough to remember," she said feeling slightly disappointed by how simple he made their association seem. Their acquaintance was simple indeed, but it felt bigger to her. More important. She shook her head.

He turned to look at her.

"May I ask you an impertinent question?" he asked.

"Of course. As you said, we are friends." If her voice sounded a bit stilted, she would never admit to it.

"Giovanni?" His lips quirked. "I'm a bit rusty in my Italian but it is a man's name, is it not? I was not wrong to assume I would be meeting a gentleman?"

"It's quite a sad story actually." Gia had never known her mother but missed her often. There were empty places in her heart and questions she had that only her mother would have had the answers to.

She'd learned all that was needed to know about womanhood from her lady's maid, but it wasn't the same.

"As you know, my mother was Italian and as my birth grew near, she considered names for both a boy and a girl. Giovanni for a boy. Verona for a girl. She repeated it to my father often to make sure he knew her wishes."

Hale nodded.

"But minutes after my birth, my mother suffered a complication. They brought my father into the room, per her instructions."

Hale had leaned closer as she spoke and she took a deep breath of the scent she had come to recognize as distinctly his. Warm leather and the sweetness of fresh hay.

She cleared her throat and continued.

"Years later he realized my mother was asking him if I was Giovanni or Verona, but at the time, my father—panicked as he was—only heard her repeating Giovanni Verona over and over until she died. And so, he named me Giovanni Verona." She laughed. "It's horrid, I know."

"It's beautifully sad that yours was the last name on her lips."

"And just as sad that because my father was too distraught and confused that she went to her grave unsure if she'd birthed a boy or a girl."

"I'm sure she knows. She must watch over you, for only

someone with a guardian angel would ride the way you do." His lips pulled up on just the one side and she got a glimpse of what he must have been like as a boy. Quiet, but not without a rebellious side.

"Perhaps you are right. I often wonder what she would think of me. Would she side with my father and try to marry me off, or would she be happy to let me be who I am?"

"Your mother, the woman who faced London society as an opera singer who married a viscount? She would want you to be yourself. With your head held high. And not worry about gossips."

"I like to think that true. Though she had another reason not to cower when the *ton* spoke ill of her." Gia looked over her shoulder and lowered her voice to a whisper. "The truth is she wasn't an opera singer. Yes, she came to London on her own and sang to make a living, but in reality, she had done so to escape her family."

"Her family?"

"My grandfather was the Prince of Carignano and my mother, Caterina, was a princess."

"*You* are a princess."

She shrugged.

"One doesn't shrug off being a bloody princess, Gia. You should tell those old crones who judge you exactly who you are." He waved toward the ballroom. "They'll stop speaking of you as if you are a harlot, and they'll realize they are not worthy to share the same air as you."

"And they'll offer friendship, or worse—marriage—that will be based on nothing but a title I've never held. My mother left Turin because she didn't want that life. She wanted to be free of who she was forced to be and find someone who loved her for herself. Why would she ever want me to assume a role she cast off?"

He frowned but nodded in agreement.

"I'm sorry. Their words shouldn't trouble me when they

clearly don't bother you," he said with a firm nod.

"They do bother me. But I've learned to ignore it. It was a hard lesson when I came to London as a hopeful girl years ago. It was unexpected. My mother had been long gone. But I had attracted the attention of the heir to the Duke of Fornwurst. I was accused of trying to lure him away from one of the other debutantes."

"I don't doubt it. You would be able to lure anyone if you wished to."

She smiled at his kind words.

"Unfortunately, the debutante's mother had known of my mother and she told all who would listen that I was spawned from an opera singer. My father wanted to defend me with the truth of my heritage, but I refused because I *am* the daughter of an opera singer, and I would not let anyone shame me for it."

⟫⟫⟩⟨⟨⟨

HALE COULD ONLY stare at the woman in front of him. He'd known she wasn't like the other women he was acquainted with. But he'd underestimated her strength and courage.

To hold her head high knowing she had information that would raze the rumors to the ground and still kept silent because she was better than that. Better than all of those who would disrespect her mother in that way.

He bowed to her. "It is an honor to call your mother's daughter my friend."

"Thank you, Your Grace."

They continued their stroll and he found it interesting that as lovely as she was, he only wished to continue conversing with her.

He couldn't remember a time he had taken a woman to the gardens for something so innocent. However, with their reputations as they were, any time in the gardens was enough to make the *ton* talk.

"Should we return to the ball?" he asked.

"Do we have to?"

"No. I only thought…" He paused to think over what he said before he made a blunder like earlier. He'd made it sound as if he didn't consider her a lady when the opposite was true. She was more of a lady than any others at this hideous party.

Despite her stripping down to buckskins in the park to ride astride and her dislike for dancing, she had more class than any woman he'd ever met. And she was so authentically herself, he truly admired her.

"You thought to avoid talk?" she said. "Isn't it too late for that? We're out in the gardens."

"Perhaps, but talk is one thing. Evidence is another. And while true we are in the gardens, we are within sight of the house and everyone is staring at us from the terrace. Should we wave?"

"No. But very well. Lydia will have probably heard the rumors spreading and will want to leave." The crease that formed between her brows made him desperate to see her smile again.

"You look quite disappointed for someone who doesn't enjoy dancing." He had exaggerated earlier by calling her a horrible dancer, but she wasn't good either. She hadn't stepped on his feet, but it was as if she wished to lead. Perhaps it would have been easier than fighting her on which direction they should turn.

"I will miss out on dancing with your handsome friends and ferreting out secrets about you."

He laughed despite the twinge of jealousy that struck him.

"And I will miss trying to wrestle you into submission on the dance floor again tonight."

She smacked him lightly in the arm and he felt a sizzle of happiness spark up his spine at her touch.

She wasn't even gone when he found himself looking forward to seeing her the next day.

CHAPTER EIGHT

SINCE HER FATHER had returned from his business in Kent late the night before, Gia sent a message to Hale letting him know she wouldn't be going out that morning for her usual ride.

She instead planned to speak to her father regarding his fruitless plans to keep her in town.

"Father," she said coldly as she entered the breakfast room.

"Still with *father* instead of *papa*? That must mean you've yet to forgive me for my slight manipulation to bring you to London." He frowned at his plate before setting in on his ham. Whatever guilt he felt obviously wasn't enough to displace his appetite.

"Your manipulation wasn't *slight*. And as Lydia will confirm when she arrives, it was all for naught. The same rumors that ran us from London years ago have prevailed and I am once again a pariah to be avoided.

"I expected as much," he said, unaffected, before taking another large bite.

"You expected me to be ignored, but yet you forced me to stay? I had not thought you a cruel man before. I see I was wrong."

"I am *not* a cruel man. It is that I regret allowing an easy escape during your come out years ago. If we'd stayed and faced the tongue-waggers back then, things might have been different. I had only wanted to get you to safety. But safety is not always the correct path when facing adversity."

She couldn't believe what she was hearing. The man had some wild fantasy that she would suddenly be accepted by society if she only stood up to them. If that were all there was to it, she would have done it. She was no coward.

She'd taken the most skittish of horses and made him a formidable racer.

But there was no winning with these people. They demanded perfection and to hell with anyone who didn't measure up.

She would never fit in. They would never accept her.

"You would have me change who I am to satisfy a group of people I have no interest in impressing? You care that little for me? Perhaps it isn't just the *ton* that rejects my existence."

"You know that isn't true. I love you the way you are. That isn't to say you couldn't bend a little. Not everyone here is bad. If you made an effort to make a friend or two, that could go a long way to moving past the gossip. Lydia will help you if you let her."

Gia thought of the friends she'd made during her come out. They hadn't turned out to be friends at all. They'd turned on her as quickly as a leaf in a breeze.

She didn't expect the fickle women of the *ton* would welcome her to their drawing rooms with open arms.

She tilted her head and stifled a smile. She had made one friend since arriving in London. Though she doubted a scandalous duke was what her father had in mind when he'd spoken of her making friends.

It was best not to bring it up. Not when she had plans to meet Hale to start training Godspell that afternoon.

"Then you plan to force me to stay here?" she asked.

"I would rather you didn't use the word 'force.' Rather I wish you to stay and show them that the daughter of Caterina Landon is not ashamed of who she is."

"I am not ashamed."

"Then show them."

GIA WAS QUIET as they set up in a field outside of the city for Godspell's first training session. Other riders were testing their horses in the same field as it was a popular place to train. There were even seats along the edge of the field for the owners to assess their investments.

Hale wasn't one to sit and watch. He preferred to be involved in how his horse performed. He wouldn't be the one riding him in the race, he had an experienced jockey for that, but he would see to the stallion's training.

"Is something bothering you?" he asked Gia when the silence had gone on too long for his liking. If he'd done something to offend her, he wanted to address it so it didn't affect their progress.

She seemed startled by his voice as if she were so intent on her thoughts, she'd forgotten he was there.

"I'm sorry, I am thinking of other things."

Obviously. He wasn't sure why it bothered him that he couldn't capture her attention. It was a ridiculous thought. Especially when she could be distracted by something very serious.

"Do you wish to discuss what is bothering you?"

"No." Her answer came quick, but the way she bit her bottom lip made him think she wished she'd answered in a different way.

"Is it a matter for women's ears only?" he pressed. He knew little about a woman's courses but knew they could cause discomfort and irritability. He needed to tread carefully.

She laughed.

"Fear not, Your Grace. I shall not speak of such things as shifts and corsets in your hearing. We wouldn't want your sensibilities to bring on a faint."

He shook his head at her teasing. It seemed she was already

improved. He would gladly take her insults so long as he could avoid the dreaded silence.

Silence bothered him. He'd dealt with too much of it in his youth.

"I should have known I would be punished for asking after your well-being. The indestructible Gia Landon doesn't need anyone's assistance or concern."

She sobered at his words and tilted her head to look up at him.

"Do you think it's possible to be accepted by the *ton* if I simply ignore the rumors and face their disapproval straight on? If I were to follow their rules and try to fit in?"

He squinted at her. Then waved a hand over him.

"This may come as a surprise to you, but I am not truly accepted by English society. I'm referred to as a savage when they assume I'm out of hearing and often ask me to repeat words I say differently than they do. I may not be the best person to ask."

"But you don't wish to fit in."

"And you do?" He squinted from the sun.

She shrugged. "Perhaps. It would be easier."

"You would prefer to spend your days with embroidery and discussions on the weather as opposed to this?" He gestured to the field beyond them where Owen was moving Godspell into position for his first run.

He couldn't imagine Gia as one of the society types. She would never fit in with them. She was so much better. He couldn't imagine why she would even want to try, and he said so. Not the part about her being better, but the latter.

"As I said, I thought it might be easier."

"Easier for whom?" He didn't know what had distressed her into thinking she should try harder to impress the foolish people who judged her. "Is this about the ball and the gossip?"

"Perhaps."

He reached toward her, wanting to offer reassurance, but pulled his hand back when he realized he wasn't quite sure how to do such a thing.

"After the failure of my come out, I retreated to Elmhurst and have been there ever since. I'm wondering now if that was the coward's way. Should I have stayed and fought for my place?"

"I don't understand what has made you question everything, but if you are truly unhappy with how things are, then I would say you need to make a change to find happiness. But if you are content with who you are, and the way you live your life, why would you want to try to fit into a world that doesn't fit you?"

"I am happy. But I don't want to disappoint my father or Lydia."

He didn't know her father, but if the man would be disappointed to have such a wonderful daughter as Gia, he didn't deserve her efforts to appease him.

"Are we going to ready this lad for a race or stand about talking in the sun?" Owen interrupted their conversation and the cloud over Gia's face lifted as she headed toward Godspell.

"We most definitely want to get this handsome boy ready to win."

She didn't seem to worry anymore over her earlier concerns as they pushed Godspell through his paces. They worked with him in a crowd of other horses. Forcing the horse to face his irrational fears.

Perhaps there was a lesson there.

GIA FELT EQUAL parts dread and excitement as she readied herself for the ball that evening. She'd already confirmed that Hale planned to attend and that he would stand ready to distract her should any of the nastier ladies of the *ton* come sniffing about.

She didn't need the duke to fight her battles. She was perfectly capable of handling them. She just wasn't sure if her way of handling them wouldn't make things even worse.

True to his word, Hale intercepted Gia and Lydia as soon as they arrived. She supplied her dance card upon his request while Lydia gave a smug smile as if telling Gia how right she was to make her pick up a card.

Gia had planned to do so anyway knowing at least two dances would be taken by the duke. As had happened the evening before, Lord Melville, Lord Penbrook, and Lord Stormont swooped in to take a dance each.

She enjoyed the sound of irritation from Hale as his friends flirted with her. She knew well enough that they were rakes with no intentions toward marriage, so she could only guess Hale was worried she'd make real her threat to ask his friends about his secrets.

Did he have any secrets?

She and Hale made their way to the dance floor for the first dance among rumors and whispers much like the night before. Except this time, Gia didn't strain to hear what was being said.

She assumed it was the normal gossip that followed her since her come out. She was the daughter of a seductress, which meant she would steal away every man she could, even two or three at a time if it suited.

Tonight, it might at least appear true since her dance card held four names. Really it was all very tedious and she decided to ignore it as best she could.

After all, it hadn't deterred Hale from visiting or asking her to dance. If he didn't care, she wouldn't either.

They chatted as normal, mostly about Godspell and his training. When the dance was over, he escorted her back to Lydia. But as soon as he stepped away, Gia was mobbed by a group of men, all asking for a spot on her dance card.

The women nearby were appalled by the attention she was receiving as Lydia made quick introductions in an organized fashion.

Fortunately, she was given an escape when Lord Melville came to claim his dance.

"My, you have quite the group of admirers, Miss Gia."

"The duke danced with me. I assume that sends a signal to the others that I am now a prize to be won. I'm sure you shall see my name in the books at your club."

Lord Melville's eyes went wide and his lips pulled up to one side.

"Hale said you were not like other ladies of the *ton*." He cleared his throat and added, "He meant it in a pleasing way, I assure you. No offense."

Gia chuckled at his discomfort, much like she had when Hale had been caught up the same tangle.

"I believe he said he appreciates that you speak your mind and do not simper or talk of the weather."

"Yes. Though I do worry what will become of our friendship if I were to actually need to speak to him of the weather. He's so adverse to the topic."

Her comment earned another laugh from the lord.

"If he gets caught in a storm, it will be his own doing. I will not fault you for not telling him."

He was laughing in earnest now. So much so that he stumbled and righted himself.

"Now I understand why he's been spending so much time with you. He generally doesn't take up company with women unless they are in his—" Lord Melville blinked down at her. "Are you a witch? How do you make men forget themselves in front of you like that? I very nearly said something completely improper."

It was her turn to laugh at his suggestion.

"If I were a witch, I assure you I would put my powers to far greater use than to get you to speak of the women who visit the duke's bed." When he looked at her in shock, she shook her head. "Perhaps you are the witch, my lord, for you made me say the improper thing you managed to avoid."

They were laughing together as the music stopped.

"Oh dear, I believe my good friend wishes me dead. At least he is glaring at me as if it were so," Lord Melville said while peering up at the balcony that overlooked the large room. "Do be a dear and be sure to enchant Kit and Graham as well, so we might finally see the limit to Hale's anger."

Hale stood with both hands clenched on the railing and a frown on his face.

"Surely he's not looking at you." She glanced around but didn't know who else the duke might be so unhappy with.

"We could put my theory to the test. Come out to the garden with me and we'll see what he does."

Gia stared at the man in surprise. Was this a ruse to get her away from everyone? How many times had men made such suggestions in an attempt to seduce her? Or rather expected her to seduce them because of her wild blood?

She'd never heard anything so ludicrous.

Not that she would have taken Lord Melville up on his offer, but even if she'd wanted to, she couldn't because her next dance partner arrived to claim his dance.

Lord Grovert was nice enough even if his gaze did drop down to her bosom more than once during the dance.

The rest of the men became a bit of a jumble. They were all handsome enough, witty enough, and polite enough even if they took as much interest in her gown as Lord Grovert had. But nothing specific stood out about any of them. Except, perhaps, Lord Duncan.

The man was tall, though not as tall or large as Hale or his friends. Maybe it was due to his smaller stature that it was easier for her to dance with him.

"You seem to have captured the attention of every man in the house tonight."

She frowned and waited for his gaze to dip to her breasts and was surprised when it did not.

"You're not pleased to be sought after?"

"I'm not a prize."

"I believe that depends on what one wishes to win."

She couldn't argue that. Lydia wouldn't be pleased with her, but Gia had had enough.

"I won't pretend not to know why men wish to dance with me. They think I am free with my favors." The man's eyes went wide. "Don't feign surprise, Lord Duncan, I know what is said about me. But I'll have you know the truth and maybe you will take it back to the others sniffing about. I am not who they think I am. I'm no great seductress nor are my skirts light, my lord."

He smiled though still looked a bit shocked.

"I don't think I've ever had such a frank conversation with a lady before."

"I didn't mean to shock you, I've just had my fill with men who want to show me the gardens."

He nodded. "I promise not to offer to show you the gardens. In fact, if you were to ask me to show them to you, I would refuse."

She smiled and counted Lord Duncan among the small group of men who were not imbeciles.

"Thank you, my lord. I am grateful for your refusal."

She was also grateful for her time with Hale's friends who, like him, had been shocked and amused by her blunt conversation.

Lord Stormont was the next of his friends to bow before her. Taller than the rest, he was leaner, with lighter blond hair.

"His Grace said you were Scottish as well, but you have no brogue," she mentioned while attempting to allow her partner to lead.

Lord Stormont, who the duke referred to as Kit gave a bright smile. She'd noticed the man seemed to give his smiles freely, but this close she saw something she'd not noticed before. An undercurrent of pain and perhaps worry.

"Ach, aye, lass," Kit said, with an exaggerated brogue. "I was born in Scotland, but my mother brought me to England as a boy. It was only when I inherited at thirteen that I returned to Scotland. Graham, Lord Penbrook, and I were friends from Eton before I moved and attended Heriot's with Hale and Julian."

"I see. That must have been chaotic at such a young age."

He shrugged. "We all have pains we must bear in silence."

"That is very true." It was strange that all of society forced themselves to hide the slightest struggle, when in truth each and every person struggled.

"And you, my dear, are about to be called on to bear one of the worst pains known to man."

Gia's eyes went wide as Kit looked over her head toward the corner of the dance floor.

"His Grace?"

Kit chuckled.

"No. Though he looks fit to be tied. I'm sure I will receive a firm dressing down for dancing too closely or smiling or looking in your general direction. It will not be pleasant, but that is not the grim future I speak of."

He nodded toward the edge of the dance floor and Gia saw Lord Penbrook waiting with a stern frown.

"I daresay the two of you dancing together will likely result in a boxing match, for neither of you will be willing to give up control."

Gia laughed. "I'm not afraid. After all, I've danced with three surly Scots and lived to tell the tale."

Kit laughed, perhaps more than the joke required. But she realized what he was doing. Riling up the duke for his entertainment.

"You are all truly the worst friends."

"That is probably the truth. But we all know we can count on the other when needed."

Gia swallowed thinking that must be a wonderful comfort.

Kit led her from the floor to hand her over to Lord Penbrook. He bowed with a smile she hadn't expected given his earlier expression. They lined up for the set and they started the dance in silence. If only it had remained that way.

Rather than the good-natured teasing she'd experienced with Hale's other two friends, the man he called Graham took a different tactic.

"A word of warning to you, Miss Gia."

"And what is that?" she asked, her brows pulling together. If he attempted to give her dancing lessons in the middle of the quadrille, she would purposefully step on his toes.

"He doesn't plan to marry. If this friendship is some elaborate ploy to trap him or—"

"Please let me stop you, Lord Penbrook. I assure you, I am not some diabolical debutante attempting to make myself into the Duchess of Roxburghe. Our friendship is only that. A mutual respect of horses."

"So you say, but as he is currently glaring at me wishing me to drop dead, I doubt he is thinking of your mutual respect of horses."

Gia glanced over to see Hale had come closer. From this distance, it was easier to see how his gaze tracked their every movement. Was the man concerned the marquess would do something improper right there on the dance floor? Or was his scrutiny something else?

"I've never seen him so enthralled with a woman. If your hope is to deceive him, I would ask you to find another mark. He's had a difficult life and doesn't need some chit turning his world upside down."

"As Lord Stormont and I were discussing during our dance, we all have some pain we carry around. I do believe yours puts you on the offensive, does it not?"

The man pressed his lips together and shook his head.

"Julian said you were a witch." The man's lip twitched and Gia thought it might be the closest she would get to earning a smile. Then he turned stoic once more. "Please have a care with him, Miss Gia."

"I promise, I will." It was an easy vow to make for if anything, she found it much too easy to care about the duke.

CHAPTER NINE

G IA WAS MORE than pleased when it was time for Hale to come lead her to the dance floor for the supper dance. She had yet to stay at an event long enough for supper, but she was happy to do so when she knew the man sitting next to her was her friend.

Except he didn't seem overly friendly when he placed his hand on her side and took her hand in his.

"What has you out of sorts?" she asked when he remained silent.

"Nothing."

She'd never heard a word sound more opposite of its meaning in her life.

"If you plan to spend the entire dance glowering at me because of nothing, then perhaps you won't mind if I change the subject. What a pleasant day today was it not? The way the sun came up and warmed the air before setting which made it—"

"For Christ's sake, all right. I was attempting to keep my anger in check, but if you wish to know the truth of it, I'm not at all happy about the men who have taken up space on your dance card. It may be hypocritical of me to say so, but they are entirely improper. You should not trust them."

"Even your friends?"

"Especially my friends. They are the worst of the lot." Hale was still frowning, but Gia knew he didn't mean what he said. She could see how close the men were. It was clear they would all do whatever necessary to ensure each other's happiness.

"You think me naïve? That I don't know what those men want? You have heard what the gossips say about me, and I told you what happened. But I guess I neglected to tell you everything."

"Then tell me now. Please, give me a reason to call the lot of them out."

"You'll do no such thing. You must promise. It is in the past and I am better for knowing. It was not pleasant, but I learned a lot about life and am stronger for it."

"What happened?"

"When a woman is assumed to be of a certain nature, the women treat her like a pariah, turning their noses up as good society does. But the men... It is a different result. They smell blood and come running for easy prey."

"They assumed the rumors were true and you would offer them favors."

"Yes. Some feigned interest, while others, well... they got directly to the point when making their propositions."

Hale's blue eyes blazed as his brows turned down.

"And why did you not assume I was one of the ones feigning interest?"

"You stumbled into Lydia's drawing room wanting to find the owner of a horse. If this has all been a ruse to lure me to your bed, it has been a most elaborate one. Besides, I've known you some time now, and I don't think you have the patience for such schemes. You would have surely attempted to advance by now."

His anger faded into surprise and perhaps even afront.

"You don't think I could maintain a dastardly plot for more than a few days?"

She laughed.

"I'm sorry if I offended you, Your Grace, for suggesting you are an honorable man and a true friend. Do you wish me to think differently?"

He twisted his mouth to the side and shook his head.

"No. I have no designs on you short of you helping my horse win at Epsom. And I *am* a true friend. Of course, I do not wish for you to paint me with the same brush as those other bounders. Your judgement is sound however, I do not appreciate how it came to be. You shouldn't have been treated like that. You are a lovely woman and I'm certain one day a man will see your true value and ask for your hand."

His smile was back and she braced herself for whatever droll thing he said next.

"And you shall kick him in the shins and run away screaming. Or something else completely unexpected."

⟫⟪

HALE'S MOOD WAS restored when he led Gia to the dining room for supper. The man next to her was ancient and focused on the woman to his right which left Gia to his company alone.

"Did your friends leave already? I don't see them at the table."

"Aye, they left shortly after their dance with you." Though not immediately. They'd made sure to seek Hale out to chide him for his jealousy.

"They have gone to seek other entertainments for the evening?" she whispered.

"Why the devil can't we ever have a conversation without it turning to improper topics?" he asked not put out at all.

"And don't forget cursing."

Yes, he'd just cursed as well. It was so easy to be with her he often forgot himself.

She let out a sigh and turned to her plate.

"There's always the weather. Or sunlight."

He shook his head and smiled at her. She always managed to bring a smile to his face.

Hale was sitting in his study the next day counting down the minutes until visiting hours so he could go see Gia. He couldn't wait to tell her how well Godspell had done on his run that morning.

She hadn't been able to join him because Lady Tomison had needed her at home that morning.

Gia would be happy to hear that her horse hadn't pulled out of the pack and seemed not to notice the other horses at all. Had he just thought of Godspell as her horse? Before he had time to dissect his comment, his butler entered.

"Lord Waverly to see you, Your Grace," Hutchinson said by the door of Hale's study.

"Please send him in," Hale answered. Having never met the man, he curiously welcomed the distraction. Anything to keep his mind from reminding him of the dances he'd shared with Gia. The feel of her in his arms. Her smile. Her laughter…

The man entered and offered a stiff smile.

"Thank you for seeing me, Your Grace." The man bowed and Hale nodded. Until he knew the nature of the visit, Hale couldn't be sure the man deserved more than that.

"Of course, please sit." Hale gestured to his decanter of brandy. It was not yet noon, but the man seemed slightly nervous. "Can I offer you anything?"

"No. Thank you."

"What might I do for you, my lord?" Hale prompted when the man remained silent. Hale took his seat behind his desk and waited.

"It is my daughter, Your Grace."

Hale's heart rate picked up. No good conversation had ever started with those words. As a bachelor, Hale was conditioned to avoid conversations with men in regard to their daughters.

"I was away from town and upon my return I've learned you've come to visit her. More than once and for some length of time, as I'm told. And then, according to Lady Tomison, you danced with Gia numerous times and even escorted her to dinner last night."

"You have received a detailed and accurate report," Hale said while trying to decipher where the man was going with this. Did he think a visit—unchaperoned as it was—and a few dances warranted a marriage proposal?

"Yes. I assumed so." Waverly nodded.

"I'm sorry we have not had the opportunity to meet until now. I purchased a horse from you through Mr. Marley in the fall."

The man frowned. "Yes, that is my understanding as well. And while it is true that we have never met, I am afraid I have heard of you. That is, I've heard of your reputation."

"I see. And you've come to warn me away from a friendship with your daughter?" Hale leaned in, lacing his fingers together on his desk, hoping he looked every bit the imposing duke. He would not be ordered around so easily, especially when it came to Gia.

The man blinked and then barked a laugh before composing himself again.

"Apologies, Your Grace. No. That is, not as you mean. If you've met my daughter, you know she is more than capable of running off any man who treats her in an unladylike way."

"As you say. And you should know that I would never attempt such a thing. And not just because she would break my nose."

"Or other important parts," the man added.

"Too true." They shared a chuckle before Hale sobered again. "Then please tell me why you've come."

"While I'm sure you have no romantic designs on my Gia." He waved his hand as if the thought were preposterous. "I have heard of the dares and wagers you and your friends make to fill the pages at White's. I've come to ask that you not use my daughter in one of your schemes. While quite sturdy on the outside, my daughter has a soft heart. If she thinks you a friend and finds out you have only used her as part of a cruel jest, she will be hurt and I… Well, I'll not make threats, but you should know the father of an injured daughter can be a formidable adversary."

Hale didn't know which part of this man's misguided comments to address first. What he did know was that he was angry. And not for anything the man assumed about Hale, but for the way he'd dismissed his daughter as being pursued for anything other than a jest.

As if Hale wouldn't find her attractive enough to seduce. Had he not been staring out the window thinking of just that thing before the man walked in?

For obvious reasons, Hale couldn't say any of that in defense of the woman. Instead, he took a calming breath and offered what assurances he could.

"I met Gia quite by accident while inquiring about a horse. In fact, she may be the only person I've met who surpasses me for equine madness—something I find astounding as well as enchanting. With your permission, I would consider her a dear friend. Though, you may not want us to be acquainted as I fear we only exacerbate each other's obsession with horses. But if you'll allow it, I can promise there is nothing nefarious about my attentions. Just two people who share a passion for horses."

The man seemed to ponder Hale's words for a moment before answering.

"I brought her to London to get her head out of the stables and give her the opportunity to meet people. Perhaps, I should consider this a compromise of sorts."

Hale smiled. "I can only hope we don't make each other worse."

"If that were possible." He shook his head. "If you could do me one thing."

"If it's in my power, consider it done."

"She's sold a few of her horses. Please don't allow her to look for them. I don't want her to go through that pain again."

Hale winced. "I'm afraid it is too late for that. The horse I purchased from you is here in London. She's already taken him for a ride and we have plans to work together to ready him for Epsom next month."

"I see." The man pressed his lips together and Hale could see how much he cared for his daughter by the concern in his expression.

"If it makes you feel any better, you should know that she didn't greet my horse with sorrow, but that of a person who was glad to find her friend happy and healthy."

Lord Waverly smiled tenderly, and Hale was happy to have given him some peace.

"I'm glad to hear it. You don't know the amount of guilt I feel that she had to sell her horses to recover my debts. She saved us and never once said a thing to make me feel bad for it. But I heard her crying in her rooms afterward, and it broke my heart."

It shocked Hale not only to hear that Gia had cried—he'd thought her impenetrable. But more so for the way his chest pulled tight at hearing of her pain. He found he wanted to track her down that instant and hold her in his arms to offer support and take away her past pain.

Not only would she not understand his sudden affection, but—as he and Lord Waverly discussed—it would surely earn Hale a broken nose if he touched her inappropriately.

"I do not pretend to know your daughter as well as you, but what I've learned thus far is that Gia is a very strong person and doesn't hold back if she needs to say something. Therefore, I have to think she truly does not blame you."

The man's smile was colored by sadness as he stood.

"Perhaps you know her better than you think." He ran a hand over his forehead. "Now that I'm certain you mean Gia no harm, I want to thank you for offering my daughter your friendship. I'm glad she's found someone who shares her interests. You are welcome in my home—or rather Lady Tomison's home—any time."

"Thank you, my lord." It was a good thing the man approved of their friendship since Gia had invited Hale to travel with her and her groom to Wiltshire for the Salisbury race the next day.

Lord Waverly had just made it to the door when Hale stopped him.

"May I ask…" Hale paused to collect his thoughts. "Why did you say you *knew* I had no romantic designs on Gia?"

The man seemed perplexed as he stared at Hale with his head tilted to the side.

"She has had many men approach her in a misguided attempt to seduce her. She knows what people say about her heritage and is on guard for such things."

"True, but why did you not think I might be considering Gia for more than seduction."

This earned another laugh from the viscount. When Hale only waited the man sobered quickly.

"You can't mean marriage."

Hale simply raised an eyebrow in a very duke-like way. Why was he pushing this?

"But you are a duke and she is a…" His brows came together in confusion. "I know my daughter is a treasure, but I am her father and as such I see her in a way others do not. Are not able to. You are a duke. If you decided to marry—and I have not heard that you plan to do so anytime soon—you surely wouldn't select a horse-mad spinster to be your duchess. As lovely as my daughter is, you have your choice of anyone."

After delivering that very reasonable explanation, Lord Waverly turned and left.

But Hale couldn't let it go. As the man had said, Hale was not looking for a wife. He had the luxury of not needing to worry over such things. In fact, he felt no real duty to carry on the title at all. It wasn't as if his father had personally tasked him with such a responsibility.

Still, at some point he thought he should at least attempt to sire an heir. And he knew, as did Lord Waverly, that Hale was considered a catch.

As a duke, with reasonably good looks and healthy finances,

he only managed to keep the mothers and their eager debutantes at bay with his seedy reputation and Scottish grumblings. That was the reason he'd gone to such great lengths to fabricate such a reputation in the first place.

But someday, when he made it known he was ready to take a wife, his past transgressions would be forgiven and any available female of marriageable age living in or around the king's realm would be thrust upon him for his selection.

So why, after hearing and agreeing with everything the man said, did he suddenly want to disregard rational thought and pursue Gia with intent to marry?

Surely it was only an effort to rebel against the man's preconceived notions. To prove that he was capable of choosing an unconventional wife that would shock the *ton*?

He didn't think he cared what anyone thought. Was he wrong?

Or did he simply want the one person he was not expected to want?

Whatever the reason, he found himself looking forward to seeing Gia the next day for their journey to Wiltshire for Godspell's first race even more than he had initially.

CHAPTER TEN

To say Gia was excited about their adventure was an understatement. Not only would she spend the day around horses and watching them race, but she would get to share her excitement with Hale as well.

Except when Hale arrived, he didn't seem excited at all.

He'd walked over to Tomison House and frowned as the carriage was brought around.

Why did he look disappointed? Perhaps he was upset that Godspell wasn't ready to race yet.

"I'm sure Godspell will be ready for Epsom. And I will cheer for him, of course. Even though Dante will also be racing, and my loyalties are split." She offered a smile and he returned it though it did not hold the same warmth as it normally did.

That must not have been the problem.

She cleared her throat, feeling strange that she was nervous.

"I apologize for the early start. Owen prefers to get on the road before the crowds."

In truth, Owen had grumbled a bit about the addition of the duke to their party, but since he didn't say any actual words that could be debated, she simply ignored her groom.

"Of course." He offered a nod and watched as Bess exited the house.

Gia's maid would need to ride with them because it wasn't proper to ride alone in the carriage with the duke. Though the duke would most likely prefer riding a horse like Owen rather than sitting in the carriage.

Oh. That must be the issue.

"If you would prefer to take a horse rather than ride in the carriage, I can have one of my mounts readied for you."

"The carriage is fine."

Gia let out a breath as her irritation grew. This was supposed to be fun. She'd thought of traveling all night. And now here he was, the man she'd looked forward to spending the next few days with and he was… brooding.

"Pardon, Your Grace, but may we dispense with this game of me trying to puzzle out what has you out of sorts? You could just tell me so we can have it out before we leave. I'd prefer not to spend the ride guessing."

She'd crossed her arms and was no doubt presenting an obstinate mien, but she couldn't help it. Or rather she didn't care to.

The duke was grinning at her as he took a step closer.

"I apologize if I seem distracted. I didn't sleep well last night and am a bit slow this morning. I assure you there is nothing to *have out.*"

"Very well, then. Shall we go?"

"Aye. Let's." He was smiling fully now and even chuckled as he helped her into the carriage.

"What is so amusing, Your Grace?"

"Nothing," he said, though it was clear he was lying. He glanced over to Bess and Gia thought he might have shared his secret if her maid hadn't been present.

Whatever it was, she didn't need to know. So long as his mood was improved and he didn't plan to ruin her adventure, he could keep it to himself if he liked.

The duke spent most of the first day looking out the window as they traveled. Occasionally, he would join in on a conversation Gia was having with Bess.

Gia rather liked the way Hale spoke to her maid as he did anyone else. Gia had noticed the way some of the nobility wouldn't deign to speak to a servant. Hale, thankfully, didn't have this affliction.

They stopped at an inn for the evening and continued on early the next morning to arrive in Wiltshire.

Unlike the last time she'd attended the race at Salisbury, the day was beautiful. Just a few non-threatening clouds to break up the blue sky. She breathed in the fresh air after the weeks spent in the city and smiled at the familiar scents of hay and horses.

Unfortunately, she wasn't able to let the sun touch her face for more than a minute before Bess was shoving a parasol into her hands.

"What the devil am I—"

"You don't want to get freckles, miss," Bess was quick to interrupt.

She was sure she saw a smirk on Hale's lips for a moment, but it was gone too quickly for her to be certain.

Gia frowned and took the contraption while Bess went to enjoy the shade of a nearby tree. Her maid had no interest at all in the race and would most likely spend the afternoon knitting.

Owen frowned at her parasol but said nothing. Hale however, couldn't seem to help himself.

"You look quite the proper lady today, Miss Gia."

"Bollocks."

He was clearly laughing as they headed for the paddocks. There were groups of people standing back from where Dante paced, but Gia preferred to move closer to see her old friend better.

She came to a stop as close as was safe and felt Hale move to stand next to her. Just as she leaned over to tell him how much she missed her horse, the rider swatted Dante's rump with a crop.

Gia's mouth fell open as the horse slipped sideways on contact. It was a slight movement, but enough to distract him from winning a race if it went unchecked.

"Why ever would they use a crop on him? He needs no encouragement to run. It only serves to divert his attention." She leaned forward to speak to Owen across Hale's chest.

"His trainers don't know him as you did. They treat every horse the same and expect the same results," Owen said.

"That's ridiculous, they are as different as you and me," she snapped.

Hale chuckled. When she turned her attention to him, he smiled and explained.

"I was just thinking the two of you couldn't be more different."

Gia and Owen exchanged a look and Hale simply held up his hand brushing away his comment.

She was too distracted to think more on it. Something had to be done immediately. She handed Owen the silly parasol.

"Excuse me!" Gia shouted toward the man watching Dante's warm up. She called louder and earned his attention only briefly before he dismissed her.

"They won't listen to ye, lass," Owen said, his normal frown deeper than usual. "Even if it would guarantee them a win, they'll not consider the words of a woman. Let them lose. Then maybe you can buy back your horse at a discounted price." He growled as he fought to close the parasol.

"You know Dante gets depressed when he loses. I'll not have it."

She called out again and this time the man turned briefly to look at her as if she were a nuisance, then turned away again. Well, if that's how he wanted to play it, she could be an utter nuisance.

As she began removing her glove, Owen growled.

"Don't do it, lass."

"Do what?" Hale watched her curiously.

"There's nothing to come of it." Owen gave another warning just as Gia placed her thumb and middle finger at the edges of her mouth and gave three shrill whistles in a distinct measure.

At the sound, Dante stopped, reared back to toss the rider from his back, and trotted over to where she stood. He tossed his head once before placing the flat of his face against her chest.

"What just happened?" Hale asked.

"He's trained to come when I call. I didn't train him to toss a rider to do so, but I can't say that I blame him since the bastard was using a crop on him." She ran a hand down his smooth sable coat, comforting her friend.

The man who had dismissed her earlier, came over quickly.

"What is the meaning of this?"

"I see I have your attention now," she said as the man tried unsuccessfully to pull Dante away from her. "You're not getting the most speed from this horse."

"He's plenty fast to win."

"Against Loiterer? No, I'm afraid not. And before you ask me how I know, I cannot say, but I can see he's not running at peak performance."

"Miss Gia Landon?" The man gasped, his eyes gone wide.

The Jockey Club did not allow horses who were trained by women to compete, so the documents submitted all had Owen's name on them as trainer. But some people knew the truth.

"Yes."

The man's demeanor changed instantly and he bowed toward her, sparing a quick glance for the duke at her elbow.

"It is an honor."

"Thank you." She brushed off the silliness and got back to business. "Do you wish to have him perform at top speed for the race today?"

"Yes, of course."

"Then get rid of the crop. He doesn't like it. It is distracting him from doing what he was trained to do. Your rider need only guide him between his opponents. Dante will run as fast as he can if your rider loosens his grip on the reins and lets him have his head a bit."

The man called the disgruntled rider over who also changed his demeanor when he learned her identity. She had no idea she was so well-known and was concerned she put the horse at risk of being disqualified since she was a woman and, therefore, unable to train a horse.

She glanced at Hale feeling slightly embarrassed to find him beaming at her with pride.

She went through her instructions again with the rider. Owen added a few suggestions as well regarding Dante's starting response.

The men thanked her and offered Gia and her guests access to their box near the finish line to watch the race. Gia would have rather watched from the starting line, but Owen had been impressed with the offer and she didn't want to disappoint him.

"I should probably have stopped you from giving them advice on Dante, so I had a better chance of winning against him with Godspell at Epsom." Hale winked, most likely to let her know he was only teasing, but the gesture made her breath catch in her chest.

His blue eyes seemed to sparkle when he laughed and she felt the warmth of his gaze melt her insides. What was happening to her? It must have been the sun.

She shook the odd feeling away to concentrate on the horses being moved to the start.

"You'll have nothing to worry about. Once we're done with Godspell he'll be as fierce as his sire."

"I need him to be fiercer," Hale said with a smile as he nodded toward Loiterer. He was quite the contender. She would be interested to see how Dante did against him now.

She wondered what drove Hale to win so badly. Did he bet on the races? Money was a strong motivator. As with most things, Gia didn't hesitate to ask. Or was he just a stubborn Scot, like Owen?

"Why do you want to win?"

"Do you know anyone who prefers to lose?" He laughed off the question, but she waited, knowing he would explain if she was patient. After a moment, he answered.

"One of my best friends died last year. Ethan, that is the Earl of Ravenwood, he called each of us into his room in private. He made me promise to find my passion. At first, I agreed without any thought, but later I realized I had to honor my word. I began thinking of what my passion was. I'd always loved horses, and decided breeding, training, and racing horses was to be my passion. I purchased Godspell that next week and Hera the week after. When she delivers, I will have the first of my stock. And if Godspell wins his race, I will consider myself a success at finding the passion to honor my promise. So, he must be ready."

"He will be," she promised. "I won't let you down and you will not let down your friend."

"I have no doubt that when you set your mind to something you always succeed. You are truly amazing."

There it was again. The heat. The fluttering in her stomach. The sun had gone behind one of those puffy clouds so she couldn't blame it for her undoing.

She was so distracted by her strange reaction to the duke, she nearly missed the start of the race.

"Look at him go," Owen shouted. The only time the man ever smiled was when he was watching a horse run. It transformed his normal gruff exterior into something that made her laugh.

Gia shouted in encouragement for Dante, though none of the other women deigned to do such a thing as to show excitement. She didn't care, she was having too much fun to spare much thought for them.

Dante pulled ahead right away and she felt her stomach tighten when they lost sight of the group. All eyes on the grounds were straining toward the last rise to see who was in front. She squealed when she saw the cluster and knew Dante was in the lead and stayed there the duration of the race to win easily.

It was only after she'd had a moment to calm down that she looked down to see she'd gripped Hale's arm with both hands. She realized how close they were when she looked up to see him smiling down at her.

"My apologies. I got carried away," she said breathless with excitement. From the race or from his closeness, she wasn't certain.

"No apology necessary," he responded with another blasted wink.

"Don't do that."

"Do what?" he asked but turned away before she could answer.

He knew very well what he had done, and no doubt also knew what it had done to her senses. She would need to be on guard as to not turn into a simpering ninny around the man.

He was her friend and nothing more.

"Perhaps you're getting overheated. Should we have Owen bring your parasol."

"So I might beat you with the bloody thing?"

They shared another laugh and her damn heart fluttered yet again.

Chapter Eleven

"IT IS A pleasant change to see you so excited to attend a society function. Usually, I have to drag you to the carriage by your ear," Lydia said with a knowing smile as Gia's father helped them into the carriage that was headed for the Flanders Ball.

Gia would not give either of them the satisfaction of confirming she was excited. It wouldn't do to allow her father to believe his machinations had actually worked.

Besides, to do so would only get their hopes up. She didn't want them to think for a moment that she was in contention for winning a duke's affections.

The idea was impossible for many reasons. The biggest of which was that the duke was not interested in having affections for just one female. He was an admitted rogue, though he'd never acted as such around her.

Which led to the second biggest reason. He had yet to attempt to lure her to his bed. Obviously, he wasn't interested in her in that way.

She wasn't sure if she was relieved or disappointed by this.

A frown tugged at her lips. There was no sense in lying to herself. She was disappointed. But only slightly so. She shook her head at her rambling thoughts.

"I hope your eagerness is not because of the Duke of Roxburghe," her father said.

"We have become good friends. Why should I not be pleased to see him again?"

Neither her father or Lydia knew she'd attended the race in Wiltshire with the Duke, though Gia thought perhaps Lydia suspected. As far as her father knew, she'd gone with Owen as was normal and with Bess as a chaperone.

"My dear, the duke is a rogue. I don't expect you to know about such things, but it is well discussed in certain circles. I worry what a friendship with such a person will do to your reputation." Her father tended to believe she was still the naïve girl she'd been during her come out and while sometimes inconvenient, she generally kept up the ruse for her advantage.

She laughed. "He's been nothing but a gentleman when with me. I'm certain he saves any roguish proclivities for the women he shares an attraction with, not horse-mad spinsters."

There it was again. Disappointment. But she pressed a smile to her lips and held it there as her father continued.

"I only wanted to make you aware of the duke's reputation, and as you say, I don't think he will trouble you in that way. But if he did, you would know he is just like the other bounders chasing after you simply for physical satisfaction."

"Thank you, Papa." She wasn't able to keep the smile in place as she pressed her lips together to keep her emotions under control. His words had been spoken with concern for her wellbeing, but they had hurt.

Specifically, the part where the duke wouldn't want her for anything more than friendship or swiving. She wouldn't speak that last word out loud. Her father was not above punishing her for using "stable vocabulary" as he called it.

Lydia must have noticed the change in her demeanor and was quick to come to her defense.

"Harold, how dare you assume what the duke wants from his relationship with Gia. He has been nothing but respectful in my presence, and I've seen interest in his gaze when she is not looking. Even the most devious of rakes can be tamed when they find the person they want to spend their life with."

Her father looked between Gia and Lydia a few times before speaking.

"You are right, Lydia. I should be the last person to tell anyone not to befriend such a person, having been called a rake, myself, in my youth. But I thumbed my nose at society to marry Caterina—and have never regretted it a day of my life, mind you. I simply wanted you to have all of the facts, my dear daughter."

Her father had been a rogue and had fallen in love. It could happen.

The question was, did she want Hale to fall in love with her?

⁂

"I WAS INFORMED by my father that you are a rogue," Gia said as soon as they'd taken their positions on the dance floor for the first dance of the evening.

Hale didn't think he'd ever get used to the way the woman just blurted things out like that. Whatever was on her mind was spoken. At least to him.

He liked that she felt comfortable enough around him to be herself, shocking as it often was.

"I see." They'd already talked about this and Hale had confessed it to be true. She didn't have a question in her comment, she was simply telling him this information had come from her father.

Hale would miss her friendship, but her father must have realized the danger Hale presented to his very lovely daughter. He did his best to prepare for what was to come next. Her apologies for no longer being able to spend time with him. Her abandonment.

He should have been expecting it all along. She was a lovely woman and had no business paying her attentions to a scandalous rake. As exaggerated as the claims may be.

Besides, everyone left him eventually.

"I've told you as much myself," he reminded her.

"You did," she said as he swept her into a turn, hoping she'd drop the subject. He should have known better. "Though I'm having trouble believing it. You have seen the way men approach me. That is the way I expect a rogue to behave. However, you have never acted outside of the rules of propriety even once. Perhaps I am too conceited to think I could attract your attention in the way I have the others."

"If you're asking me if I find you attractive, I do. But before I had the chance to consider other behaviors, you spoke to me of horses, and I was forced to like you. Once I found that I liked you, I couldn't do anything to jeopardize that."

That was more truth than he'd planned to share, but it was out and she seemed to accept it easily.

He'd worked tirelessly in obtaining his reputation to scare off women of the *ton*. Gia was a woman of the *ton*. More importantly, she was a woman her companion and father hoped to marry off. Hale would do well to remember the danger such a relationship posed for him. Yet he couldn't stop from wanting to be around her.

She frowned. "I must admit, I'm not versed in the ways of being a rake, but I would expect you to have sexual relations with a lot of women."

"Don't say *sexual relations* so loudly." He glanced around them and only saw one gentleman lift a brow.

"Fine," she whispered. "Do you or do you not bed many women."

"I do not bed *many* women," he practically shouted which called the attention of more people than she had.

"You are not a rogue then. I was wrong when I initially made that assumption, and you didn't wish to correct me. My father has been misinformed." She settled her statement with a single nod.

"You were not wrong."

"Please explain. How could you be a rogue without sleeping with hordes of women?"

"Good lord, it has escalated from *a lot*, to *many*, to *hordes*." He shook his head at the absurdity of this conversation. And that they were having it in the middle of Flanders' ballroom.

"Which is it?" she pressed.

"A *few*. Possibly *some*. Maybe even *several* depending on the timeframe we're discussing. But not *a lot* and definitely not *hordes*."

"I don't think one warrants a reputation as a rogue for sleeping with merely *several* women at your advanced age."

"I am not even thirty, and…" She was too clever. He might as well come clean. "Very well, I may have allowed the actual quantity to be exaggerated."

She tilted her head as she studied him. He glanced away, embarrassed by his confession.

Gia laughed, almost snorted but she cut off the sound quickly, no doubt remembering that Lady Tomison would scold her for doing something so vulgar as to have fun at a ball.

"You have created your reputation to frighten off proper ladies, haven't you?" She was whispering again and had leaned closer. He felt her breath on his neck.

"Aye," he admitted with a grin.

"You are a *fogue*."

"Excuse me?" Was that some exotic animal that used a façade to hide from predators? If so, it was a most apt description.

"A faux rogue. A *fogue*."

He couldn't stop the loud bark of laughter that escaped, causing the other dancers to scowl at him. Forgive him for not exhibiting the proper look of boredom when in Gia's company. It was impossible to be bored when he was near her.

"You are too clever by half."

"Not as clever as you. You are bloody brilliant," she enthused, and he felt warm from her praise.

"I'm glad you approve." More than glad.

"Strange how I am in a similar situation—a reputation that is entirely untrue. Yet mine is unwanted while yours was purposeful. And my reputation doesn't seem to frighten men away. Perhaps only honorable men are deterred by my scandalous heritage."

"Have a care with my feelings, Gia." He chuckled at her inference he was dishonorable to want to spend time with her. Her cheeks turned a lovely shade of pink.

When their dance was over, he reluctantly returned her to her father and Lady Tomison then took a spot in the corner of the room where he could watch the other men who asked her to dance until it was his turn again.

Fortunately, he would be spared from watching her dance with his friends as they were not in attendance. Most likely because he had neglected to tell them he was coming.

He frowned as Lord Duncan led her into a dance with a smile. More unsettling was that Gia was smiling back at the man. Hale wished Lord Duncan had a reputation, faux or otherwise, so Hale might warn Gia away from him, but in truth the man would be considered a respectable suitor.

The look on Lady Tomison's face when Duncan returned Gia to her side confirmed it.

He watched Gia's face to see her reaction, hoping she might seem bored. Would it be too much to wish for a yawn? But there was nothing there but a polite smile.

Until the man laughed.

Damn the man for finding Gia as humorous and enchanting as he did.

After watching her dance with a few other men, he found himself eager to speak with her even though it had only been an hour since he'd last heard her voice. When the supper dance was announced, he made his way to her side to find her biting her bottom lip, concern clear in her warm brown eyes.

"What is it?" he asked, wanting to protect her from anything that caused her a moment of unhappiness.

"It appears our reputations have shifted slightly through the course of the evening."

He recalled the evening the gossips assumed he was seeking pleasures from Gia and that she was offering them freely.

"Oh? What is being said?"

"You may not want to stand too close or dance with me again."

He had been counting down the minutes until he could dance with her again. Not so much the dancing, but the privilege of holding her in his arms. No lewd whispers by the old crows of the *ton* would stop him.

"And why is that?"

"It appears the *ton* has the idea you are courting me."

It was not so surprising. His friends had warned him of such a possibility. For whatever reason, Hale had done nothing to dissuade such an insinuation. He wanted to tell himself it was because he was above caring about what these people thought. But the way his insides warmed by the misunderstanding that he was courting her, he was forced to look at another reason he hadn't taken their advisement more seriously.

Gia went on while he picked at his motives.

"I didn't think we were in danger of such a rumor, why would they think you would consider me for marriage?"

He turned to look at her more closely. She genuinely believed she was above or rather *under* the *ton's* notice. Did this thinking come from her father's perception of her, or her own?

She didn't say it as if she should be pitied for not being considered for a duke, but rather as if it were merely fact. The sky is blue, and no one would ever think he would be interested in her as his duchess.

If he were forced to marry, he would not find a more pleasing candidate. She might not be suited for hosting grand balls or soirees, but she would fill his home with laughter. She might not hold interests that conformed to acceptable *ton* activities, but Hale would never be in danger of boredom a day in his life with her by his side.

He found himself in the peculiar position of being in defense of Gia against herself. How did someone proceed in this situation?

"We have danced on more than one occasion. We go riding in the mornings. Someone might have seen us. Not to mention at Tattersall's or at Salisbury. Why do you think it is such a leap for them to assume we are courting?"

And more importantly, why did he suddenly wish they were?

CHAPTER TWELVE

GIA BLINKED AT Hale much in the same way her father had during his visit to Hale's home.

Was Hale the only person who could see the beauty she was? No. He knew for certain every man in London with a working penis had noticed as well.

"But we're not courting," she said.

"But to the casual bystander, would it not look that way?"

Her eyes went wide. "I hadn't considered. Please forgive me. I never meant for anyone to think that you would actually…" Her cheeks flushed and her eyes darted quickly around the room. "What should we do to put things right? I should leave you alone."

"No. Please don't leave me alone. You are the only thing keeping these events from being tedious." He watched her for a few more seconds, hating how she was distressed by this. "In truth, if I *were* looking to actually court someone, I would be hard-pressed to find anyone more lovely than you."

She looked back at him incredulously.

"Are you mad? Just against that wall alone are six young ladies who would be better suited for a duke. They've probably been training for such a thing since they slipped from their mother's womb. And if you needed any further proof I am not of the same caliber as them, I can guarantee none of them would be so gauche as to speak of such a thing as wombs at a ball."

He was laughing once again. "And that is the very reason why I find you so charming. You intrigue me. Every time you open your mouth, I have no idea what will come out, but I'm sure it will be vulgar or amusing. Generally, both."

"Are you suggesting you welcome this rumor that we are courting?"

"I can't say that I have an opinion. London is filled with gossip, half of which is not even close to the truth. I don't feel the need to correct anyone who thinks we're more than friends. As long as you and I are in understanding as to what our relationship is and isn't, then why should we care what the rest of the *ton* thinks?"

She let out a breath and visibly relaxed.

"I suppose you're right. I never care what they say about *me*. It's just that when they implicated you, I wished to spare you the embarrassment."

"I am not embarrassed to be your friend, Gia, and I do not appreciate that you think it is *my* reputation that is at risk here. You've met my other friends. They are far more of an embarrassment. Besides, as we've discussed, I am known to be a rake and a scoundrel. And don't forget a savage from Scotland. If anyone should worry about being seen with the other, it is *you* who should not want to be found in the shadow of my character."

"Are you angry?" she asked bending forward to look at him closer. He caught a whiff of something warm and inviting. Jasmine? Honey? Or just her?

"Aye. As a matter of fact, I am." Though he couldn't be sure why.

"Not because you've been caught up in a possible scandal, but because I am apologizing for it?"

"Yes." He answered before thinking, that was exactly it.

"That makes no sense."

"Just the same." He'd found recently that many of his feelings made no sense.

"I'm not sure if I should apologize for my apologizing or if doing so would just make you angrier."

She glanced at him and he could see the smile that played at the corner of her lips.

"You are utterly ridiculous," he said, not hiding his grin.

"Your Grace, I'm offended." She might have convinced him if she'd not been laughing.

Keeping up the charade, he took her hand in his and stared deep into her dark eyes.

"Forgive me, my lady."

She returned his gaze and shrugged.

"I would never hold a grudge against one of my dearest friends."

They had been teasing one another a moment ago, but he could tell she was sincere now. That she thought of him as her dearest friend warmed his heart.

He had friends. Ones so close he thought of them as brothers. But what he had with Gia was different. Easier somehow. Necessary.

He found he wanted to know her better. Not better. He wanted to know *everything*.

"Can we speak about something other than horses or scandals?" he asked as the song ended and he led her toward the dining room for supper.

"What else would one talk about *except* horses?" she answered.

Once again, she pulled a laugh from his rusty chest.

"I'll come up with something."

"You realize if the mamas think you are courting me, they will leave you alone and you no longer need your title of *fogue*."

He chuckled. "I believe I will make an excellent *fuiter* instead."

She giggled at his made-up word for a faux suiter.

"You are quite clever yourself, Your Grace."

THE NEXT MORNING, Gia dressed quickly and met a frowning Owen at Tattersall's where he waited with Arabella in a regular saddle and a palfrey named Rosey wearing a side saddle.

This had been their routine every morning so long as the weather was fit for riding, but this morning Owen was frowning more than usual.

"What is it? And be warned, if you plan to try to dissuade me from meeting the duke, I will not listen. He has confirmed he thinks of me as a dear friend, so riding with him is really no different than riding with you, whom I have always considered a friend. You even grumble and snort in the same Scottish manner so I can assure you it is no different."

Owen let out a grumpy sound and rolled his eyes.

"Of course, lass. It's quite clear you feel nothing but friendship for the duke. Nothing at all." There was more, but he mumbled it so low she couldn't hear what he said and didn't particularly want to.

Whether she thought more of the duke than friendship was of no import, for friendship was all he was offering and all she would ask for.

"Shall we?"

She climbed up on the silly saddle and pushed Rosey faster so she could get to Hale quicker.

He was waiting astride the tall stallion with a smile. He hopped down as she came closer.

"Please allow me to assist you down from this temperamental beast," he teased, but stepped back as she jumped down without any help.

It was amazing how well he'd come to know her in just a few weeks.

He did however assist her with the hooks of her riding habit to remove the skirts so she could ride in her buckskins. Moments ago, she'd assured Owen there was no difference between him and the duke, but the fumbling in Gia's fingers said otherwise. And the grumpy sound Owen made proved he knew it.

Arabella greeted her brother as she and Hale started out on a path. He would run Godspell later during his training. This morning was just for enjoyment and warming up.

As they rode, they laughed and taunted one another; too soon it was time to return.

"Will you be attending the Rochester ball this evening?" he asked casually.

She winced and shook her head. "No. Lydia is set on going to the Barnett musicale."

"And you do not like music?"

"I do like music. I just don't like sitting for long periods of time to listen to music," she explained. Even in the country, she and her father were often invited to performances at a neighboring estate.

It was truly horrible to be forced to sit for so long regardless of the skill of the performer. Gia preferred to be moving. It was probably the reason why she'd never taken to other activities suitable for a gently bred lady such as embroidery. Even reading, as much as she enjoyed it, was reserved for rainy days when she couldn't be outside.

Hale was still smiling at her with a grin that gave her a glimpse of the naughty boy he must have been in his youth.

"Then I shall come just so I can watch you squirm."

"You are the devil," she accused.

"As you'll recall, I've never claimed otherwise." He tipped his hat and rode away.

Without realizing it, she stood there smiling until she lost sight of the intriguing man. She was pulled from her gawking by a gruff voice from behind her.

"Ach, aye. 'Tis just friendship ye feel for the duke. Clear as day," Owen said with his bushy brow raised.

Gia whacked her surly groom in the arm, causing a rusty

laugh from the older man.

Was she actually looking forward to attending a musicale?

Apparently, she was.

⇥⟫⟫⟨⟨⇤

LATER THAT EVENING, Gia was still excited as she took her seat next to Lydia in their carriage.

"I know you're still cross with me for tricking you into coming to London, but at least I never forced you to sing in front of a large group of people." Her father nodded sagely as the carriage set off for the Barnett home where they were to be entertained that evening.

The mid-April evening was damp and chilly, and Gia had hoped it would dissuade Lydia from wanting to leave the warmth of the drawing room, but alas they were on their way.

As much as she disliked balls, at least one had the ability to move about as one pleased. They weren't expected to sit still for long lengths of time.

"I believe, father, the reason you've refrained from having me sing is more out of mercy for you and your friends since you know I can't sing."

He leaned over from where he sat in the rear-facing bench and patted her knee.

"I'm afraid you were given my singing voice rather than your dear mother's. Such a tragedy for her gift to have been lost. Instead, I have a child who sounds like a goose being plucked for stew when she sings."

"Papa," she feigned insult, though he wasn't wrong.

"Indeed," Lydia said in defense. "Everyone knows they do not pluck a goose while it's still alive."

"Thank you, Lydia," Gia offered flatly. Some defense that had been.

She didn't see Hale when they arrived, so she assumed he had thought the musicale the limit of their friendship. She couldn't blame him.

The music started up and she was forced to take her seat and be quiet. And sit still.

Quiet and stillness were not things she did exceedingly well. Many a governess had lost her temper when it came to the challenge of getting Gia to sit still for any length of time.

As an adult it should have been easier, but it wasn't. Now she could almost feel each second of her life drifting away. She was aging. Her life was passing by. And she would never get this time back. Time spent in agonizing stillness.

She might as well be dead for the life was being sucked from her with each note. Not that the nervous young lady singing was bad. In fact, she had a pleasant voice, but not pleasant enough to keep Gia from wanting to escape the room.

"Stop fidgeting," Lydia whispered.

"Was I?" Gia truly thought she'd been hiding her unrest well enough. Hopefully, Lydia was the only one who'd noticed.

She turned to look over her shoulder to ensure no one was watching her and locked gazes with the large man standing in the back of the room.

Hale.

He should have looked severe. His size and wash of tartan across his chest. But then he winked.

Instantly, she felt the peace his presence seemed to inspire, and she felt her face light up in a smile.

He smiled back. Not a grin or a smirk, but an actual smile offered just for her. She turned back to the front of the room when Lydia nudged her, but as she did, Gia realized this was no longer just a friendship.

Her heart was in danger.

HALE FELT HER gaze like a jolt of lightning and his body respond-ed in a way that was most inconvenient while in a room filled with other people watching a musicale.

For the first time since coming to London, he wished for a kilt to hide his reaction.

"Dear God, the girl is in love with you," Julian whispered louder than he should have.

There was so much wrong with the man's statement.

Firstly, and most importantly, she wasn't a girl. She was most definitely a woman. Secondly, she wasn't in love with Hale. She was smart, and he'd warned her of the dangers in getting attached to him.

He'd told her not to expect more than friendship from their arrangement. But the way her face lit up when their gazes met told of something more brewing between them that shouldn't be. *Couldn't* be.

It was clear she'd forgotten his warning.

Perhaps they'd both forgotten.

"Are you ready to go?" Hale asked his friend. Hale needed to retreat. He wasn't prepared for this battle.

"Ready to go?" Julian made a sound of indignation. "I dinna want to come here in the first place. You made me."

"Then we should be off. Let's go meet Kit and Graham at the club and maybe a gaming hell after that. We'll make a night of it."

Julian cast him a look as they left the house.

"You wish to stay out all night? But you'll miss your early morning ride with your dearest friend of whom you just ran away from as if she were the devil herself."

"I think it's for the best that I don't go riding tomorrow."

"Very well. Let's get you ripped so you don't notice how badly you are falling for that woman."

Hale opened his mouth to argue but knew there was no use. Not only would Julian never relent if he thought he was right, but...

Bloody hell, what if he was right?

IT TURNED OUT to be a very bad idea to go carousing with his friends. He felt like hell, and not just because his head pounded and his stomach roiled.

Feeling as though he was getting too close to Gia, he'd made sure he wouldn't be tempted to go riding with her that morning. He wouldn't allow himself to pull her into his arms and think things he shouldn't be thinking. Do things he shouldn't be doing.

He'd been the one who made it clear they were only friends. That neither of them could expect anything more from their relationship. He'd set the rules and she'd accepted them easily.

And now here he was thinking of her in a most unfriend-like way.

He didn't understand why he hadn't grown bored or found something she did an annoyance. Or just found himself distracted by something or someone else by now. It had been weeks and none of those things had happened.

Instead, he couldn't wait to see her.

Except he couldn't see her. Not until he got his head on straight.

Instead, he woke late and ended up in his study tending to his accounts, but soon he was staring out the window wondering if Gia was upset he hadn't joined her that morning. And wouldn't be visiting that afternoon. Perhaps he should have sent a note. But a note would make it seem as if he'd missed their meeting on purpose. Which he had.

He'd never worried over someone so much in his life.

He missed riding with her. Missed her smile. Her laugh. The way the sun gleamed off her dark glossy hair when it broke through the trees to start the day.

He missed her conversation and the things she blurted out that never ceased to surprise him.

He would miss their visit as well. Would miss all of his visits.

But this was the right thing to do before whatever this was in danger of becoming went too far. Before it was too late to save her.

To save himself.

It was near two o'clock in the afternoon when Hutchinson came into the study while Hale was resting his forehead on his arm contemplating what he should do.

"You have a visitor, Your Gra—"

"A visitor? Is it a woman?"

"Er, yes."

Before Hutch could finish, Hale jumped up and rushed for the drawing room where his butler would have put her.

The dark-haired beauty turned her head and Hale's stomach plummeted.

"My, don't you look disappointed."

"Lady Flemming, so wonderful to see you today."

The young widow had warmed his bed a number of times—not *a lot* or *many*, but a few. She had not been well attended by her former husband, and Hale had shown her how good bed sport could be with the right partner.

He thought briefly of how wonderful it would be to share that knowledge with a different woman and shook it off to show the lady who had come to visit the respect she deserved.

Lady Flemming was a welcome distraction. He knew why she had come. She only visited him when she required his *attentions*. He was always happy to oblige. Her timing today had been perfect. They would both get what they needed.

He gestured toward the corner of the room where a particularly comfortable settee awaited. But before he could close the door, he was interrupted by his butler.

"A message has arrived for you, Your Grace."

He had half a mind to send Hutchinson away without looking at it, but he'd seen his name on the note, and recognized the handwriting. It was from Gia.

He opened it so fast he risked a sprain.

Hale,

You must come right away. I have received something from America and you won't want to miss seeing it.

Your friend always,
G

He'd expected it to be an inquiry regarding his absence. Perhaps a serving of guilt for not coming to visit at his regular time. But instead, it was a simple invitation to share something she thought he would want to see.

Maybe not so simple, he could almost feel her excitement dripping from the parchment. It was happy news and she wanted him to be there for it. As a friend would.

And he was avoiding her. He would continue to do so until any unfriend-like feelings had been vanquished. But while he wasn't ready to see Gia, he also didn't want to fall back on his old ways either.

He glanced over at the woman who'd come to him for sex and knew he couldn't possibly go through with it.

"I'm afraid I've been called away. I'm sorry, Diana. I must go."

"Very well. Then I'll call on you again tomorrow."

She could, but he feared he wouldn't be in any better position to be with her the next day. He owed her the respect of ending their association properly.

"Actually, I must end our acquaintance. At least the physical portion of it."

She smiled.

"I had heard a rumor that your heart was otherwise engaged. I hadn't believed it when I was told who had captured your attentions. Miss Landon is lovely, but a bit of a hellion."

Diana was correct in one aspect. Gia was indeed a hellion, but his heart was not engaged. He wasn't quite sure he had one to engage.

"I assure you; it is not because of any feelings for anyone else that I must decline your offer. It is just a matter of my time and other duties that call for it."

She smiled but didn't argue further. He didn't care for the way she looked at him, as if she saw through his excuse. But he didn't care to argue with the woman.

Lady Flemming had barely left before Hale felt the need to leave the house. He needed air to clear his head. He set off on a brisk walk, not really paying attention to where he was going.

Before he realized it, he had arrived at Tomison House and had knocked on the door.

It had been his feet that took him there and his hand that had knocked. His *heart* had played no part whatsoever.

CHAPTER THIRTEEN

GIA HAD BEEN disappointed the night before when she'd realized Hale had left the musicale without her having a chance to speak to him.

This morning when he didn't meet her for their morning ride, she was left to assume something was truly wrong. Was he ill?

He'd seemed fit and hearty when he'd winked at her. The warmth of his smile had caused her to tingle in places she'd long ignored.

She wondered if he would come today.

If he wasn't ill, it could only mean he wished their friendship to come to an end.

It was sad really, but she understood. Men didn't want to marry as a rule. She didn't want to marry either, despite it looming as her father and Lydia attempted to guide her in that direction. And when or *if* the duke ever decided to take a wife, he would certainly pick someone more suitable than her.

She didn't know the first thing about being a duchess and truth be told, didn't care to. She only wanted a quiet life where she could spend her days with her horses. And if she wished to spend her nights with a certain man... she would keep those thoughts to herself.

Not even an hour had passed from the time she'd sent out the footman with her note that the duke arrived at Tomison House.

"I came right away," Hale said as Gia met him on the path from the house to the stables. "Luther said you were out here."

"Yes. It is so exciting. You won't believe it." She turned back toward the stables then stopped abruptly causing him to run into her. "I should have asked after your health. Are you well? You left the musicale early last night and didn't come riding this morning."

"Oh. Aye. I'm well. I... should have sent a note." He appeared unsure and she didn't know why.

"You surely don't need to account to me. I just wanted to be sure you weren't ill. It's not my business what kept you." Though she did wonder.

"Still, I told you I would see you at the musicale and then I dinna stay."

She shrugged and headed for the stables, not wanting to delve any deeper. It felt as if she had plucked at a thread and if she continued to tug at it, the whole garment might unravel. And it was her very favorite garment. "Wait until you see her."

"Her?"

"Yes. She only arrived this morning and I wanted you to be here." Hale was the only person besides Owen who would express the proper amount of excitement over the beast that was waiting in the stable. And excitement was not Owen's forte.

She hadn't realized she'd taken Hale's hand until she felt his warm fingers wrap around hers. It felt strange, but nice. Wonderful, actually. She released him to open the stable door.

With a bit of fanfare, Gia waved her hand gesturing toward the horse.

"She's beautiful," Hale said as soon as his gaze landed on Gia's new mare.

"A mustang from America." Gia pointed toward the brown and white spotted horse. Shorter than her Thoroughbreds and Arabians, the sturdy horse was somewhat wild or rather, without trust. Gia looked forward to winning the lass over with respect and kindness.

"She has spirit," Hale said next to her. "She rather reminds me of you."

Gia turned to Hale to find him smiling at her in a way she'd never seen before. She might have scolded him for comparing her to a horse, but she felt certain he'd meant it as a compliment.

She'd never seen him so at ease. And that smile. It was something that needed to be captured. She knew as soon as she was alone in her rooms, she would put it down on paper so she could remember this moment always.

"I got her on a trade. A man in Virginia wanted one of Goliath's sons to breed hearty workhorses. I sent him two stallions for her, and he paid to transport them all."

"You are a skilled negotiator." His smile hadn't dimmed one bit.

"What should I name her?" she asked to distract herself from the thought of moving her paintbrush to form the curve of his lips. It was a ridiculous notion. He was a friend and nothing more. She needed to remember that.

They shared an interest in horses and, yes, they'd shared some other information. But she would do herself no favors to develop a tendre for the man.

He could never be hers.

"Xandra is the goddess of adventure, and this lass must have had quite an adventure to arrive here, don't you think?" he suggested.

"That is beautiful." Gia turned back to the horse and held out her hand. "Welcome home, Xandra." With a few more tosses of her head to make her displeasure clear, the mare placed her nose briefly to Gia's hand before settling and turning away. It was a good start toward friendship.

"Thank you for giving me the honor of naming her," Hale whispered.

"If you'd picked something horrible, I would have only pretended to consider it," she admitted and they shared a laugh. He was standing just behind her and she could feel the heat of his body spread into her back as his breath touched her neck, sending a shiver through her.

"I have no doubt. I'm glad I didn't disappoint you."

"You rarely do."

This time when she looked at him, the smile was gone. As was the laughter. The look on his face held something quite different. Something she was unfamiliar with until the moment his gaze dropped to her lips for a heartbeat before returning to her eyes.

She remembered one of the younger grooms doing such a thing years ago, just before he'd kissed her.

Surely Hale didn't think to kiss her. She had most likely projected her own desires onto him. Just because she might want to kiss him did not mean he shared the same idea.

"I'm grateful you were able to come over so quickly before I'd named her something wretchedly unoriginal like Spot or Sally. You didn't have plans?"

He shook his head. "No. Nothing more interesting than answering your call."

He hid something in the way he pressed his lips together. A secret he would never share with her, even if she'd asked.

"Well, Xandra is grateful as well."

"I'm sure she is. Sally, indeed. How could you think to give such a majestic creature such a banal name?" He frowned. "Should we have some tea while she rests from her travels and you can tell me what you have planned for her?"

"Yes. Let's." They headed into the house as if nothing had ever happened.

It was best to move on and be content with what they had. Wanting more would be unwise and would only lead to disappointment.

HALE GAVE UP his plans to stay away from Gia almost immediately after seeing her on the path to the stable.

He realized it was a doomed effort, so he'd surrendered. At least for now.

But he knew he needed to be careful. He'd nearly kissed her in the stables there in front of her surly groom and a restless mustang from America.

Gia was a beautiful woman. He'd known as much already. However, it wasn't until she'd given him the honor of naming her new horse, that he saw what they might have together. A life filled with horses and laughter.

Until their happiness ended in anger and disgust and they were trapped with one another for the rest of their lives. No. He couldn't allow that to happen.

They were friends, but if he did not keep watch he could very well lose his heart. He had never fallen prey to such a thing before, but he was aware that caring for a woman he also found attractive were the very ingredients for disaster.

But he was not a coward. Hiding was not the way. He would hold control of his feelings and desires. Proving it meant staying with her when his instincts told him to run.

It was in this vein that he stood before her now requesting a dance.

"I'm afraid I only have one dance left and it's the supper dance." She seemed almost surprised as she held out the otherwise full card at her wrist.

"I will soon need to carry a stick to these affairs to keep the men away from you."

"I've also had numerous offers of escort to see the gardens." She frowned.

"Oh?" He had been joking a moment ago, but this was serious. Seeing the disappointment on her face made him livid enough to want to hunt down those undeserving swine and break their noses. "It is ridiculous that society does not allow a woman to reject an offer of a dance. Why do men bother to ask if a woman is at risk of being a prude if she turns him down? Why not just yank you onto the floor by your hair? It's nearly the same thing."

"Well, I believe the danger in that is all the sharp pins, Your Grace." She was smiling now and as glad as he was to have cheered her, he still wanted answers to his questions.

When he remained angry, she nudged him with her elbow.

"Don't worry. I'm well aware of what they really want. As I'm sure it wouldn't be five minutes before a tour of the gardens would find me in some shadowy corner being pawed at."

His hands clenched into fists at the very idea of someone touching her in that manner. The hypocrisy was not lost on him. How many nights had he spent thinking of the very thing with his own cock in his grip? He was no better than these rakes that feigned interest in polite company when contriving to get under her skirts.

It was a testament to her intelligence that she had yet to fall for such trickery.

"You are wise to be weary of a dashing smile and valiant propositions."

She frowned again and looked away.

"Of course. No one could actually be interested in more from me, Your Grace."

He'd never heard the honorific said with such unhappiness. He caressed her arm with his thumb, cursing the blasted gloves that kept him from feeling her skin.

He wanted to believe his touch was his attempt to soothe her prickled feelings, but the way his body tightened betrayed the truth. He simply wanted to touch her.

Clearing his throat he pushed away all thoughts of her warm, soft skin and focused.

"I did not mean it that way. They should want more. You're per—"

"If you'll excuse me," she cut him off. "The first of my fake suitors awaits."

With that she stormed off to grab the lanky man's arm and drag him to the dance floor.

She was well out of his hearing, but he finished what he'd been saying anyway.

"You, Gia Landon, are utterly perfect."

GIA SMILED AT Lord Rhinehart, and he smiled back. His prominent Adam's apple bobbed in his skinny throat. She didn't need to look up to see him as he was nearly the same height as her. She couldn't help but think of how she had to crane her neck to look at Hale.

This position was much easier on her posture.

Despite them being of the same height, she had noticed the man's gaze dip lower on more than one occasion as they fumbled about the dance floor.

The memory of Hale's lack of argument still burned in the back of her throat. That she was right to be cautious of anyone who would seek to be close to her. Because she had nothing to offer other than the possibility of physical pleasure. And upon finding that she wouldn't part with her virtue so easily every man would quickly pass her over.

She was aware not all of that was said aloud, but it was the spirit of the conversation, and he hadn't reassured her that perhaps some man might actually like her or want to marry her.

She knew why *he* might not be interested. But he assumed no man would want her. After all, she was not polished enough to run a home. She was not eloquent enough to host guests. She was not biddable enough to produce heirs on command. She was not perfect enough to be considered for the duty of wife.

But he was the one man who did know her and accepted the things about her she knew others found odd, but didn't consider her suitable for marriage to someone else either.

She'd thought maybe if these men knew the real her, they would see her as more than just an object to be trifled with and might actually care for her. But Hale was evidence that was untrue. He knew her better than anyone.

"I'm afraid I don't feel well," she said to her dance partner.

His beady eyes flared.

"Perhaps some air would restore you. I would be honored to escort you outside. We could stroll the gardens," he suggested.

She came down on his foot rather forcefully earning a satisfying yelp from Lord Rhinehart.

"Oh, dear. It appears you are unable to walk the distance to the gardens. I will leave you to tend to your injury."

She headed toward Lydia and her father. "I must go."

For once, Lydia didn't argue or protest. She simply looked at Gia and gave a curt nod. "Harold, please have them bring the carriage around."

Her father shot into action walking ahead of them.

She caught sight of Hale who watched in concern as she tugged Lydia along. Just as they made their way to the door, Hale managed to push his way through the crowd to cut them off in the foyer.

"Gia? What's wrong? You're pale."

"She doesn't feel well. Please excuse us," Lydia snapped and Gia was grateful for the way the countess kept Hale at a distance. It didn't stop the tears she'd been holding back from falling down her cheeks as she turned away from him and left the house.

She was being dramatic. She hadn't learned anything tonight she hadn't already known, but for once, Hale had made her feel worse about her situation instead of better. Knowing no one wanted to marry her was acceptable.

Knowing he didn't—while no real surprise—hurt her considerably.

Chapter Fourteen

Hale stood in the foyer minutes after Gia had left, unable to swallow. The pain he'd seen in her eyes had burrowed straight into his chest making it difficult to breathe. She'd been hurt to the point of tears and if he was not permitted to help her, he would seek vengeance instead.

Turning sharply, he made his way back into the overheated room and sought his prey limping off toward the back balcony.

The man was no sooner outside before Hale grabbed him by his scrawny arm and dragged him down the few stone steps that led to the dim garden.

"Ow." Lord Rhinehart yanked himself free of Hale's grip and stumbled to the ground, staining his fancy breeches.

"What did you say to her?" Hale demanded.

"Say?"

"To Miss Gia."

"I didn't say anything. She nearly maimed me though." He got up and brushed the grass from his clothing. "She said she was feeling ill. I offered to escort her outside to get some air. That is all, I swear it."

Exactly what every other cad had said to her. Their ruse to get her alone.

"Hear me and tell the other slimy bastards who think to escort Miss Gia to the gardens in the future. She is an innocent. A lady. Trifle with her at your peril."

"Slimy bastards? Do you mean like you?" For a man of such slim stature, Lord Rhinehart surprised Hale with his courage.

"Whatever I may or may not be is only of concern to you in as much as that I do not dally with innocent ladies. And you will cease trying to get Miss Gia alone in the gardens. Is that understood?"

"Or you'll call me out?" He chuckled. "For a half-Italian bit of mutton?"

Hale's fist flew before he'd consciously decided to hit the man. Rhinehart dropped like a stone, getting the other leg of his fancy breeches stained in the process. The man was beyond hearing, but Hale answered for his own benefit.

"Aye. I will call you out for her honor."

LYDIA CAME IN carrying a tray of chocolate.

"I thought you could use something warm to comfort you."

"Thank you." Gia took a sip and offered a smile before setting the cup aside.

"Do you wish to talk about it?" Lydia perched on the edge of Gia's bed waiting with a hopeful look on her face. The countess had gone out of her way to offer guidance, understanding, and friendship while Gia had been living in her home.

Gia shook her head and then nodded. As much as she didn't want to hurt again, she understood the importance of draining a wound of poison so it could heal.

"The men think I'm some wanton seductress because of who my mother was. My father told me of their courtship. I know it was rushed, but that was because they couldn't wait to be together."

"I know. People often confuse the reasons for marrying quickly. Either the couple has already presumed their vows and is in danger of an accelerated pregnancy, or the couple doesn't wish to presume their vows and is jumping at the bit to do so." She smiled. "In reality, it is only the most dispassionate marriages that make it through the banns."

Gia patted Lydia's hand knowing she spoke of her own nuptials and the passionless marriage she'd shared with her late husband.

"Your father and I are very close and while he would probably burst from embarrassment to have you know this, I think you should. Both of your parents were chaste when they went into their marriage."

"Truly?"

"Yes. They were very much in love and couldn't wait to share that love in a physical way. Thus, the speedy marriage."

Gia nodded. "That must be a wonderful feeling."

Lydia tilted her head to the side. "I believe Lord Rhinehart acted ungentlemanly this evening, but I don't think he has caused this deep pain. He's no one important enough to touch you this way."

Gia let out a breath. "It is ridiculous, but I think I have feelings for Hale. That is, the Duke of Roxburghe."

"Why is that ridiculous?"

"Because I know he doesn't wish to marry. I know he doesn't think of me as anything other than a friend. He may not be as much of a rogue as everyone expects, but I'm certain he seeks out only experienced women to take to his bed. Why would I expect him to want any more than friendship from our acquaintance? It's something a silly girl would hope for. I'm not silly and I'm not a girl. How could I have let this happen? I don't even want to marry."

She winced and squeezed Lydia's hand.

"I know you want that for me, but I am happy to be in the country with my horses. I don't wish for more than that."

"Are you certain?" Lydia asked.

"Yes." Gia tried to sound certain, but heard her voice waver.

The tears returned and Gia wrapped her arms around her

stomach to hold herself together.

"You seem to think we have a choice in who we allow into our hearts. And in many cases, you might even be right. We can put up walls to protect ourselves. We can keep certain people at a distance. But others... I think the people who are meant to be in our lives are impossible to hold back. They find all the weaknesses in our walls and simply stroll in. There is nothing to be done for it, but to hope they realize what an honor they have been given and love us back."

"He cannot."

"He might."

"He won't."

"We'll see." Lydia patted Gia's leg under the covers and smiled before standing. "Get some rest. I have a feeling he will be calling on you tomorrow."

Gia managed a fitful sleep. She was too tired to go riding in the morning. And she knew she was not ready to see Hale. If he even came.

She couldn't decide if she wanted to confront him or would rather hide away. She'd never been a coward before. She could face down the most irritable stallion with a calm hand. But Hale...

She didn't want this.

No. She didn't want to want this.

Throwing back the covers, she called for Bess to help her get ready for the day. The duke had done nothing wrong. He hadn't promised anything more than friendship.

He had not hurt her. She had allowed herself to be hurt. He was not to be punished.

By the time she was ready, she felt strong enough to handle her reaction to him if he were to visit. She decided somewhere between the tightening of her corset and the restraining of her hair, that she wasn't willing to lose Hale as a friend because she was too weak to accept what he was willing to offer. He was the best friend she'd ever had and she wouldn't want anything more.

THE DRAWING ROOM at Tomison House was overflowing with men and the sweet, cloying scent of dozens of flowers with rivaling fragrances.

What the devil was all of this?

It was one thing for these men to attempt to lure Gia from the ballroom to the gardens, but to go to the next step of calling on her? It was too much.

Lord Duncan was sitting entirely too close to Gia on the settee. Why was Lady Tomison allowing such a thing?

"Good day, Your Grace." Lady Tomison noticed him by the door and offered a rather stiff welcome.

"Good day, ladies." He moved to come closer, but it was no use, the seats in the room were all filled and no one seemed willing to budge. Not even for a duke.

He generally wasn't one to use his title to intimidate others, but in this case he couldn't resist. Not if it meant having Gia to himself.

"If you'll excuse us gentlemen?" He didn't try to disguise his brogue as he cast a look about the room that would not be tested. He was only grateful he was of the highest rank or he might not have been successful at clearing the room as effectively.

Fortunately, it only took a few minutes for them all to get to their feet, pay their final wishes to see Gia at a future event, and leave. When they were gone, he took a seat in front of her, fighting the desire to reach for her hands. To reassure her of something he couldn't name. But whatever this unease was he felt coming from her, he wanted to vanquish it immediately.

"Are you well? You weren't in the park this morning. I do believe Godspell was put out," he said as Lady Tomison rolled her eyes in a most unladylike fashion before she rose and left the room. Leaving them alone.

It wasn't uncommon. Since the first day he'd come to

Tomison house, they'd been left alone often. The door always open enough to hint at propriety. He didn't know whether to be grateful, or to be offended that he was not considered a threat to Gia's reputation.

And didn't that conflicting thought sum up his feelings for Gia perfectly?

"I am fine. I was just not up for a ride this morning," she said.

"I see." He sat straighter and looked her over. Had he inadvertently stumbled into some female situation?

She chuckled. "You look as if you are about to bolt for the door."

He shook his head at his idiocy.

"I only just realized there could be a reason you are unhappy that is not quite illness." What had he just said? He'd spent too much time with Gia if his thoughts were to start blurting out of him unfiltered.

She smiled and leaned closer to whisper.

"Do you wish to talk about a woman's courses, Your Grace?"

"Good God, no." He rubbed at his temples. "Unless you wish to—bloody hell." He winced and shifted uncomfortably. Why was the room so blazing hot?

She was nearly to the point of falling from her chair and losing her breath she was laughing so hard.

"Ungrateful witch," he said as he gave her a playful shove before he broke out laughing with her. "I was going to make an attempt to speak of it if you needed to, but forget it now."

"I'm sorry. I do appreciate it. But it is unnecessary."

He gave a curt nod. And they sat in silence for a moment.

"You've become quite popular," he noted, looking toward the door her suitors had left through.

She dismissed his comment with a wave of her hand.

"They will lose interest soon enough when they don't get what they want. I could save them all a bit of time if it wasn't impertinent to do so."

In a very Gia-like gesture she shrugged.

He looked away remembering his impertinent conversation with Lord Rhinehart the evening before.

"As you say, I'm sure they will find out the truth of things soon enough."

"And what is the truth?" she asked.

"That you're too good for all of them."

She blinked. "Do you truly think so?"

"Of course. You're too good for me as well, but fortunately we share a madness for horses and you permit me to exacerbate your condition."

"I do." She smiled.

He felt whatever unease he'd noticed between them fade away in that moment. He had his friend back. He wasn't certain how long he'd be able to maintain this relationship, but he'd never felt the need for something—or someone—more in his life.

CHAPTER FIFTEEN

G IA AND HALE shared sandwiches and went over Godspell's feeding schedule and training regimen. The tension that had sizzled between her and Hale over the last few days had eased. And Godspell was coming along nicely in his training which gave them something else to focus on.

"I think he'll be ready for Epsom. I believe he has a chance to win," she said.

"If he does, it will be solely because of you. Both what you did with him in the past and what you've done now."

She smiled at his praise.

"I love working with them. Seeing them thrive. I imagine it would be similar to watching a child take their first steps."

A shadow came over Hale's face. He did his best to cover it with a smile, but she knew him well enough to know she'd said something that gave him pause.

"What did I say?" she asked. Without thinking she reached out and rested her hand on his arm. It was meant to comfort him, but as soon as they touched, she felt something quite different from comfort. Yet, she didn't withdraw her hand.

He looked down to where her touch lingered, and then up into her eyes, his gaze heated.

She swallowed and stared back at him, unable to look away or move.

Except she had moved. She'd leaned closer to him. And he'd

leaned closer to her.

She waited for something to happen. Something wonderful.

Footsteps in the hall outside the door startled them free of whatever snare they'd been caught in.

He pulled back, dislodging her hand and clearing his throat before answering her question.

"'Tis nothing."

She tilted her head to the side, still rather stunned, and decided whether it would be best to back off or pry.

Needing a distraction, she chose the latter.

"You've never mentioned your parents. From things you've said, it didn't sound as if you had an easy childhood."

"It's obvious by my title that my father is dead. That is the end of the story."

"Do you miss him?" she pushed when it was clear he didn't want to speak of his family. A proper lady wouldn't have pushed the issue, but it was quite clear to anyone who knew her, she wasn't a proper lady.

He shook his head. "We don't need to discuss this."

"I know. But I want to know."

"There is nothing to know. My parents married because they were expected to. It was no love match, in fact from what I understand they hated each other immensely. I never saw them together. I interacted with my mother a handful of times and met my father only twice. I was merely the result of them performing their duties successfully and nothing more. They spent all their time with other people. I was an heir left to the wilds of Scotland. Never a son."

"I'm sorry."

"Don't be. It's not as if I lost something I once had. I never had it to begin with so—"

"I don't believe for one moment it matters. I miss my mother every day, yet I don't remember her."

"Your father kept her alive for you in memories. You miss her because you know she would have loved you and you missed that opportunity. I have no such memories to hold onto or anyone to tell me of them. My father loved pleasure and took it from anyone willing to give it. My mother was filled with anger and jealousy for the love she could never have and sought to drown her pain in drink and took lovers in an attempt to replace what she'd lost. They were never anything to me other than these few facts."

"A child deserves to be loved by at least one parent if it can't be both."

"Love is unrealistic, unattainable, untrustworthy, and unbelievable."

"My, that is quite a lot of words beginning with *un* stuffed into one sentence." Her joke to lighten the moment worked. She was too close to telling him the truth about love.

That it came unsolicited while one was unprepared and was both unfathomable and unwilling to relent. It seemed she had her fair share of *un* words to describe the feeling as well.

⇥⇥⇥✕⇤⇤⇤

IT WAS RAINING the next morning and Gia sent a note she wouldn't be going to ride. After not seeing her the night before, or that morning, he was barely able to wait until visiting hours before taking the steps at Tomison House two at a time to knock on the door.

He was greeted by Luther, Lady Tomison's pleasant butler, but Hale was not shown into the drawing room.

"Miss Gia is not at home for visitors today, Your Grace."

"Is she unwell?"

"I believe she grew a sensitivity to the flowers presented by the hapless fops who feign an interest, Your Grace. But I see you have not brought any offending blooms with you so I can tell you, she's in the back garden painting."

"Thank you, Luther." Hale smiled as he made his way

through the house as if he was part of the household. Over the last several weeks, it had seemed as much.

The butler's description of Gia's ailment might have been more believable if the woman wasn't currently in the garden surrounded by flowers.

Hale was pleased he had been given access when others had not.

He stopped when he saw her sitting on a bench with her easel propped in front of her. She had her back to him and hadn't heard him approach so he was able to stand there and watch her paint.

Her hair was pulled up on her head in a messy knot that suited her despite its inability to hold all of her hair in place. A few tendrils had fallen free and curled gently against her elegant neck that was bent toward her work.

Her hand gripped a brush that moved effortlessly over the thick paper where the shape of a horse came into focus. If he were to guess, he would say she was painting Xandra. Simply because it was the only horse she hadn't yet recorded in her art.

He found he couldn't wait to see it when she finished. He knew she would capture every subtle characteristic of the mustang in meticulous detail.

He took in the smock she wore that hid the shape of her body while protecting her clothes.

He knew that when she eventually noticed him, she would offer a smile filled with everything he'd searched for and never found. Companionship, acceptance, and comfort.

Knowing what awaited him, he took a step toward her. Hearing him, she turned. She had a bit of brown paint on her cheek and a smear of blue in her hair.

And then she smiled and he was unable to categorize anything else.

"Lovely," he said.

Her smile grew and she shook her head.

"I've barely even started." She thought he'd been speaking of the painting, and after hearing his thought spoken out loud, he went along with her misconception.

"I'm sure it will be lovely. Your paintings always are." That was true enough. He pulled out the copy of the book he'd purchased for her.

"The General Stud Book, by James Weatherby? You got it!" Gia exclaimed and fairly ripped it from his fingers.

"I did." He'd gladly spend his entire life earning her smiles if given the opportunity. The thought should have sent him running, but he was too lost in the moment to be frightened.

⟫⟫⟫⟪⟪⟪

GIA EXCITEDLY FLIPPED through the book Hale had brought, looking for one of her horses to be documented within its pages. She found Dante right away and may have squealed in a rather feminine fashion.

Hale didn't seem to mind as he watched her with a grin of satisfaction on his face.

"Look. Dante has multiple pages," she said, flipping through.

"I would say so. He is a most noteworthy racehorse."

"Except, they have this wrong." She pointed to the information.

"I'm sure they check and double-check everything before printing."

Was he doubting her? She raised an eyebrow and he chuckled before recanting.

"I'm sure you are correct. What do they have wrong?" He leaned closer and she caught a whiff of his scent which had become as familiar to her as her own. Leather, sunshine, and the sweetness of hay. He'd gone riding that morning without her. Had he missed her company?

"The description," she said, focusing on the book once more. "I'm sure he has a white sock on his front foot not his back."

"Well, you can verify it easily enough." He waved toward the door and she knew right away he was referring to her other paintings.

"You're quite right."

"As I generally am," he said in a lazy way befitting a duke. Only she knew him well enough to know he wasn't as arrogant as he pretended to be. She was fortunate enough to know the real Hale.

She didn't address his comment, instead, she entered the drawing room from the terrace and went to the door to call for Luther. She asked him to get her paintings from Bess and bring them down for her, then thanked him as he left for the stairs.

Hale had followed her inside and sat by the table to wait with her.

It was only a few minutes longer before the stack arrived and they were sorting through the paintings. Each of them focusing on their own pile seeking for the page with Dante's image.

"Oh," Hale said in surprise.

She looked up to see a grin pulling up both corners of his mouth. His dimple popped out and she was unable to look away. At least until he spoke again.

"I thought you said you reserve your talent for painting magnificent creatures?"

"That's right." She tilted her head to the side waiting for him to make a joke.

When he turned the painting toward her, she felt her breath catch at the same time her whole body went hot then cold. It couldn't be. She hadn't had that painting with the others. At least she hadn't thought so. Had she tucked it away when Bess came into the room so her maid wouldn't see it?

Had she forgotten it was there? Bollocks.

Obviously, something had gone wrong because Hale was holding a drawing of himself. Not just himself, but himself smiling at the artist the way he had the day Xandra had arrived.

"I can explain," she said on instinct, though there was really not an explanation that would keep her from dying of embarrassment.

Best just to go with the truth then.

"I did this after Xandra arrived. You were so happy that day. I had never seen you smile like that before, and I thought it would be a good idea to capture your... exuberance, since I'm sure it doesn't happen often."

"Exuberance?" he said with a laugh. "I don't recall being overcome with such an emotion."

"But you were happy. Happy to see her, that is. And it's not every day that you will happen across a breed of horse you've not met before."

She stood and began pacing as her mind flitted from thought to thought, desperately trying to get herself out of this awkward situation and put them back to rights.

If he thought for a moment she had feelings for him, he would surely end their friendship immediately. And she would...

She would very possibly fall to pieces.

She handled skittish horses all the time, but Hale was beyond skittish.

Despite his strength and sturdiness, he'd been broken and not put back together to heal properly. In fact, he was so damaged and in so much pain, if he were a horse, she would have had to have him put down to spare him.

She closed her eyes. She couldn't say any of that. Obviously.

"It is nothing really. In fact, I was going to give it to you. I'm glad it was brought with the others." She would paint another one for herself later that day and make sure it was kept some-where safe. He would never know.

"So, it is a gift? For me?" He raised his brow in challenge. She would need to lie and she was horrible at it. Especially with him.

"Yes." There it was, impossible to decipher a lie from a single word. Wasn't it? Perhaps it would have worked, but instead of waiting to see the result of her subterfuge, more words poured from her lips. "I didn't paint it for myself. It's not like I'm besotted or smitten with you."

He stood and came closer. Why were her legs shaking? For once she was glad to be wearing a dress so no one could see.

He stared at her for a full minute, his eyes darkened as he stood unmoving. She felt as if he could see right into her soul.

If so, he would know. He would see how she felt and then he would tell her it couldn't be that way between them. As if she didn't already know.

She waited, as immobilized as a rabbit locked in the gaze of a wolf. If she remained still, it would be fine. He would move on and she would live another day.

"Perhaps," he said, his voice low and rough. "It wouldna be such a bad thing if you were smitten. Just a wee bit."

Her lips opened on a gasp a second before his mouth came down on hers. With her lips still parted, it was an easy thing for him to slip his warm tongue into her mouth.

She was swept away by heat and emotion. Her fingers clenched and she realized her hands were filled with his silky blond hair. He moaned—not in pain but approval—and she pressed closer.

Or would have pressed closer if there had been any space left between them. His arms had already wound around her body and pulled her to him tightly. There was no room to breathe or even for her heart to beat without him feeling it.

And yet, as close as he was and as much as she felt, she somehow still wanted… more.

As if hearing what she craved and deciding to do the exact opposite, Hale pulled away from her, leaving her chilled and bewildered. Then he seemed to decide it wasn't yet far enough so he pushed her to arm's length.

He stood before her with wide eyes, his chest heaving.

He'd never been more beautiful. But she knew even before he spoke that she'd just ruined everything.

CHAPTER SIXTEEN

HALE WAS SURPRISED by the strength it took to pull himself from Gia. He'd known from the moment their lips touched how wrong it was.

Perhaps not the *very* moment.

Indeed, for a full second—perhaps two—he may have even been swept away in the rightness of how wonderful she felt against him. But definitely by the third or maybe the fourth second, he had realized.

He was no better than the men who had filled her parlor the day before.

They'd wanted her body and had no intention of marrying her afterward. Or more importantly, *before* they touched her.

He had warned her. She well knew his reputation. Her chaperone had thought he wouldn't take advantage of their friendship. What an error that had been.

Shame twisted his stomach. Was he any better than his parents who had taken what they'd wanted for their pleasure without a care of who they hurt?

"I'm sorry," she said quietly. Her warm brown eyes filled with fear, and her shoulders had pulled in as if preparing for the weight of his rejection.

Any emotion besides the one he grasped onto would have been better. But anger for himself and for whomever had rejected her in her past fired through him.

"You have nothing to apologize for. This was all my doing," he snapped harshly and ran a hand through his hair, remembering the way it had felt when her hands had been gripping his locks moments ago. She'd held him too tightly. Pain to the point of pleasure.

The pain in his trousers offered no pleasure where he still throbbed for her.

Had he allowed the kiss to go on much longer, he might not have stopped until the discomfort had been sated. It was clear, she had no intention of stopping him. She would have let him do what he'd wanted.

She would have let him ruin her. Because she thought him a friend. Because she thought he cared about her. Because she trusted him.

He'd thought she could trust him.

He was horribly mistaken.

This was not how a friend behaved.

⊁⟫⟩✦⟨⟪⊰

GIA SLUMPED TO the nearest chair when Hale left the room. She knew he wasn't angry at her, but what did it matter if the end result was the same?

She'd kissed him and ruined everything.

Picking up the painting of him, she took in a shaky breath. The difference between the smiling image in her hands and the man who'd fled after whispering an agonized "Forgive me" were incomprehensible.

She'd known her feelings for him had grown beyond friendship. And she'd known she'd needed to keep those feelings restrained so she wouldn't lose him.

Her fingers brushed over her lips that still tingled from his kiss.

Yes, she'd painted him. But he'd smiled rather than been

appalled.

Yes, she'd offered a flimsy excuse. But he'd offered a flirtatious retort. Even encouraging her to cross the line from friendship to more.

Yes, she'd kissed him. But it was he who had kissed her first.

It was his tongue that had reached for hers.

It was his hands that had explored her body.

And it was his feet that had walked out the door.

They'd been equal. Both wanting what the other was so willing to give. But what was she to do now?

Over the next week, things went back to normal for the most part.

That is, the way they'd been before she'd met the Duke of Roxburghe.

Gia went riding in Hyde Park alone. She spent her days painting until visiting hours when she entertained the few remaining men who flirted and attempted to get her alone for this reason or that. She expected their attentions would wane soon enough when they finally realized she wasn't interested in an affair.

She worked with Xandra, building the mare's trust. She'd even managed to encourage the mare into a bridle while making sure it came off as Xandra's own idea.

When the horse had walked with the lead without throwing her head or stomping, Gia had been most pleased. Until she'd looked over to share the moment with Hale and remembered he wasn't there.

But this was how she'd wanted things. Just her and her horses.

She didn't wish to marry. Not that Hale would be a candidate for her husband. He was merely a distraction.

He'd kissed her and moved on. In the end, he was no better than the other men attempting to lure her to seduction. He'd simply grown weary of the game after a kiss.

She'd mistakenly allowed such liberties and might have allowed a few others if he'd not had at least enough honor to stop them. She shook her head. It was likely the risk of being caught in the drawing room and forced into marriage, rather than honor.

After all, he was a rogue. Less *rogue* than she'd originally thought. Had that been part of his ruse?

She should have known better than to trust him. But despite knowing their separation was for the best, a large part of her still missed him.

He wasn't at any of the entertainments she attended. She had stopped looking for him after the second ball, knowing he was avoiding her.

She thought she might have seen him when she'd visited the training paddocks, but if he was there, he managed to stay out of view.

Determined to move on, she'd attempted to engage the other men she danced with in actual conversation.

Casting off discussions of the weather as Lydia had instructed, Gia smiled up at Lord Peterson. After he finished telling her how skilled he was on a hunt, she interjected.

"Do you have many horses?" she asked.

"Horses? Yes, of course." His brows pulled together in confusion.

"Do you only have hunters or do you have racehorses as well?"

It was only when his confusion turned to surprise that Gia considered that perhaps Lord Peterson wasn't speaking of an actual hunt when he'd mentioned the heat of the chase. His gaze flared anew.

"Do you wish to play the lady at the race? Will you drop your handkerchief and I will retrieve it for you and you shall reward my chivalry when you visit me in the stables?"

"Oh. Uh—"

"Should I go now and wait for you in the mews?"

Gia nearly fell over as the man abruptly stopped the dance and walked away.

"Wherever did Lord Peterson go?" Lydia asked when Gia

returned to her side.

"He had an urgent matter to attend to," Gia explained with a frown. There was no way she could explain the man's behavior to Lydia.

She tried again to talk of her love of horses with the other men she danced with. While those conversations didn't end with a proposition in the stables, they certainly didn't end in friendship either. In fact, none of the men cared much for horses outside of exulting over their pedigrees. They all preferred to turn over their care to their grooms rather than be involved themselves.

Gia could only assume they would be equally discerning when selecting a wife and show equal care of them once acquired. Which was to say, none at all.

She once again returned to Lydia's side with a frown and a shake of her head.

"Might I have your next dance, Miss Landon?"

Gia smiled at Lord Duncan. While the man didn't make her pulse quicken, he was a steady man who had yet to propose anything indecent.

"Thank you, my lord."

On the dance floor, Gia tried once again to engage in conversation regarding her interests with a potential suitor.

"Do you have many horses, my lord?"

He seemed surprised for a moment, but then answered. "Why, yes. I enjoy riding immensely though I prefer to do so in the country rather than here in the park."

"And what of racing?"

Again, his eyes showed his surprise.

"I do not wager large sums on horses, if that is what you are asking."

"No. I enjoy taking in the races. I only wondered if you did as well."

He smiled. "Yes, in fact, I do."

While she enjoyed their conversation, Gia didn't feel at ease enough to tell Lord Duncan of her hobby of training racehorses.

She didn't think he would approve.

He returned her to Lydia and went on his way. She could not say she was sorry to see him go. He was pleasant enough, but there was something missing.

Or maybe it was just that he wasn't Hale.

The worst of it was that neither her father or Lydia even acted surprised that Hale had stopped calling on Gia. As if it was expected that she'd have scared him off at some point.

They were joined a little while later by Lady Archer and Lady Foxley. The odious pair shared a bit of gossip with Lydia who smiled politely, but did nothing to encourage them to continue.

Gia hoped the women would grow bored with Lydia's lack of excitement, but instead they shifted their gaze to her.

"You'll certainly be a late riser tomorrow, after all of the dancing you've done this evening, Miss Gia."

Gia wasn't sure what reaction was expected from this comment, so she simply followed Lydia's cue and smiled politely.

"I do wonder where the Duke of Roxburghe has been of late. The two of you cut a fine line on the dance floor earlier in the Season. I thought perhaps you would bring him up to scratch."

"Perhaps His Grace has already gotten what he wanted from the Season and is content to turn his attentions to other things," Lady Archer said with a tilt to her head.

Lady Foxley's brows rose in speculation while Lady Archer smiled dangerously. "Indeed."

Gia opened her mouth to say… something. She wasn't certain what exactly she would say, but surely, she should refute their veiled insinuations that Hale had had his way with her and moved on.

But the truth seemed worse. She'd kissed him and scared him off. No, that would do no good.

Lydia squared her shoulders and came to Gia's rescue.

"I believe the duke mentioned something about being bored at events attended by ruthless, old crows."

Bravo, Lydia.

The two women frowned and walked away as Lydia muttered under her breath. Gia wasn't able to hear everything she said, but some words were clearer. Mostly curses.

"I'm sorry. I didn't realize people would jump to that conclusion."

"Not everyone would. Just the gossipmongers. It's been a light season for scandal thus far, they are desperate for anything to spice up their dreary lives. Pay no mind to them, Gia. They are not worth your concern."

"Thank you for defending me. I wasn't sure what to say that wouldn't make it worse."

"It's best not to say anything. I should have remained silent rather than bait them, but I couldn't hold my tongue. I'm sure I shall be punished for engaging with them, but it was worth it."

She gave Gia's arm a consoling pat.

"When and if you wish to talk about the real reason the duke is no longer visiting or attending events, I will listen without judgement."

"I don't want my father involved."

"So long as the duke has done nothing dishonorable, I will keep it in confidence. But if he has done what those awful women have assumed, he needs to do the honorable thing."

"It is nothing so dire as that. He was only flirting with me, and I got carried away in the moment and his smile and I… Well, I kissed him. I thought it was wonderful, he apologized and left the house. I haven't seen him since. Do you think the kiss could have been that horrible? I didn't bite him. No blood was shed. How bad could it have been?"

Lydia offered a sympathetic smile and shook her head.

"I would guess the kiss was so good it has shaken his world, and he is feeling unsteady on his feet."

Gia couldn't help but roll her eyes at Lydia's ridiculous claim. She'd hoped the woman would prove honest enough to guide her in the steps Gia should take to get Hale to speak to her again and repair their friendship. But it seemed Lydia planned to take after

Gia's father in offering empty platitudes.

As if Gia was such an excellent kisser the duke was overwhelmed by her skill.

"Pfft."

"We don't make those noises when out in society," Lydia reminded her.

"Then you shouldn't say things to warrant such sounds."

That evening after she was settled in her bed, Gia thought of the kiss as she had every evening since it had happened.

In her mind, it seemed quite lovely. Better than the two other kisses she'd had hence. Those other boys had bumbled their way through it, while Hale was a man and handled the exchange with skill and confidence.

She decided maybe she did want to speak to Lydia about it. The woman had been married. Certainly, she knew a good kiss from a terrible one. Gia wrapped her dressing gown around her and padded down the hall toward Lydia's room.

Lifting her hand to knock, she jumped back from the door when she heard a man's voice from within. Not any man, either. It was her father.

She couldn't make out his words, but she knew the rumble of his voice well enough.

Whatever he'd said must have been amusing because Lydia giggled.

Giggled? The woman was rarely prone to smiling let alone giggling.

"Oh, God." Gia froze as all the droplets of information collected to form a deluge of evidence. Turning, she hurried back to her room as fast as her bare feet would allow her to go and only when she was inside, safely behind her closed door, did she contemplate what had just occurred.

She ran through a number of emotions. Revulsion being first and foremost. Her father was in Lydia's bedchamber. And the woman was *giggling*.

But as Gia managed to put the memory of the giggling to the

side, she considered that her father was a charming, handsome man and Lydia was an elegant, beautiful woman. They had been friends for a long time. An attraction seemed expected.

By the time she finally settled back in her bed she found she was happy for them. So long as she never needed to think about the giggling again.

Ever.

CHAPTER SEVENTEEN

Hale spent most of his time working with Godspell. He'd decided to put him in the Newmarket race even though he wasn't completely ready, it would be a good test to see where he was so far.

He'd thought of reaching out to Gia for her opinion several times, but then he remembered he couldn't. *Shouldn't.*

He wasn't hiding in an attempt to avoid speaking of their kiss. He was staying away out of concern for her. He'd never been so swept away by a kiss before and he worried if he was with her, he might kiss her again without any care as to where they were or who might see.

He needed to make sure it was safe before he put himself in that situation. Until then… well… he was hiding after all.

Rather than stay in town and wish he could see her, he would be leaving the next day to journey to Suffolk for the race.

He did wonder if she might be there. The possibility made his blood race.

He had only settled in his study a few minutes when he was interrupted by his butler.

"You have a caller, Your Grace," Hutchinson announced while Hale was reviewing his estate books for the third time that week. Everything was in order, but he needed the distraction and one couldn't be too careful when leaving for a few days.

"I put her in the parlor."

Her? Hale's heart was pounding. He wanted it to be Gia. No doubt if she was calling it was to give him a piece of her mind and he would accept it gladly as deserved. But he didn't move toward the door.

If it was Gia, he would send her away. He would tell Hutchinson to make an excuse. He feared seeing her again would churn up all the feelings and desires he'd worked so hard to control. Or attempt to.

"Who is calling?" he managed to ask.

"Pardon, Your Grace, it is Lady Tomison."

Lady Tomison? Perhaps Gia was ill or worse, and Lydia had come to give him the grave news.

"Is she wearing black?" he whispered.

"Black? No, Your Grace. I believe she is wearing a green frock today." If Hutchinson thought it an odd question, he didn't show it.

"I'll see her." If for no other reason than curiosity.

He paused long enough to take a breath before entering the room with a smile fixed upon his face that he hoped looked sincere. Not that he didn't like Lady Tomison.

She didn't hover when he visited Gia. However, had she been a more attentive chaperone, that kiss with Gia would not have happened.

"Good day, my lady. How wonderful of you to call. May I ring for refreshment? Tea?"

"No, thank you, Your Grace." She looked rather irritated. He was certain she would not be irritated if Gia were ill or injured and he breathed easier knowing that she was alright.

"Then how may I help you today?" He gestured toward the settee and she looked at it for a moment before deciding to sit. Interesting, she must have originally planned to drop whatever information she held and leave.

He took the chair opposite her and waited.

"You must know your absence at recent entertainments has been noted."

"I see. By whom exactly?"

"The gossips. With no facts to discern the reason for your withdrawal from society they have been left to speculate."

"As is common."

"They are speculating that you were paying your attentions to Gia only to entice her into your bed, and now that you are no longer speaking to her you have succeeded in your efforts and have moved on. As you can imagine, this gossip borders on ruinous for Gia."

"Those vicious crones," Hale stood and paced about the small room. Why hadn't he met Lady Tomison in his study where he would have had access to whisky. He felt this conversation would have been better handled with whisky.

"I don't disagree. However, even I have to admit it does seem a reasonable explanation for your absence. I know about the kiss. That's all Gia spoke of. I'm asking you, Your Grace, if anything else happened."

"Nothing. It was only a kiss." He felt foolish confessing his sins to Lady Tomison, but it was important that she knew he hadn't defiled Gia. Though he felt a twinge of guilt knowing he had defiled her in his mind many, many times.

But thinking and doing were two different things. Thank goodness.

"I know your reputation as a rogue is exaggerated."

"A *fogue*," he muttered as a small smile came to his lips.

"I believe the new name she came up with was even more clever. When I called you a rake, she said you were a 'fake' for faux rake."

He chuckled and nodded. "It does seem fitting."

"Still, some of the reputation is warranted. I just thought Gia would be safe from your intentions."

"Why does everyone assume I would not be attracted to Gia?" he nearly shouted. "She is a beautiful woman."

"I didn't say you wouldn't be attracted to her and she is quite lovely. I meant she should be safe because I didn't think you to be the kind of man who would defile an innocent, especially one you think of as a friend."

"I see. Thank you." He rubbed his temples feeling like a monster.

"Regardless, this kiss… Gia is terrified it is the reason you have not seen or spoken to her. She thinks it was so awful it frightened you away." She squinted at him. "I wouldn't have expected a man like you would have been felled by a mere kiss."

"I didn't find the kiss lacking. It was truly wonderful." The best kiss he'd ever experienced and while he was a *fogue*, he still had enough skill with kissing to make an adequate comparison.

"I see," Lady Tomison said.

"What do you see?"

"I was right. The kiss… It wasn't bad. It was too good. It shook you. It frightened you."

"I am a man of honor, and that kiss made me want to keep going without any thought to what that would mean. It was no *mere* kiss," he argued her earlier assumption.

"You think you pose a real danger."

"I know I do." He looked her in the eye hating to admit to such a failing, but needing her to understand what was at stake.

"Then there is only one thing to do." She let out a breath as if they'd come to a mutual conclusion, though he had missed a vital piece of the plan.

She folded her arms over her chest and gave him a formidable look.

Oh.

"You think to force us into marriage because of one kiss?"

"You just said it was more than one kiss, or rather that you wanted it to be more than one kiss. And no, that is not what I was implying. I know you don't wish to marry Gia. She would not make a good choice for a duchess. She shouldn't have to change who she is to fit herself into a marriage."

He frowned at the woman.

"You do not give her or myself enough credit. First, to think that I would want an ordinary duchess and second, to think even if I did, Gia wouldn't be able to do her duties and still manage to retain the essence of herself while doing so."

"Are you saying you *do* wish to marry her then?"

"Er…" He wasn't sure how the conversation had become so twisted to the point that he was now arguing all the reasons why Gia would make him a fine wife.

"I know she's a bit odd," Lydia said as she walked over to the window.

"She isn't *odd*. She's intriguing. She may have different interests than most women of the *ton*, but that isn't a bad thing. Not for the right person."

When she smiled this time, he realized she'd baited him and he'd fallen right into her trap.

"*Someone?*" She tapped her index finger against her chin. "You mean a man who doesn't care about having embroidered linens or someone to entertain him in the evenings with music?"

"Exactly."

"Someone who shares her interests in horses, you mean?"

"Aye."

"Someone like *you?*"

"Aye, but… Nay. Not me."

"Someone *like* you, but *not* you?"

"Right." Except the idea of this person, who was like him but not him, touching Gia and making her laugh caused him to clench his hands into fists. "I see what you are attempting to do here, Lady Tomison, and it won't work."

"I'm certain it already has." She smiled cheerfully as if she hadn't just dragged him along on her maddening train of thought.

Rather than entangle himself worse in her trap, he remained silent.

After a full minute, she finally let out a huff and spoke. "You will need to come to the Worthington ball tonight and dance with Gia. Talk and laugh as cheerful acquaintances. Give the impression that everything is as it was before. Make it known that you had other things keeping you from attending activities the past week. Set things right."

"But… I am leaving in the morning for a trip."

"Good. Then you will be available tonight."

What was happening? Speaking with Lady Tomison was like being caught up in a cyclone and put down somewhere far from where you'd been.

"If you no longer wish to visit her or go riding in the mornings, no one will notice, but your evenings for the time being need to be spent as they had before. I will increase my efforts to find a man who would wish to marry her. Lord Duncan seems pleasant enough."

Lord Duncan *was* pleasant enough, but he wasn't for Gia.

"Very well. But make sure this man is able to properly appreciate her."

"And you're certain you don't want the honor for yourself?" She cocked her head to the side, inspecting him carefully. He felt as if she could see into all the dark corners of his soul.

"I—no."

"Very well. Thank you for your time. I will see you this evening."

He saw her to the door and returned to his study, suddenly feeling exhausted.

CHAPTER EIGHTEEN

"**I** REALLY DON'T think I should attend the ball this evening. I believe it would be better if I stayed out of the eye of the *ton* until people stop speculating about the reason Hale is not speaking to me."

Gia had her fingers clenched together in front of her chest in a gesture of begging and yet Lydia didn't even consider it.

"You need to attend tonight. I believe everything will work out for the best."

"What do you mean?" Gia squinted at her friend. "You don't have a plan to match me up with someone odious, do you?"

Lydia gasped in mock affront. "Who have I ever matched you up with that was odious?"

Gia shook her head. "I'm sorry. You've been wonderful, and I've been so difficult. You probably wish my father would have left me in Surrey while he visited London."

"And miss the theatrics upon your arrival? Surely not."

It was quite humorous now to remember how her father had performed so terribly to get her to London. Though it hadn't been very funny at the time.

"I can't believe I fell for his ruse." Gia frowned. "Perhaps I'm not as adept at seeing a man's true intentions as I once thought."

"You miss the duke?"

"He was my only friend here, aside from you, of course."

"Let us go to the ball and see if we can't find you a new

friend."

Gia didn't want to disappoint Lydia again so she walked into the Worthington ball with every expectation she would find the first woman her age and make her acquaintance. But before she had the chance, her gaze met warm blue eyes she knew all too well.

"The duke is here," she whispered to Lydia. "He's coming this way. What should I do?"

"You should stand still and allow him to approach and see what he has to say."

Gia fought the urge to run from the room and stood fast, waiting the excruciating hours it seemed to take Hale to arrive in front of her.

"Good evening, Your Grace," she said and dipped into a curtsey.

"Miss Gia, you look lovely as always. Would you honor me with a dance?"

"Oh. Of course." She held out her hand so he could jot his name on her dance card. "Are you certain?" she whispered so only he could hear.

"Surely no harm can come from a simple dance."

"No. I imagine not."

He nodded and walked away.

As awful as the past week had been without him, tonight seemed so much worse that he was there but she didn't know what to expect.

By the time it was their turn on the dance floor, she wanted to run from the room and go home. But she was an adult, and adults did not run away from uncomfortable situations. No matter how much they wanted to.

"He's not going to bite you. You must relax," Lydia said as Hale headed in her direction to collect Gia for their dance. "Smile. You look as if you are heading to the gallows."

Gia wasn't so sure she wasn't, for Hale looked like he was being forced to eat slugs.

"Shall we?" He nodded so formally it hurt. Even on their first encounter he hadn't treated her like a chore.

"Yes, Your Grace," she answered stiffly. She'd always enjoyed dancing with him but this time she wished her dance card would have been full by the time he'd asked.

He offered his arm and led her to the dance floor where they waited for the music to begin. Instead of a waltz like he'd usually claimed, he chose a quadrille which gave them little time to speak before moving out of range.

"How have you been?" he asked.

"Well. And you?"

"Fine."

"That's good."

She spun away and tried to come up with something to say by the time they came together again. Perhaps in the hour and a half she had been waiting for her dance with him she might have used her time more wisely and devised a few topics of conversation. But she had nothing.

They spent all the time they were paired up in silence and Gia wanted to run from the room, adult or no. This wasn't just uncomfortable, it was incredibly painful.

It was clear she had truly ruined the easy camaraderie they'd once shared.

Even if she'd thought of something to say, her throat was too clogged with emotion to speak. She was relieved to be pulled away from him for another turn and didn't attempt to make eye contact when they returned to each other.

Finally, *finally*, the horrid dance was over and he returned her to Lydia's side.

"Thank you for the dance."

She swallowed and managed to say, "Of course."

As soon as he turned away, she whispered to Lydia, "I'm so sorry. I just need a moment." Then she hurried from the room so as to not cause a scene when the tears came.

HALE HAD KNOWN it was a bad idea to come tonight. Seeing the sadness in Gia's eyes as he danced with her only confirmed how badly he'd destroyed the friendship they'd shared.

If it weren't bad enough to have Lady Tomison glare at him, seeing Gia rush from the room with unshed tears in her eyes nearly broke him. Unable to help himself, he followed Gia from the ballroom, down the hall, and into a parlor overly done in floral décor.

Leaving the door wide open so not to cause more harm to her reputation, he went to stand next to her by the window where she attempted to wipe away the tears that had fallen.

His chest seized in pain and he worried he wouldn't survive it.

Holding out his handkerchief, he opened his mouth to speak but she beat him to it.

"I'm sorry for kissing you. I've ruined everything."

"Please stop apologizing for the kiss. Has it escaped your notice that I returned the kiss? It wasn't one-sided, Gia. We were both involved."

She shrugged.

"I wanted to kiss you. But now it isn't safe for you to be with me, because that kiss forced me to see that I didn't want to stop with one kiss. I wanted so much more. And that would lead to your ruin. I would rather end our friendship than risk hurting you like that. I care about you too much to endanger your reputation."

He took a breath and frowned.

"Why are you smiling?" he asked when he noticed the tears were gone and she now looked happy.

She was beautiful, but when she smiled it was like the sun had risen just for him. Seeing that smile with tears still glistening on her lashes was too much.

"You didn't hate the kiss. I didn't do it poorly," she said, as if amazed by this fact.

He stared at her for a few breaths. How could she have thought such a thing? He felt his lips pull up and realized he hadn't smiled since he'd been with her that day. It had only been a week, but it felt strange. Like he was already out of practice.

"I didn't hate it. You are quite an accomplished kisser."

She fairly beamed for a few moments, but the smile faded again.

"But we cannot be friends because we'll want to do it again?" she whispered.

"Aye."

The way she caught her bottom lip between her teeth made him want to go shut the door and claim her lips once more, but he took a step back. He wanted to ask what she was thinking.

It seemed she was contemplating something. But he knew Gia well enough by now. She always told him her thoughts without him having to ask.

"I think I will still want to kiss you, whether we are friends or not. In the last week, I've thought of it many times and wished I hadn't made a muck of it so I could do it again and again."

"Gia…" He nearly groaned. She was killing him with her honesty and innocence. "I must go now."

"Will you think of our kiss?" she asked.

He glanced toward the door a second before he placed his hands on her jaw and tipped her chin up to place a kiss on her lips.

Why did it have to be as perfect as the kiss last week? Why did it have to feel so right, like a promise of everything he wanted and thought he couldn't have.

Why did she have to look up at him as if they were made for one another?

"I must go," he heard himself saying before he turned and rushed from the room before he did something they would both regret.

GIA WAS NEARLY as surly as Owen as they left the tavern that morning for the Newmarket racecourse. The day before had been spent in silence as Gia and Bess bounced along in the carriage.

"It looks like it might clear up in time for the race today, miss," Bess said.

Gia smiled sadly as she looked out the window. Bess was correct. The sun appeared to be making an effort to fight off the clouds. But what amused Gia was that she was conversing about the weather. Something Hale would have found appalling. It was what was expected of proper ladies.

As she had since she set out for the race, Gia wondered if Hale would attend the race.

When they arrived, Gia passed on taking the parasol Bess offered and headed for the starting area. She saw Dante easily but was shocked to see Godspell standing beside him.

"Godspell is racing?" she said to Owen, who shrugged.

"It doesna hurt to see what the old boy does," her groom answered, but Gia was no longer looking at the horse but at the crowd. If Godspell was here, Hale was as well.

As the riders mounted, she spotted Hale toward the back of the crowd, but he wasn't watching his horse. He was studying her with a frown on the lips she'd kissed just two nights ago.

At the sound of the starting shot, his head snapped up as the horses were set off on the race.

"Maybe if the two of you spoke you could get all of this over with," Owen surprised her. He never spoke of things like this. And she surely didn't wish to speak of them with him.

"I'm sure I don't know what you're talking about."

"I'm sure you do. You've been moping around for over a week and the duke has been suspiciously absent during that time. Something set you two off. You were in each other's pockets and now you can barely look at each other."

"It's none of your business."

"Did he do something he shouldna done?"

"As if I would tell you and have you rush off to defend me."

"If you're needing defending, I'll do what I'm called upon to do."

"To a duke? And be hauled off to hang in front of Newgate? No. Besides, he didn't do anything I didn't want."

Owen winced and shook his head.

"I've never been happier to see the end of a conversation. Here they come," he nodded toward a group of horses coming into sight.

"Dante is in the lead," she said excitedly, though she hoped Godspell was close by.

As they got closer, she was able to make out the horses better.

"Damn. Loiterer is gaining on Dante and Godspell is behind him. I can't tell if he's third or fourth," she said and remembered her language when the two men beside her frowned in her direction.

"Not bad for the lad's first run," Owen said.

As the horses ended the race, Gia wanted nothing more than to go over to Hale and congratulate him for coming in fourth place. As Owen had said, it was a decent showing for the horse's first official race. If Hale kept up with his training, he'd have a chance of winning at Epsom.

Not that she would be able to help.

Rather than go to him, she watched as the men around him patted his back and he offered smiles to the well-wishers. She caught his gaze for a moment, and he gave a brief nod before turning to someone else.

"Hmmph," Owen said, or rather grumped. "I'll go see to the carriage so we can leave immediately. It doesna look like this rain is going to hold off much longer. You'll want to get out of here."

"Yes. Thank you." Though it wasn't the rain that had her wanting to leave. It was the proof that her friendship with Hale was officially over. He couldn't give her more than a nod?

They had shared so much in the last month. But one kiss—make that two kisses—and he could barely look at her.

"Let's go," she ordered and headed off in the direction of the carriage. She was done with this race, done with Hale, and done with men in general.

CHAPTER NINETEEN

A FEW NIGHTS after getting back to London, Gia was shaken awake by Bess. Her room was still dark and she was muddled with sleep. She didn't know what time it was, but it couldn't yet be time to wake.

"You've received an urgent letter, miss," Bess whispered quickly as she lit a lamp by Gia's bed.

"What? What is it?"

"I'm not sure, but my guess is something is amiss, and the letter will explain it. Luther woke me so I could wake you. The rest of the house is still asleep. A footman from Roxburghe waits for your reply."

Roxburghe?

Whyever would Hale send for her? He was no longer speaking to her.

Gia rubbed the sleep from her eyes and stared at the missive Bess had placed in her hands. She recognized the seal and snapped it immediately, to open the letter.

There were only a few words on the page and what little there were had been scribbled in a hurry. She held it closer to the light and squinted to focus.

Gia,

Please come. I need you. It's Hera. She's in distress.

Hale

Gia was out of bed and reaching for the shirt Bess held out for her.

As if instinctively knowing Gia wouldn't want a gown, a pair of buckskins were thrust at her next. As she tugged them on, Bess braided Gia's hair back and ran a cold cloth over her face.

And as Gia pulled on her boots, Bess packed a fresh shirt and trousers in a bag and handed them over. A few swallows of the tea Bess had brought, and Gia hurried from her room.

Only a few minutes had passed from the time she'd been woken until she was downstairs being helped into the waiting carriage by Hale's footman.

She was amazed by how quickly she could shift from deep sleep to being wide awake.

She didn't know what was wrong with Hera, but the lack of details in Hale's summons didn't bode well.

She was taken directly to the mews and led into the stables where over a dozen lamps blazed in the small space. The sweet scents of horses and leather welcomed her.

Glancing around she counted seven men including Hale. Hera was standing which was a good sign, but she was agitated. Gia could feel it hovering around the horse.

"Thank you for coming," Hale said, his eyes a bit frantic. "I didn't know who else might be able to help. The foal isn't coming. Her water broke over an hour ago."

"Of course. I'll do what I can," Gia promised. "Let me check her over."

She didn't miss the sniff of dismissal from one of the men as she passed between Hera and the group to get to the horse's head.

It wasn't the first occasion men had underestimated her abilities when it came to horses. They most likely wouldn't think much of her techniques. She didn't care. Hale had called for her, and she would do her best to help the mare deliver.

"What's wrong lass?" she whispered to the horse.

Hera put her head under Gia's chin and breathed out. A gesture Gia liked to think was the horse's way of saying, "Thank you for coming."

One of the men laughed and she felt Hera shift slightly away from the loud group. Four men stood in a huddle discussing the option of tying a rope to the hoof they could reach and tugging until it came out.

A deplorable idea if the foal was breech. They could end up killing both the foal and the mare that way.

But she could tell by Hera's unease it wouldn't be the first time someone in that group had hurt this horse.

On the other side, two boys—brothers, she guessed—stood eager for instructions. The fact that Hera had no issues moving closer to the boys spoke volumes in regard to who she trusted and who she did not.

Gia only had to convince Hale to do what needed to be done. With a flick of her head, he came over from where he watched her perform the evaluation.

"Do you trust me?" she asked quietly.

"With my very life. What is it?"

"One of these men have hurt this horse. We don't have time to figure out which of them it was. They all need to leave. Immediately."

"I'll see it done," he said without hesitation.

While he handled that, Gia called to the two boys. "My name is Gia. What are yours?"

"I'm Robbie, and this is my little brother Sam."

They looked to be around fourteen and ten. Slight of build, but strong enough for what she needed.

"Very good. I need Sam to run to the kitchens and have them bring several buckets of hot water and towels. Be quick about it."

Sam nodded and ran off toward the house.

"Robbie, I need you to move Hera around so she is facing the opposite way. It will make her more comfortable."

Gia had sensed the horse didn't like having her head in the corner. She was skittish with the men at her back as anyone would be.

Hale was still arguing with the men. She heard the larger man blustering.

"You think this chit is going to deliver that foal. She's no bigger than Robbie."

"What I think is no longer your concern. I asked you to leave the premises. I'll call for you if I need you."

"And I might not be available when you call."

"I'm willing to take that chance. Go on." He waved and the men shared their disagreement with a few more disgruntled curses before leaving for good.

Gia had her hand on Hera's neck and felt the horse relax at their exit and her ability to protect her flanks.

"Let's move her up a bit more. Yes, that's perfect. Right there." They now had room behind her to work. "Move some of those lamps around to this side," she instructed.

Hale had heard and helped Robbie with the lighting. Positioning it carefully so it would illuminate the area without risk of catching something on fire.

"Robbie, I want you to hold her, not too tight. Talk to her and brush her neck." He nodded and started to soothe the horse. A natural with Hera.

Gia felt the horse relax even more allowing Gia to perform a more thorough examination.

"Let's see what we have here, lass." Gia spoke just loud enough not to startle her patient as she began feeling Hera's belly, pressing here and there to determine where the head might be. "Oh, I see," she said after counting her fifth hoof and then the sixth.

"What is it?"

"It appears you have two racehorses in there and they are both of a mind to win who comes out first."

"Two? Are you certain?"

She didn't take offense to his question. Twins among horses were uncommon. And even when it happened it was rare for both foals to be born healthy. She took a moment to show Hale how she had come to that conclusion.

"Can we save them?"

"I believe they are both alive. We will certainly try to keep them that way. But we must hurry."

Sam had returned with two footmen who carried two buckets of water each. She thanked the men and instructed Sam to help his brother. "You'll both need to keep her still as His Grace and I try to move the foals around. Don't scare her, but don't let her back up or lie down. She may want to move around but we must keep her in this position."

Both boys gave a determined nod.

Gia checked Hera again, positioning Hale's hands where she needed him to help support the mare's abdomen. She told him which direction he should push when she gave him the word then she pulled a stool behind the horse, rolled up her sleeves, and washed her hands before she stood on the stool and reached in.

Hale shook his head and offered a nervous smile.

"If the *ton* could see you now."

"You know well enough what I think of them." She turned her focus back to the horse. "Ah, I see you are winning this race by a nose, so we will bring you out first, little one."

She took a breath and looked to the terrified duke on her right.

"Hale, on my mark, push the way I instructed you to with your right hand first. Then when you feel it give way, push with your left. Just as I showed you. Boys, get ready. She isn't going to appreciate this very much. But she'll live to thank us all later." Gia took another deep breath to prepare and then said, "Now."

Things moved rather quickly then. The other horse slipped back as if conceding to his sibling and the first horse slid from its mother in a wet splat upon the thick straw.

The second foal was not far behind now that its way had become clear. The twin was much smaller than the first and Gia helped to clear away the birthing sac.

She gestured to Hale to give her a wet cloth and used it to clear away the horse's nose so it could breathe.

The larger twin was already struggling to remove the sac from its head and Gia and Hale worked together to hold her and clean her up enough to assure she was breathing.

"She's impatient. But her younger brother is going to give her a run for her money," Gia said as the smaller horse had positioned his foot to stand.

"What should we name them?" he asked, bestowing the same honor to her that she had when he'd picked the name for Xandra.

"They weren't born to Leto, but they are twins so it seems right they should be Artemis and Apollo."

He smiled. "It does seem fitting. They both gave a valiant god-like effort to get to us safely."

Gia wished his smile didn't force one of her own to her lips. Taking care of Hera was not even a question. She would never allow her feelings for the owner to keep her from helping a horse.

But with the danger over, she didn't know where they stood. Were they friends again? Would he go back to avoiding her? Did she wish to speak to him, or should she just duck out and go home?

Despite their inability to speak, understanding horses was always easier for Gia. It was human men that were impossible to fathom.

The little boys cheered when Apollo beat his sister to his feet and stepped up to be inspected by his mother. Artemis didn't take long to make her way and instead of waiting to greet her mother, dipped her head under the mare to start nursing.

Gia—still running on excitement—spent the next hour tending to the mother and her babies. All of which seemed healthy enough. Robbie and Sam were exhausted and Hale sent them to find their beds.

Using some of the water that had cooled, Gia cleaned up and reached for the bag containing fresh clothes.

"I'm going to change before returning home."

"You can come into the house," he offered.

"No need. I'll just be a moment. I would just go home and change, but I fear if my father or Lydia saw me like this, they would have an apoplexy." She gestured to her shirt now spattered with blood and other questionable things.

"Of course. That stall is empty and clean. No one is around so…" He swallowed as if only just realizing the impropriety of their situation. Not that they hadn't been alone many times before.

This, however, would be the first time they would be alone since they'd kissed and while she was in a state of undress.

She carried the clean water into the stall he'd pointed to and closed the door behind her. She made quick work of stripping off her clothes and washing.

It seemed intimate to be naked while being close enough to hear him move about the room outside. He had muttered something to himself and huffed out a breath.

The thick stall door seemed too thin to block his sounds.

When she attempted to pull on her clean breeches, she realized her plans were hindered by her damp skin.

Instead of struggling and ending up on her arse, she pulled the shirt over her head and used the fabric to fan her bare legs.

Her usual impatience mixed with exhaustion proved fatal as words rolled out of her mouth without thought.

"What happens now?" she asked.

"What do you mean?" When he spoke, it sounded as if he was speaking from just the other side of the stall door.

"I mean between us. Shall we take up as friends again, or will you go back to avoiding me?"

She heard him take a breath. "You saved my horses. I can't very well go back to avoiding you."

"So, you admit you were avoiding me?"

"I didn't think it was in question. Of course, I was avoiding you."

She heard the scuff of his boots and guessed he was pacing as he did sometimes.

"All because I kissed you? What if I promised it wouldn't happen again?" She didn't know if she had the strength to adhere to such a promise, but she missed him and was desperate for any way to have him as her friend again.

"I don't think you have the power to promise such a thing when you have control over only one of the participants." His voice was quiet and strained.

"To be honest, I probably shouldn't have made that promise. I can't say I have any control at all. I think I proved that already."

He chuckled and she smiled. This was better. The safety of the door between them allowed them freedom to speak without the awkwardness of facing each other.

Gia gave up on her trousers for the moment and leaned against the stall by the door. Merely a few inches of wood separated them.

"I am equally unsure if I can be trusted," he finally said.

"Really?" It came out as a whisper, but because she was so close to where he stood on the other side of the door he heard. That single word might have been said with more excitement than a regular question.

She wanted him to lose control again. She wanted to kiss him.

No. Kissing wouldn't be enough.

When they'd kissed the last time, he'd started them down a path to something more. That was what she truly wanted.

More.

As if she'd wished it, the latch on the stall popped up and the door opened. There he was.

CHAPTER TWENTY

HIS FACE WAS so close to hers. His eyes flared with surprise or desire, she wasn't sure which it was.

"Yes, really," he answered her earlier question. "I have thought of little else but kissing you since that day."

His gaze dropped and it was then they both realized she wasn't wearing anything but a thin lawn shirt. Her breeches hung on the other side of the stall.

Of course, she'd known she wasn't wearing anything on the lower half of her body but had somehow forgotten when he'd first entered the stall. Now, seeing the need on his face, she was glad she'd waited to put them on.

He didn't move anything but his eyes for maybe twenty beats of her thumping heart. Then it seemed everything moved at once. He stepped closer, latching the door behind him as his other hand reached for her. She lurched the short distance between them and their lips met, relentless and urgent.

She'd thought their first kiss had consumed her, but this was raw and desperate passion. She couldn't get close enough.

"Gia," he said in what she thought might be a question. She wasn't certain what he was asking, but the answer was most definitely *yes*.

"Yes," she said repeatedly until his hands moved along her body. When they dropped below the hem of her long shirt and came up under the fabric, her breath caught. He was touching her bare skin. Not just any bare skin but that of her thigh and her buttocks.

"We need to stop before we can't," he whispered. "Tell me to stop."

"I don't want to stop." Stopping was the last thing she wanted. "Please."

"I need you to be the strong one. I can't. I'm too far gone," he said, desperation clear in his voice.

"I hate to disappoint you, but… I am not very strong at the moment."

She felt his smile against the skin of her throat as he placed kisses down her neck to her collarbone.

"It seems neither of us wants to stop." He pulled away enough to look her in the eye then he moved again.

She answered with a sound, rather than words, as his lips enveloped her nipple. She tugged at his shirt, grateful he hadn't bothered with a waist coat or cravat. He was so accessible. When the fabric pulled free of his trousers, she laid her hands against the warm skin of his back, feeling as if she had caught fire.

"Jeremy," she whispered and felt his body shudder. "May I call you that?"

It seemed wrong to use his formal name when she had worked her fingers to his falls and was trying to get them open. Hale wasn't his title, it was his family name, but still it wasn't his name alone.

"No one ever has," he said, pulling away enough to stare at her.

"It's either Jeremy or Your Grace," she teased. "You choose." She noticed his body responded again—a brief shiver—when she'd said his name. He liked it. "Never mind. I already have my answer, *Jeremy*."

"Christ. I never considered how much I would enjoy hearing my name on your lips. Especially when your hand is down my breeches."

Except, her hand had not made it down his breeches, she was

still struggling with the blasted falls. She wore breeches and knew how to go about undoing them, but it was much more difficult with her hands shaking the way they were.

He was probably used to experienced women who knew how to get a man out of his clothing. While she'd thought of this moment in many different ways, actually touching a man's skin was making her clumsy.

She nearly cried in relief when the buttons gave way and then she paused. The next step would be to touch him. There.

She closed her eyes and gathered her courage.

They shared a brief laugh that shifted to a moan when her hand found his length and she wrapped her fingers around him. His skin was so hot and the strange body part twitched in her grip.

He pulled her shirt over her head leaving her in nothing but the short corset she used when wearing men's clothing. She worked at the laces as he pulled off his boots and breeches.

When they were both free of their clothes, they stood staring and panting.

"Hmm," she said without meaning to.

"What does that mean?" he asked.

"I've only ever seen a horse's member before. You are much smaller."

His eyes went wide and he laughed.

"I've always heard maidens were put off by the size of a man. All worry over whether or not it should fit but you..." He laughed. "Of course, you would say something completely unexpected."

"Well, I know it will fit, don't I? How would humanity continue on if male and female parts didn't align correctly?"

He was really laughing now and she realized this was probably not the way experienced women seduced their lovers. With their odd ramblings of procreation. She'd wanted him to lose control, not break down in hysterics.

"I'm sorry. I shouldn't have said anything. I don't know all of what should happen between us, but I'm sure you shouldn't be laughing."

He was still smiling though the laughter had faded as he placed his hand against her cheek.

"Why should you and I do what is expected when we can be so much better?"

He kissed her deeper.

"Promise me one thing," she whispered as his lips moved to her neck.

"Anything." His voice shook and she thought he was on the precipice of losing control. She felt the power rising in her.

"Don't stay away from me anymore. Please, Jeremy?"

"I only did so to try to protect you. But now… Even if I should wish to, I'm afraid I lack the strength."

"Good." Very good, in fact. She needed him.

She had missed his friendship horribly. His dry wit and the way he was often amused at her antics rather than put off by them. Sometimes even encouraging her.

But this… this physical element of their friendship was so much more than expected.

His kisses had moved lower, across her stomach and as her legs began to tremble, he lifted her enough to settle them in the hay atop the plaid he'd laid there.

When she shifted and let out a restless sound, he clearly knew what she needed even if she didn't. His fingers slid over her most intimate place twice before diving within.

She had touched herself in the past, but it had not been like this. She'd had nothing to go on but what felt good. He, however, was skilled in knowing what felt extraordinary.

She gasped and remembered she should also be touching him. After all, it was for both of them and so far, he had made it all about her.

Her hand caressed over his broad shoulder, up his neck and through the silky, blond locks of his hair. But when his lips touched her core and his tongue teased at her, caressing gave way to grasping and clinging until he reached up to tug her fingers free from where she was pulling at him.

Another chuckle, but this time the breath of his laugher reached out to touch her center and she moaned in want of something only he could give her.

"Please." Was she begging? She didn't care if she was.

"Aye, lass," he promised and she relaxed only slightly, knowing that he would take care of her, even if he wasn't doing it fast enough for her liking as he lapped at her lazily.

"Please," she said again in a long groan.

"Impatient." He shook his head. "I should have expected as much."

Yes, he should have.

They had been friends for some time now, and she was never pleased to have to wait for anything. Definitely not something so exquisite.

He relented. Slipping two fingers into her, he curved them just so to touch a blessedly wonderful place inside her she hadn't known existed. His tongue moved in concert with what his fingers were doing and it resulted in a quick building of pleasure.

But unlike the shallow pulses she'd managed to eke out of her body while alone in her bed, this grew to become something much bigger. Crashing waves of desire rolling over her. Sweeping her away. When she thought it was over, another would strike until finally the storm of waves settled into a more peaceful tide. Her breathing calmed and her body felt heavy.

But as the passion waned, she knew she had not experienced everything. His cock lay hard and heavy against her hip as he repositioned himself to kiss her.

"We should stop now, before it is too late," he said the exact opposite of what she'd been thinking.

She shook her head.

"No. I want you. All of you. Please."

"There would be no going back. I can't—"

"Please. This is what I want."

She may not have known the proper way to seduce a man, but this man—her Jeremy—responded immediately. And when he rolled on top of her, and she felt him enter her body she knew this could not have been stopped.

She didn't want to stop.

⟫⟪

HALE HAD NEVER had a home to speak of. Not really.

He'd been moved about from property to property strategically situated so not to become attached to anyone or anyplace.

Even the house in which he lived now—just a few steps away—wasn't a real home. It was another property, entailed to him with his title. But as empty as those he'd grown up in, despite all the people about.

It wasn't until he'd joined his body with Gia's that he finally knew what coming home was like. How it felt to be the complete opposite of alone.

Hearing her gasps and his name—his real name—on her lips opened him up and allowed her inside where no one had ever been. He felt vulnerable, but alive.

He had someone. He had Gia. She knew him and wanted him. Accepted him when so few had.

As much as his primal need urged him to claim her as his, he realized he knew Gia just as intimately. She would never belong to anyone else. She would give herself to him, but remain her own person. Always.

He smiled at the thought, his lips brushing her neck where her pulse beat.

This was what he wanted. Needed.

Her.

"Jeremy," she whispered. "I think it is going to happen again."

His smile grew. Pride warred with happiness.

"Then let's see that it does, shall we?" Putting his hand between them he found the place where his touch would launch her into oblivion.

She cried his name repeatedly as she throbbed around him and he knew he was too close to prolong this pleasure any longer, no matter how much he might wish to.

He wanted nothing more than to bury himself deep in her body as he climaxed, but his larger concern was her.

With an effort that could only come from protecting someone who one loved, he pulled out of her in time to spend in the straw.

Rolling to the other side, he stared up at the wooden beams and grinned lazily. He'd pulled her close so her head rested on his chest and her fingers grazed across his stomach, just this side of ticklish.

His fingers roamed absently up and down her spine and he thought the moment would be perfect if the straw wasn't so itchy and if they weren't lying in the stables where anyone could happen across them.

He blinked and then blinked again. The haze of passion was quickly being replaced by the fog of unease.

He sat up, displacing his lover as he looked around almost surprised to find himself exactly where they had begun.

"Bloody hell," he muttered.

"What's wrong?" she whispered.

What was wrong? Did she not see?

He gestured to the stall.

"I just took your virtue in a fucking stable, Gia."

She giggled and shrugged.

"I think it a most fitting place actually."

He felt his eyes go wide at her comment.

"Gia, the stable is for drunkards to strop barmaids. It's no place for an untried proper lady." He ran his hand down his face, feeling the heat of shame on his cheeks. "I'm terribly sorry, Gia. How could I have been so barbaric?"

He knew the answer, he'd lost his head completely. Seeing

her in nothing but a thin shirt. Her bare legs, toned and begging for his touch.

Even now, he was getting hard again. As if he hadn't done enough damage.

He'd taken her virtue in a stable.

He'd taken her virtue.

"Bloody hell. Gia… I…"

She laughed again.

"It was wonderful, Jeremy. Perfect. Though I do think you're making more of it than is warranted."

Oh, there was much more to it than she realized.

"We should discuss what happens next," he said, swallowing loudly. He'd never thought he would do such a thing. But here he was in the very situation that he'd promised himself he'd never find himself in.

"More sex?" she suggested with a hot grin.

He didn't think he'd mind that at all, but no. One of them had to be the voice of reason, and God help them both, it seemed it would fall to him.

"Not now."

"Oh. Yes. You're right. I should get home. Dawn is only a few hours away."

Just like that? As if she'd come for tea and visiting hours were over. As if he hadn't just ruined her in the most improper location.

He'd ruined her. The woman he thought more highly of than any other. She deserved so much more than this. He would see that she had it.

"Aye. And later I'll come to your house and speak to your father."

"My father? What do wish to speak to him about?"

"Marriage."

"What? Why?" She jumped up.

"Gia, I took your virtue in a pile of hay. I have a duty to your honor and I'll not ignore it."

"But why can't we just enjoy this? Neither of us wants to marry. I'm not a debutante hanging all my hopes on finding a titled husband. I know what I want. I also know what you want—or rather what you don't want. I surely didn't do any of this to trap you—"

"Of course, I know that," he reassured her. They'd both been consenting adults, but he still had responsibilities. Instead of being terrified of the consequences, he found he wasn't all that worried about the possibility of marrying Gia.

Perhaps that fact should have terrified him.

"You said you weren't ready to marry," she continued. "And you definitely don't want to live in the country. I surely don't want to have to stay in town, and neither of us would be happy with a marriage in name only. So, let's just have this."

"Have this? Sex in stables?"

"Maybe not a stable the next time, but it wasn't unpleasant."

"Gia. It's not done," he reminded her. She was not conventional in any way, but she certainly understood this was far beyond propriety.

"Why Jeremy? Why should we do what is expected when we can be so much better?" She threw his words back at him.

He studied her. Looking for any indication she was simply saying this to appease him.

"If your father were to find out…"

She laughed. "My father and Lydia are having an affair. What can they say?"

"This is truly what you want?"

"Yes. Truly."

"And if it isn't what you want any longer, you'll tell me immediately?"

"Of course."

He smiled and brushed a piece of straw from her hair.

"Then I will trust you to know your own mind and what you want. I'll not hold you to a different standard or impose the rules of society upon you."

"We'll be friends. And lovers. We'll enjoy each other's company both in and out of bed."

"Speaking of a bed. Get dressed and come with me." He held out his hand and placed a kiss across her knuckles in the way a man does when paying respect to a lady he didn't just tup in a barn. "If we're going to do this, we will at least do it properly."

Christ almighty, he'd done her so wrong. But if they didn't get out of here soon, he'd do it all over again.

CHAPTER TWENTY-ONE

"HURRY," HE SAID as he tossed her shirt at her.

They dressed quickly and, taking her hand, he led her from the stables and into the back of the house. The kitchens were empty as he and Gia passed through and turned for the servants' stairs. He had to duck to keep from hitting his head, but this was not the first time he'd sneaked into his own home.

He led her up to the second floor and quickly made a left to his rooms.

Chauncey, Hale's valet, was already in bed but Hale locked the door just to be safe. Then he turned to Gia.

"Take off your clothes."

"What is it? Get dressed or take off my clothes?" she said with a laugh.

"If you don't take them off, I'll do it for you and you'll be left to explain to your maid why there is so much mending needed after the birthing of a horse."

She made quick work of her shirt and trousers and he thought it a wonder more women didn't go around like this instead of with all the layers of gowns and petticoats. This was so much simpler. At least for him.

He pulled her naked body against his and kissed her, ready for her again.

But then he remembered this had been her first time. Perhaps she was not so ready as he.

"Wait. Are you sore?"

"What?" She blinked as if her mind was elsewhere.

"It was your first time. If you are sore, we can stop."

"No. I'm fine."

He searched her face and found only honesty. She would tell him if she didn't want him. He could relax knowing he didn't have to puzzle out her feelings in addition to his own.

He trusted her.

"Very well," he said falling into his bed and pulling her down with him.

THE BED WAS surely more comfortable than the straw, but she hadn't minded it at all. In fact, all of it had been perfect.

It was clear Jeremy was concerned he hadn't made the experience pleasant enough for her, but he needn't fear. He had been wonderful.

And there was more to come.

When he shifted to roll on top of her, she slipped from underneath him so she could straddle him while sitting up.

"I saw it done this way in a book. Shall we try?" she asked, wondering if he would mind her making a suggestion. It seemed men were to set the pace and select the position, but was that always how it was done? Could a woman not recommend alternatives?

He laughed.

"Gia, it's nearly three in the morning and I'm fair exhausted. If you care to do all the work, I'm certainly not going to stop you."

She grinned and sat forward feeling as powerful as a goddess.

"Help me," she said with a hint of frustration as she fumbled between them. It had seemed easy enough in the pages of a book, but getting his parts aligned with hers was not as simple.

"Up a little further and then—Ah. Christ."

When she sank down, taking him completely, he shuddered and closed his eyes as if in pain. He stilled her with a firm grip on her hips as he took a few breaths.

"Did I hurt you?" she asked.

"Only in the best way. I just need a moment." After a few more breaths that caused his taught stomach to move against her palm in a delightful ripple, he released her again.

Her rhythm was uneven at first, but it didn't take her long to find her stride.

"Slow," he pleaded.

"But I want to go faster." She was new to this, but her body seemed to know instinctually what to do.

"Do you want it to be over?" He opened his eyes, the blue brighter because his pupils had drawn to tiny dots.

"No."

"Then slow. Let it build."

He reached between them and touched her in that spot that coaxed her into a quick orgasm. Feeling her body clasp onto his in her climax was the most perfect experience of her life.

"You feel… too good." He gasped and it only took a few more strokes before he picked her up and flipped her over so he could take over. A few thrusts and he pulled out of her before his release as he had in the stable.

She knew the way children were created whether they be equine or human and was grateful that he took such a precaution.

They lay together in a tangled, sticky heap, grasping for breath and touching for a few wonderful moments before he practically jumped from the bed to get a cloth to clean her.

When she reached for him to join her in bed, he shook his head, instead leaning down to kiss her swollen lips.

"If I lie down with you, I will fall asleep in no more than two seconds. And you will fall asleep as well and your family will wake to find you missing come morning."

"Bess and Luther know where I am. They'll just assume it

took longer for the foaling."

He studied her. "Truly? You can stay? We can sleep together."

"Unless you want me to leave."

"No," he answered quickly. She thought as she drifted off, she heard him add the word, "Never." Or maybe it was her own thoughts echoing in his voice.

The light coming through Jeremy's windows an hour later was still pale when Gia woke in his bed.

She shifted to look at him and smiled. He was still asleep, his mouth open slightly, his wavy blond hair seemed to change colors before her eyes as the sun touched each strand.

He was beautiful. Even with the bronze stubble on his chin and upper lip. She couldn't resist the urge to touch it to see if it was soft or rough.

With only two fingers she traced the line of his jaw, smiling at the raspy sound it made against her skin. It tickled. Or would have if it were applied to a different part of her body.

"What are you doing?" he asked, his eyes still closed.

"Inspecting you." He was everything a man should be. Not just attractive physically, but kind and funny.

And he'd asked her to marry him.

Actually, he hadn't asked. He'd assumed it should be because of what they had done. It was simply the act of an honorable man. It wasn't because he loved her or wanted to spend his life with her.

She knew the strength it had taken for him to make such an offer. He was against marriage. Especially marriages of convenience.

She had not made love with him to lure him into the trappings of marriage and would not allow him to make that sacrifice.

"We've only been sleeping a few minutes," he groaned.

"It's been longer than that."

"Not long enough."

"I need to go."

He let out a long breath and opened one eye. A moment later he opened the other and then he smiled. And she realized that she didn't care if every gossip in London saw her sneaking out of his house, it was worth it for this time with him.

"You are beautiful," he said.

She only had to reach up and touch the mess that was her hair to know that wasn't true. *Was that a piece of straw poking her palm?*

Regardless of her state, she didn't argue because the way he stared at her made it clear he believed what he'd said.

Couldn't one find beauty in things others didn't? She'd often used the word when watching a foal stand for the first time, still covered in fluids from birth. To many, it would not be worthy of the word.

Knowing this, she allowed him to determine what he used the word for.

"Thank you for saying so." She kissed his chin, laughing at the way the hair tickled her lips. "You are rather lovely and if I didn't need to get home, I would want you again."

He wrapped his arms around her and she felt the evidence of his answering interest press into her hip.

"Oh."

"It is a thing that happens in the mornings. Though even worse when there is an incredibly desirable, naked woman in bed with me."

"It feels a shame to waste it." She bit her lip deliberating on the best way to proceed while he laughed.

"You always surprise me, Gia. You never say the expected thing. My life is so much better for having you in it." He frowned and she thought he was probably remembering how she hadn't been in his life of late.

"I've missed you," she admitted the feeling she'd kept from putting to words even in her mind. But now she just blurted it out.

"I've missed you too. And it was even worse because it was

my own doing. I thought it was the right thing."

"You should have asked me. I would have gladly told you how wrong you were."

They laughed together and he pulled her close to kiss her neck. She pulled away giggling. "Your whiskers tickle."

"Oh? You shouldn't have told me that." He rolled on top of her and made to tickle her breathless, but the naked wiggling distracted him from his torture and soon he was making her breathless for an entirely different reason.

When he was sleeping once more, she slipped quietly out of his bed to go home before he could distract her yet again.

With her clothing back in order, she stepped out into the gray mist of dawn. How strange to know she looked just as she had when she'd come to his home hours earlier, but inside she felt completely different.

How was she supposed to go about her day as if she was the same? How did others treat such an amazing thing so casually? And more importantly how would she manage to be in a room with him and act as if she didn't wish they were naked in his bed? It would be impossible.

Tradespeople would be moving about soon, but dressed as a boy she could move about without question. She tugged her hat down on her messy hair and rushed down the street.

Bess would grumble at the state of her hair. Would her maid know what she'd done? It felt as if the truth were written plainly on her face.

She was forever changed.

CHAPTER TWENTY-TWO

Hale woke in his empty bed with sunlight streaming in through the windows. It was later than he was used to sleeping, but after their night together, there was no way either of them would be up for a ride in the park.

Their night together…

Hale smiled as he pulled the pillow across him, filling the void where Gia's body had been just hours earlier. Letting out a sigh of disappointment he breathed in the scent of her still clinging to the pillowcase.

She should have woken him, he would have seen her home. But, of course, Gia wouldn't need his assistance.

He wished she'd still been there.

In truth, he didn't know that he ever wanted her to leave. If there was ever a person he enjoyed being with, it was Gia Landon.

She was fun, full of life and now with this new aspect of their physical relationship to consider, he found he was actually regretting that she'd turned down his offer of marriage. Not that it had been an offer. More of an expectation.

Still, it was strange that he would even be considering it now when at the time he'd suggested it, he'd thought he might be ill to be forced into marriage.

How quickly things could change.

He sat up and took in the room. The only evidence of what

had happened the night before were a few pieces of hay in his bed and across his floor.

How beautiful she'd been with her hair rumpled with straw in it and her warm naked body against his.

Yes, he could learn to be quite happy with her in his bed every morning.

He frowned to think of her going back to her home alone.

He would apologize for not escorting her later this afternoon when he went to visit. He was glad he could spend the latter part of the day with her rather than have to wait to see her at a ball.

At Tomison house they would be left alone to talk about horses. He already planned to use the time to steal a few kisses.

And if they were caught, and her father demanded they marry to save her reputation, Hale would gladly accept the consequences of their actions, so he might continue with those actions for the rest of his life.

After breakfast, he spent a few hours in the stables looking after the new additions, but mostly counting down the minutes until he could see Gia again and thank her for what she'd done.

Hale was just getting ready to leave for Tomison House when Hutchinson came to tell him he had a visitor. Lord Waverly.

Perhaps the man had caught Gia sneaking in and she'd confessed to what happened. It was no matter. He was ready to do what was necessary.

Hale swallowed before squaring his shoulders and entering the drawing room where Gia's father waited.

"My lord, it is good to see you."

The man looked almost surprised to see him. Simply blinked.

Hale went on. "Is there something I can do for you?"

"Gia said she was here last night helping foal your horse."

"Aye. That's correct." Hale was tense because Waverly was tense. What accusations did he plan to make? Whatever they were, Hale was most certainly guilty. There's not been much he hadn't done to the man's daughter.

When the man said nothing else, Hale went on.

"In fact, I was just heading over to Tomison House to thank her again for her help. I'm afraid both foals and probably my mare would have been lost if not for her."

"I see."

The man glanced away with his brows pinched together. Hale was glad the man could "see," for Hale certainly couldn't see what was happening here.

"Is there a problem?" Hale asked, ready to have out with this one way or the other.

"You and my daughter have become friends in recent weeks and I've not said anything because I didn't see the harm. But if you are helping my daughter plan an escape back to the country, I would ask you to reconsider."

Hale had considered many things the man might say, but that hadn't been one of them.

Hale opened his mouth to assure the man he had no plans to help Gia leave London, but then, because of his friendship with Gia, he changed tact.

"You plan to keep her prisoner here in London, then? Despite her wishes?"

"I don't expect you to understand, but a father knows what is best for his children."

Hale couldn't dispute that his own father had not only not known best but not known anything about Hale at all.

"If Gia were a flighty, timid, debutante who avoided society out of unjustified fear, I would say I agreed with you. But Gia is a strong woman of sound mind. I have never seen her waver even once in her desire to spend her future in the country with her horses. How can you be certain what you want is better than what she wants for herself?"

"Loneliness? Surely you of all people wouldn't want that for someone after the way you were brought up."

Hale swallowed and tugged at his coat, a nervous habit he despised.

"I am not helping her plan an escape, Lord Waverly. She hasn't asked. If she does, I'm afraid my loyalty would have to fall with the lady as she has become a dear friend." It was true she was a dear friend. She was also much more, but he couldn't say that.

"I will not be around forever. Gia has no brothers to inherit my title and lands, both will go to a distant cousin who seems willing to take on a spinster relation at the moment, but there are no guarantees are there? What would you have your dear friend do then, Your Grace? I wish to see her settled and even more to see her happy. I would ask, if you care for my daughter as you seem to, please do not interfere."

He turned for the door and only stopped when Hale called his name.

Hale came to stand before him shaking his head.

"I don't understand why you don't push for *me* to marry her. You know we are friends. I spend more time than is acceptable in her company, yet you've not even hinted at such a thing. Do you find me unworthy of her?"

Hale wished he hadn't asked that last question for it was one he'd been asking himself and worried at the answer.

Waverly clasped Hale's shoulder.

"I've enough on my plate trying to wrestle Gia into marriage. I'm afraid I'm not up for such a battle as to herd the both of you to the alter."

"Lord Waverly, I have an idea." In fact, as the seconds ticked by, Hale devised a plan that would please everyone. Well, almost everyone.

⇛⇛✳⇚⇚

AFTER SPENDING MOST of the morning arguing with her father over her plans for the future, Gia was more than a little suspicious when her father stepped into the library where she was painting with a smile on his face.

He had been gone for some time and she'd hoped when he returned, he would drop this ridiculous plan to marry her off in some grand love match.

It was on the tip of her tongue to tell him she was ruined so he would give up, but she realized he would only set his sights on marrying her off even sooner.

The fact he was relaxed and smiling didn't bode well for Gia's freedom. Had he found someone to offer for her?

"Whatever has you looking so pleased?" she asked when he sat and steepled his hands in silence.

"I have sent Bess to pack a bag for you. Roxburghe will be coming for you at dawn tomorrow."

She swallowed, but made sure to keep her face unreadable. Had Jeremy spoken to her father and agreed to marry her? Were they heading for Scotland to elope? Why was she not more terrified of such a possibility?

"Where will we be going?" she asked, seeming only slightly curious despite her frantic heartbeat.

"Elmhurst."

Gia was certainly not expecting that.

"You've agreed to let me return home in the middle of the Season?"

"Yes." He tapped his index fingers against his lip and eventually gave up on his silence. "For a week. Roxburghe has requested your help to train his horse for Epsom and I've agreed it makes more sense to do so in the country where it is less likely you'll be seen."

She tilted her head and pushed for more information. There was no way her father would agree to this unless there was a concession made to his advantage.

"Why have you agreed?" Gia tilted her head, hiding her eagerness to leave this instant for home.

"Roxburghe will be bringing a friend. An unattached, titled friend. The Earl of Melville."

"I see." Gia wasn't sure she understood what Hale was doing, but she was certain he had no intentions of creating a match between Gia and his friend. Not when he'd just taken Gia to his bed the night before.

She had danced with Lord Melville and was certain he was even less interested in marriage than Jeremy.

"I think this could be the match for you, dear. Roxburghe says Melville shares an interest in horses and he's not declared he'd never marry unlike a certain duke you've befriended. And, of course, there's the matter of the betting books. If I can make a killing on both your marriage and Roxburghe's horse taking Epsom, all the better for me. If it doesn't work out with Melville, we'll only lose a week and there's still much of the Season left."

"But Lady Tomison won't be able to go with me. She is preparing to host her ball in two weeks' time. I should stay to help."

"I will stay with her, and Bess will go with you to the country to chaperone."

"My, it seems you've thought of everything," she said, knowing her father hadn't come up with any of this. Though Hale probably made sure her father would think he had. "I guess I have no say in the matter? It is only a week, I'm certain Lord Melville will not be overcome in a week's time and I'll be back here soon enough."

"I see no reason to rush home if everyone is enjoying the country. Perhaps two weeks would give you and Lord Melville more time to get to know one another."

Gia opened her mouth to ask if his sudden plan to send her away had anything to do with his wanting to have Lydia alone to himself but refrained.

However the situation came about didn't matter as much as the fact she was given permission to be away from the Season for two weeks.

And would have Jeremy to herself as well. It seemed everyone had what they wanted.

"THIS IS AN absolute nightmare," Julian complained as they trundled toward Tomison House in the early hours of dawn the next day.

With much to prepare, Hale hadn't made it to visit yesterday, hoping Gia would be pleased with his plan to get out of town for a week or so.

Julian, however, was the only person Hale had made unhappy with his hasty strategy.

"A nightmare, I'll remind you, I've agreed to compensate you for."

Julian's response was a displeased sound Scottish men were taught at birth. He'd tried to get Kit and Graham to join them as well, but in the end, only Julian was willing to give up sleep for Hale's benefit.

"I don't want your blasted coin, I want to be in my bed."

"If you don't want my coin, what is it you want?"

"I prefer to wait until I have you further over this barrel."

Whatever it was, Hale would gladly pay his friend for doing him this favor.

"I don't understand why I actually had to come along. You have no intentions of truly matching me to the lass."

"The staff at Elmhurst will certainly speak of the visit. I couldn't readily explain your absence without questions being asked."

"Very well, but did we need to leave at such an ungodly hour?"

Hale couldn't say that he wanted to be alone with Gia as soon as possible, so instead he muttered something about the transport of his prized racehorse which Julian didn't have the knowledge to dispute.

As soon as they stopped in front of Tomison House, two footmen carried out a small trunk and Gia and her maid descended the steps.

"My, it seems someone is eager to be in our company," Julian said with a brow lifted.

Rather than respond, Hale hopped down from the carriage and helped the ladies into the carriage. His hand lingered too long on Gia's waist and she held his hand longer than was proper which caused Julian's brow to raise a bit higher.

"I cannot wait to get out of this city and this bloody corset," Gia said as she settled in the seat next to him. Her maid, Bess, taking the seat opposite her, next to Julian.

"Careful, you'll make Julian blush," Hale teased her for her language.

Gia winced and turned toward the other man who had shifted into an easy smile.

"My apologies, Lord Melville."

"Not to worry. Your language is much deserved and quite accurate. Corsets are the devil's work. Besides, my blushes are not so easily won."

Gia's maid cleared her throat, expressing her displeasure on the topic, but said nothing directly.

"And now I must warn you, Julian, that you may have just created a challenge for her."

Gia smiled. "Unfortunately, my attempts to shock Lord Melville further will have to wait. I'm afraid I'm not up for such tasks thanks to Jeremy, for having us all up at this hour."

The carriage had barely pulled away from the house before Bess had fallen asleep leaning against the side of the carriage. As they reached the city limits, Gia joined her, but he was delighted when she'd leaned against him.

He shifted and wrapped his arm around her in an effort to make her more comfortable.

"*Jeremy?*" Julian said. Would his brow ever come down from its judgmental perch? "No one calls you by your Christian name."

"She does." Obviously.

Without thinking, Hale leaned down to press his lips to the

edge of her hairline as his fingers brushed through her hair.

"My God. You *love* her," Julian whispered. The smile on his face revealed he finally had a grasp of both pieces of the puzzle he was trying to solve.

"You know I have no concept of such things." Hale was quick to reject Julian's assumption. Though if ever Hale thought himself capable of such an emotion, it would most definitely be with this woman.

"Do you ever find it odd how we both suffer the same affliction, but for entirely opposite reasons?" Julian tilted his head before explaining further.

"You were abandoned by everyone who should have taught you about love and therefore you find yourself incapable of it, while *my* father was obsessively immersed in my upbringing and found fault in every speck of my existence, to the point I find I avoid anything to do with love as well."

"Perhaps it is why we are such close friends." Julian, Kit and Hale were three Scottish nobles, educated in Edinburgh before being launched on London. That alone would have drawn them together. Allies amongst the *ton*.

But it was more that had made them friends. Each broken and in need of someone to help distract them from noticing how many pieces were missing.

"Perhaps I am the only person who you might believe when I tell you we have been misled." Julian said, sadness clear in his voice.

"You want to love someone? Offer up your throat to the wolves?" Hale could hardly believe it.

"Nay. I would not attempt such a thing. But I wouldn't mind being loved by someone the way she clearly loves you." He nodded his head at the woman drooling on his coat.

Was Julian correct? Did she love him? How had he allowed her to do such a dangerous thing? He didn't want her to be hurt in any way, especially not like this.

"You're wrong, Jules." Hale shook his head. "She knows

better. She doesn't want marriage any more than I do."

Julian sniffed. "Maybe not now. But eventually you'll want it so much you'll do the unthinkable to get it."

"Do you think it would be so bad?"

"Which part? Marriage? Love? Opening your heart to someone?"

"All of it?"

His friend slid down in his seat and tugged his hat over his face, getting ready to join the women in slumber. Hale thought he might not answer, but after a few moments of silence, Julian said, "We would need to possess a heart in order to open it to someone, now wouldn't we?"

CHAPTER TWENTY-THREE

IT WAS NEAR dark when they pulled into the drive leading to Elmhurst.

Gia sat up from where she'd been leaning against Jeremy and felt a blush as Lord Melville smiled knowingly, yet kindly, at her.

"Welcome to Elmhurst, Your Grace, my lord," she said courteously.

Jeremy blinked, probably at her formal greeting.

They had remained rather silent on the day's journey, but she could tell Lord Melville and Jeremy were close. As well as Lord Sinclair, or Kit as they referred to him. The two shared tales of their school days and the trouble they got into. It was quite entertaining if also a bit sad.

She was helped down from the carriage and upon entering the foyer, Gia could tell the staff had been prepared for her arrival.

Jennings, the butler, was directing everyone about. A battalion of footmen were already carrying hot water up the stairs for a bath she would be most grateful for.

Mrs. Kempt bustled about as well.

"It is late, but I'll have trays sent up straightaway so you all might have a bite before retiring for the evening."

"I will see our guests to their rooms personally."

"Of course, miss."

"Thank you, Mrs. Kempt."

Upstairs Gia showed Lord Melville to his room first and then escorted Jeremy to the room closest to her own.

"I am right next door in case you are frightened by all the country noises and need assistance."

He glanced down the hall before wrapping an arm around her and pulling her close. He captured her lips and trailed kisses down her neck. A noise from her room forced them apart. Bess would be setting out things for her bath.

"I will most definitely take you up on your offer," he said before placing one more quick kiss on her mouth. "As soon as your maid has retired."

With that, he went into his own room.

She pressed her fingertips to her lips that tingled from his touch. Her cheeks were still warm when she went into her room and of course, Bess noticed.

"You and the duke seem quite close. I have a feeling there will be no match with Lord Melville," Bess smiled. Of course, she would have noticed how closely Gia sat to Jeremy, even leaning against him.

Bess could be trusted to keep her secrets and in truth, Gia wanted to confide in someone about what had happened.

"The night … After Hera delivered… Well… I was intimate with Jeremy. That is, the duke."

Bess's eyes went wide and then a smile spread slowly over her face.

"You're to be a duchess then? How exciting, miss."

"Oh. No."

Bess frowned. "He took your virtue and didn't offer for you? I thought the duke to be better bred than that, even for a Scot."

"No. He did offer. But only out of honor."

"As he should."

"I refused his offer."

"Refused? Miss, pardon me for being so bold, but you could be increasing this very moment and what then?"

Gia had of course known the way of things and the risk she'd taken.

"If it comes to that, I would certainly reexamine the situation, but so long as I'm not in the family way, I would prefer not to marry. You know that isn't what I wish for."

"You wish to remain here at Elmhurst with your horses." Bess didn't say the word "still" but Gia heard it nonetheless.

"Yes." Though as Bess said it, the thought didn't have the same satisfaction it once held. It sounded rather... empty.

She shook her head and focused on her future. The one she'd always planned on.

"Yes," she repeated, more forcefully this time.

Bess was not convinced if her raised brow was any indication.

"It is a long life ahead of you. And a lonely one if you get your wish."

"But it is my life, is it not? And I have a right to live it the way I want."

"With horses instead of a husband and children?" Bess shook her head as if the idea was absurd.

"Yes." Gia gave up on sounding convincing.

In truth, the more she thought of a life filled with the pleasure and happiness she felt with Jeremy, the more she considered that option. She would like nothing more than to spend her life doing the things they'd done before and would most likely do this night.

To have a husband who adored her.

She blinked and sighed.

He didn't adore her. He respected her. He offered marriage out of a sense of honor, not love.

"What put that sadness in your eyes?" Bess asked.

"There is nothing forcing me to make any decisions this minute. There is plenty of time to decide what is best. And I think some rose oil in my bath would be best."

Bess mumbled a few other things Gia didn't hear and didn't think she wanted to.

Gia sank into the warm water and allowed her mind to drift. Whether Jeremy would become her husband, remain her lover, or go back to being just a friend, she wasn't certain.

Time would tell.

⟫⟫⟫⟪⟪⟪

WHEN ALL WAS quiet, Hale slipped into Gia's room like a specter and found her at the open window. She cast a look over her shoulder and he felt his body respond to her silent invitation.

"You should be careful standing by this open window, you could catch a chill," he warned quietly as his fingertips played with her hardened nipples.

She turned to him and lifted up on her tiptoes to kiss him. It was the easiest thing he'd ever done to pick her up with his hands under her arse and carry her to the bed.

He was desperate for her, despite spending the day together in the carriage. It had been a pleasing torment. Slight touches as the carriage swayed. Hearing her voice, feeling the weight of her body as she slept against his side.

As he slid into her warmth he thought again of his earlier dilemma. He wanted this woman more than he should and not just to satisfy his carnal desires. Though she was quite good at that as well.

He didn't want to have to wait for secret moments to be with her. He wanted to share… his life with her.

As this realization settled over him like a warm blanket, he kissed her, wanting her to feel the emotions that were shifting in him. He wanted her to feel the same.

"Jeremy, please," she begged for him to give her the pleasure he'd exposed her to a few nights ago.

"Aye, lass," he promised and thrust in her again, deeper, harder as he reached between them to stroke that part of her that would bring her what she needed.

She cried out his name as she throbbed around him pulling him over the edge to join her in ecstasy.

But unlike other encounters, the joy didn't dissipate when he and his partner had climaxed. Pulling the counterpane over his sated lover and holding her close pulled a smile to his lips.

"I want this," he said into her hair.

"Hmm?" she said in response.

"I said I am happy here with you." While not exactly what he'd said, it was also true.

"Are you sure you wish to stay?" she asked. "I can train Godspell alone if you wish to return to London."

Did she want him to leave? He couldn't imagine having to leave her here alone. He wasn't sure he could.

"I know how much you detest the country," she went on when he'd remained silent. "Being forced to take in all this fresh air, sweet scents, and quiet? It's quite cruel, really." She smiled at her own joke and he joined in, glad he was not being dismissed.

He kissed the top of her head.

"Nay. Perhaps it is the company, or that I have not been here for more than a few hours, but I don't feel uncomfortable here. There is no sense of overwhelming loneliness when I have you in my arms."

"I shall make sure you are never lonely during your visit," she promised.

He shouldn't be pressing for more from her. At least not until he'd made sense of these new feelings. He only knew that he didn't feel the least bit lonely with her in his arms.

⧽⧽⧽⧼⧼⧼

ALMOST A WEEK after she'd arrived at Elmhurst, Gia was pleased with Godspell's progress. But it was not all she was pleased about. She loved being home. The house was large, but comfortable. And she enjoyed strolling through the fields of oats or the path through the woods.

Owen had arrived a few days ago to assist her in training

Godspell. And Godspell had a good shot at winning, according to her groom.

But it was her nights spent with Jeremy that brought her the most joy.

Jeremy seemed pleased to spend the days with her as they had in the past, talking of horses and Godspell's training. But their nights… there was no talk of horses.

In fact, there was not much talk at all as he taught her all the ways a man could satisfy a woman. She wanted to ask if this was normal, this constant desire, but she didn't want to pressure him into sparing her feelings. She did not need promises of a future together, though more than a few times, Gia had wondered what it might be like to have this for the rest of her days.

In the morning, she opened her eyes to find Jeremy already awake and watching her.

"What are you doing?" she asked while trying to hide her face. She felt thoroughly rumpled from their activities the night before.

"Waiting for you to wake so we can go eat. I'm rather famished after you made me do all the work last night."

"It is too early in the morning for jokes, Your Grace."

He chuckled, the sound deeper than usual in the mornings.

"The fact that you woke earlier than me clearly proves that I exerted more energy than you."

She loved teasing him and watching him burst into a fit of laughter. She'd felt a certain power as she'd made love to him the night before riding astride him as she would in the saddle of a horse, but earning his laughter held a different kind of power.

She had the ability to push away all the sadness and pain of his past and make him happy, if only for a few moments before he shrugged that weight back onto his broad shoulders.

As she had the night before, she rolled on top of him and settled herself on his length, earning a hiss of delight.

"You know very well I enjoy a morning ride, Your Grace."

He closed his eyes and tucked his hands behind his head,

ceding control to her.

"I am a lucky man, indeed, for I know well how hard and fast you prefer to ride in the mornings."

She bent to kiss his lips. And when he opened his eyes and turned that molten blue gaze on her, she knew it was she that was lucky.

CHAPTER TWENTY-FOUR

HALE HADN'T HAD a moment to concern himself about being in the country. While the sunlight filled the sky, he spent his time with Gia in the field with the horses. And when it set, he spent every waking hour in bed with her.

He couldn't get enough of her.

Even when they spent the necessary time in the dining room eating, or in the drawing room with Julian, he enjoyed being with her. He hadn't laughed so much in all his life.

The things he was most afraid of—marriage—were no longer scary. And each day he fell for her a little bit more.

He expected there would be a moment when he would be jerked from her spell, but for the moment he only wanted to fall deeper.

"I think he's ready," Gia said as he sipped his claret over dinner. Julian had chosen to stay in his room to pack for their departure the next day, so he had Gia to himself.

"Pardon?" Hale said.

"Your horse. Godspell. Remember the reason why we've come to Surrey?"

The reason he'd come to Surrey was to be with her. But she was correct. There was another reason as well.

"He'd better be. The race is in two days. Whether he's ready or not, he'll be out there. I think the old chap will give his best, but Dante will as well."

"Godspell is a little taller than Dante. Longer in the leg. It could make a difference in this situation."

They fell into a weighted silence as he looked at her. When would they be together like this again? He would have to go back to pretending she was merely a friend. He would only have stolen moments to kiss or touch her skin.

Eventually she looked up and caught him watching her.

"What?" She wiped at her chin self-consciously.

"You are beautiful," he said, the words just came out of his mouth. The truth as easy as breathing.

She must have considered arguing for a moment but instead of dismissing his comment she sat a bit straighter and picked up her fork once again and simply said, "Thank you."

And that was when he realized he was in love with Giovanni Verona Landon. While he wasn't sure how such a thing had happened, he didn't feel the fear he expected.

At least not yet.

⇛⇚

SOON ENOUGH RACE day was upon them, bringing a close to the week and a half they'd been hidden away from everyone in their own small paradise.

In mid-May, everyone who loved horses traveled to Surrey for the Epsom Derby. Gia had been many times, but this year she would be watching two of her horses compete. Rather two of her former horses.

A nervous Jeremy was waiting to help her down from the carriage when they arrived. Not that anyone else would know he was nervous.

"He will be splendid, you'll see," she reassured him as she looked over the grounds and took in all the colors. The gorgeous blue sky and the thick green grass that would soon bear the weight of ten thoroughbreds at full speed.

The ladies in their colorful frocks did not distract from the natural beauty of the day especially when the man she loved was smiling at her.

"And if he isn't?" he asked.

"Then you will tell him he did a fine job and take him home. And we will make sure he is better prepared for the next race." She shrugged, unsure what else there was to do.

"You seem to forget that men wager on these races."

"Oh." She frowned. Women were not permitted to place bets, and she wouldn't have done so anyway. "Well, in that case, if you lose your shirt, I will certainly appreciate the view."

He chuckled and leaned closer. "Do not say things that stir my arousal when we're out in public. I do not want to have to walk around with an uncomfortable and embarrassing erection," he whispered.

She felt the flare of power once more that her words had roused him physically.

"I would surely appreciate that view as well."

"Minx. You shall pay for that." He glanced down and while she wanted so much to look, she knew it would be highly improper. "Who knew you were so naughty?"

"If I am, it is all your doing. You have awoken my wanton desires."

He widened his eyes and looked away. Apparently speaking of her wanton desires was one of those topics to be avoided if the bulge in his breeches was anything to go on. And, yes, she looked even though she'd tried not to.

"If you don't behave, I will have to find a discreet shrub or a tree to take you behind."

She chuckled quietly as he led them to the edge of the racecourse so they would be in position to see the start of the race.

Owen came up and gave a curt nod which served to tell them the horses were ready and on the line to start. Jeremy offered a return nod of thanks. Gia felt as if they spoke another language that hadn't been offered by her tutors.

The language of Scottish men. And what a complicated communication it was since they preferred not to use actual words.

She took a moment to peruse the crowd and waved at her father and Lydia. She kept the smile on her face despite knowing she would be leaving with them to return to London.

Her time alone with Jeremy was over.

"You suddenly look quite sad. Are you well?"

"Yes. Let us focus on enjoying the race. Which appears to be ready to start."

Before she'd said the last word, the horses were off. The thunder of hooves made the ground tremble beneath her half boots. She wished she could be one of those jockeys, but women weren't permitted to participate in any part of horse racing. At least not officially.

When the horses were out of range, Jeremy stepped away to pace in a circle.

"Do you have a large amount wagered on this race?" she worried. Surely, he wouldn't have risked so much on a horse running only his second race.

He shook his head. Gia couldn't interpret if that meant too much to speak of or nothing at all.

"It isn't about the money," Owen said to her as Jeremy continued to pace.

The crowd had grown quiet as they waited for the first sign of the horses to reappear on the horizon. Gia focused intently, hating to so much as blink until she saw the first horse crest the hill.

"There," she said while pointing.

"Is it him?" Jeremy asked.

"I think it is." Though she felt it was Godspell more than saw that it was. As the pack grew closer, she was sure Godspell was in the front with Dante right behind him. She reached out to squeeze Jeremy's forearm in an effort to keep from jumping and shouting in a most unladylike manner. "It's him. I'm sure of it."

With each second the horses grew closer, until they were better able to see their horse was in the lead.

"I'll be damned. It is him," Hale whispered. "He's going to win."

When Godspell crossed the finish line and was declared the winner, they merely looked at each other with wide smiles on their faces.

"You don't know how much I wish I could kiss you and twirl you around in my arms right now," he said quietly.

She felt the loss of such a celebration and realized it was a mere sample of what was to come when their time together was over.

She didn't know if she would survive it.

IT WAS NEARLY torture to be so close to Jeremy and not be able to kiss him. Not be permitted to touch his skin and pull him against her so the heat from his body warmed her own.

But they were on a dance floor with all of society watching. As such, she stiffened her spine and refrained from doing anything untoward.

"You smell delicious and I want for nothing more than to lead you away from here so I might have my way with you."

"What is it you always say about me saying things to make you aroused, Your Grace?" She raised a brow. "I can feel you have been most unsuccessful tonight in avoiding such a situation." She knew it wasn't coincidence that had him brushing that part of his body against hers.

"Then let us change the subject until later tonight. Perhaps I might find myself outside your home after everyone else has gone to bed."

"And perhaps I might need to take some air and could find you in the garden?"

"Yes, the garden. That might be a place where you would find someone while taking in the cooler evening air."

They shared a knowing smile and she shook away the thoughts that came unbidden. Memories of his touch and the feelings he brought to the surface.

The night wore on and eventually they returned home. In her bed chamber, she waited in a chair by the window for her rendezvous with Jeremy.

When the house went still, she left her room and made her way outside to the garden where he was waiting. The silvery moonlight cast a glow upon all it touched.

His hair looked almost white as he bent to kiss her.

They both groaned in happiness.

"I wanted to do that so many times this evening, and the past few days since we've returned to London."

"Just kissing?" she asked, doing an adequate job of playing coy.

"Shall I show you the other things I thought of doing to you?"

Her heart pounded as he placed a kiss near her throat. His lips burning the skin that had chilled in the night air. She wanted his lips everywhere.

"Yes, Jeremy. Show me every single one."

⇒⇒⇒⇐⇐⇐

"I FEAR I'M becoming used to you coming to my room each night," he said as he kissed her and slid off the cloak she wore over her thin night rail. He stripped her in his usual efficient manner before leading her to a bench.

Once there, he opened his trousers enough to pull his hardened length away from the fabric. She straddled him, taking him inside of her in one easy glide causing them to moan in relief.

She rocked against him in their stolen moment.

Despite the happiness she felt when joined with him, she felt something else now. The cool chill of reality caused a shiver.

This was all they would ever have. Stolen moments. She was merely his lover. And while she believed he was faithful, and thought her a friend, what would become of her when this affair ended?

But the only other option was marriage.

She'd never wanted that. Or at least she hadn't thought so.

She'd refused his proposal made for the sake of her honor that morning after she'd given him her virtue.

When she'd first arrived in London for her come out years ago, she'd thought of marriage a great deal. She'd imagined every man she met playing the role of her doting husband. The proud father to her passel of children. But as time went by, she'd realized they never planned to marry her.

Perhaps she'd grown jaded after her first season—no, she was certain she had—she painted every man with the same brush. Rake, rogue, scoundrel.

It had been easier to protect herself. She'd once wanted a love match like her parents had, but had given up on that dream.

She should be happy with this. What they had now, whatever it might be called. It was more than just sex. They were good friends who shared physical pleasure whenever possible.

Except it had grown to be more than that. At least for her.

She was in love with Jeremy. She did her best to hide her feelings from him, but in their intimate moments it became nearly impossible to keep them in check. She so badly wanted to say the words and hear him say them in return.

I love you.

But this was planned to end. Most likely at the end of the Season.

She would return to Elmhurst with many fond memories of her time with him, and he would stay there in London doing whatever he'd done before she came along and disrupted his life.

She would miss him terribly. Maybe even severely. But they couldn't carry on after the Season ended. To do so would just make it more difficult for the both of them.

"I'll miss you," she admitted quietly against his skin, hoping he hadn't heard her confession.

"I wish we could…" he said, but she kissed him before he could finish that wish.

She wished as well. And perhaps they wished for the same thing.

He'd told her how his parents despised one another and left him alone. Of course, it made sense that he wouldn't want to end up in the similar situation of an unhappy marriage.

He'd been neglected and unloved simply because his parents couldn't stand to be near each other. The innocent victim of his parents' hatred.

But what if in protecting themselves they missed out on happiness by trying to avoid unhappiness?

She got caught up in their love making, as his eyes bore into hers communicating all he could not say aloud. When they broke, they did so just as silently, allowing the other person to see them at their most vulnerable moment. When their hearts were exposed.

He let out a breath and pulled her close once more.

"We don't need to have the answer tonight," he whispered as if he'd heard everything that had passed through her thoughts.

An hour later, Gia climbed the servants' stairs and sneaked into her room. And she knew as she slivered into the cool sheets, she didn't want to lie in a cold lonely bed the rest of her life.

She wanted a husband.

CHAPTER TWENTY-FIVE

HALE RETURNED HOME at only half ten, feeling as if he'd left a rather important part of himself back in the Tomison gardens.

Apparently, their time together was not just about satisfying their physical desires. If it had ever been simple lust—which he doubted—it had grown to be more. He felt empty to have to return to his home alone when he wanted to sleep next to her and wake in the morning to her teasing.

There was only one way to ensure he would always have that.

Marriage.

The word no longer held the revulsion it once had. It wasn't something to be feared or avoided. Not if it was engaged with the right person.

He'd not wanted to be forced into a marriage like his parents had. But a life with Gia would be so far from that.

If he chose her because he didn't want to spend a day without her, it would not be the same at all.

He'd thought them incompatible. She who hated the city and flourished in the country. He who clung to London and the distractions it offered so he'd never be alone.

But no distraction of the *ton* would ever make him as happy as seeing Gia in her breeches, smiling and laughing in the sun.

And suddenly he knew exactly how it could be with them,

and everything he wanted turned on its axis. Plans clicked into place and before he realized it, he was knocking on his valet's door.

"Yes, Your Grace?"

"Pack my trunks, we leave at first light tomorrow."

"Yes, Your Grace. And where are we going?"

"Home." That wasn't quite right. It wasn't a home yet, but he wouldn't stop until he made it in to one. At Chauncey's confusion, Hale clarified. "To Scotland."

⇉⇇

THREE WEEKS HAD gone by since Gia had last seen Jeremy.

He'd left without so much as a mention of where he'd gone or what important business had called him away—not that it was her right to know—but she did wonder what made him flee so abruptly.

Part of her worried she'd spoken too much of her feelings out loud that night when she'd stumbled across the knowledge she wanted to marry. It would explain why Jeremy had run off to the country of all places.

For all she knew, he could have been set upon by pirates—though he hadn't said anything about a sea voyage.

She had even made certain to bump into Lord Melville and Lord Stormont in order to ask them if they'd heard anything, but they only said he'd told them both he had business in the country. So at least he hadn't kept the details from just her. His other friends knew as little as she.

Maybe he was trussed up in some hamlet to be ransomed off, only no one in his household had responded to the request.

Her mind had no shortage of dangerous scenarios as to why Jeremy had not returned in time to comfort her when her world had suddenly turned upside down.

Just a few days after Jeremy had left, her father and Lydia

shared some shocking news. Not only were they getting married, but Lydia was with child.

That last part was, of course, not common knowledge and was only shared with Gia after she'd noticed how frequently Lydia had been ill in the mornings.

Gia couldn't help but be happy for them. It was clear they were in love.

And, yes, she may have taken more than a few moments to wonder as to the chances that her father would find *two* wonderful women to love in his lifetime, while others never found anyone.

And yes, she selfishly meant herself, which was why she'd kept the thought private. And even more so because Gia had in fact found love, only the object of that love was at present missing and had no plans to marry.

In truth, her father was adorable in the way he doted over Lydia and would excitedly declare that he was to have an heir. Obviously, there was no proof to his claim that the child was a male, but Gia hoped he would get the son he'd always wanted.

As the days went on, and the wedding plans were coming together, Gia contemplated how these changes would affect her life.

At first, she thought the pending nuptials would give her leave to return to Elmhurst after the wedding and allow the new family their own space in London.

But soon other thoughts filtered through her mind.

How long would they want to support her? She could sell more of her horses to cover her expenses, but the truth of the matter was, she would be a burden. Perhaps not a financial one, but the dreaded spinster daughter.

Her father had brought her to London to marry her off so she would no longer be his responsibility. How had she not realized the reason? Yes, she believed he wanted her to find a love match, and he wished for her happiness, but she was supposed to move on.

And if her new sibling was a girl, instead of the heir her father expected…

Gia rubbed her temples as she contemplated how having a spinster sister would hurt the girl's chances to marry well. It would be many years until that came to fruition, but each year she remained unmarried it would be all the more difficult to marry.

She barely slept the night before the wedding, stressed as she was by her situation. She knew neither her father nor Lydia would push her from her home, but she did need to consider her options.

She had already invested a great deal of time into the Season and had no desire to have to do so again next year. She could possibly fan the flames of interest with one of the men who still visited occasionally. Though she hadn't felt even the smallest amount of attraction or affection for any of them. Not when she'd had Hale to distract her.

But Hale wasn't here and she didn't know when he would return. And if he did, what would it matter? He didn't wish to marry. And though he'd proposed after they'd made love the first time, it was clear it wasn't what he truly wanted.

He'd asked her to marry him out of duty rather than any true interest to be married. He'd told her on more than one occasion why he had no interest in marrying. He hadn't wanted a cold marriage of convenience. But would it have to be like that for them? He was her best friend and lover.

He was also a man.

She'd experienced how easily men could pretend to care for her in the hopes of getting what they wanted. She hadn't thought Hale was toying with her. He'd not pushed for anything until she was ready. He cared for her, didn't he?

What if his seemingly unyielding patience had all been part of the game?

It seemed they were well suited in all things including their lack of plans for their futures. She had been of the same mind, with no desire to marry.

Until now.

Just because Gia's circumstances had changed didn't mean Hale was interested in changing his plans. There was also the matter of their difference of opinions in where they wished to live. Despite his extended stay in the country currently, he preferred town life. While she felt suffocated under the rules of society in London.

She put on her best smile during the wedding the following morning and kept it there throughout the breakfast despite the comments tossed her way.

"Surely the newlyweds will want their privacy when they return from their honeymoon. Do you have a relative you could visit?"

"The Season is not over yet. There's still time to find a husband, dear."

Gia stepped out into the garden to get some air. Only when she was alone did she feel the need to cry. And it was becoming more and more obvious that she would be alone for the rest of her life if she didn't do something drastic, like marry. As soon as possible.

"Here you are," her father said as he came up behind her.

She felt ridiculous crying about her own issues on such a joyous occasion.

"What is this?" he asked, proving she'd done a poor job of hiding her tears.

"I'm so happy for you and Lydia, Papa."

He frowned and put his arm around her. Her head fit perfectly against his shoulder as it had since she'd been fourteen. But she was no longer a girl. She was a woman. And women married and left their father's homes. Generally, they did so way before they'd reached the age of five and twenty.

"I've seen tears of joy before and I daresay, they don't look like this."

"Apparently I inherited your deplorable acting skills." She

laughed through the tears and he offered a chuckle before patting her arm.

"I *am* happy for you. Truly," she repeated with more emphasis and fewer tears. "I love Lydia. She may now have the title of stepmother, but she shall always be my friend.

"I know you are not unhappy about our marriage. But something is wrong."

"Nothing is wrong." *I'm wrong.* "I'm so sorry I've disappointed you, Papa. You brought me here to find a husband and I didn't take it seriously. I didn't realize…"

"Gia, I didn't bring you here to find *any* husband. I could have found you a proper husband without all the dramatics to get you to London. I wanted you to meet people, and I'd hoped you would meet someone who made you happy. Someone who *wanted* to marry. I'd hoped Lord Melville…well, never mind that."

She'd told him she and Julian were not well suited. And she was sure his mention of someone who *wanted* to marry was in relation to Hale.

He cleared his throat and went on.

"Sharing your life with someone you care for makes it so much sweeter. I only want that for you."

"Would I even know if I found the right person? Like you did when you met mama?" She'd always heard theirs was a love at first sight. While she had admired Hale's fine looks when they'd met, she hadn't been stricken with any great emotion until recently.

"Sometimes it happens like that. A lightning strike. Other times it can be a friendship that builds over the years." He smiled and she knew he spoke now of Lydia. This was more similar to how it had been with Hale, but their friendship had not lasted years.

"For others, they might start off with something as simple as respect, and one day they realize it has grown into love somewhere along the way. However, it comes about, having someone by your side brings peace to your days."

"It sounds lovely." And it did seem wonderful. But unfortunately, when she thought of the person she wanted by her side for the rest of her days, all she could envision was Jeremy.

How his dark, blond waves would turn lighter until they bleached to white. How the creases at the corners of his blue eyes would deepen from years of laughter. She imagined children and later, grandchildren, to love.

And she wanted it so badly, it brought another batch of tears to her eyes.

How could she possibly miss something she'd been certain she'd never wanted. She felt all kinds of silly for not seeing why others wished for this.

"Here you two are," Lydia called as she came out and wrapped an arm around her new husband's waist. "They are bringing the carriage around. We should say our farewells."

Her father's brow creased in worry and she knew he was considering pushing back his honeymoon to stay with her. She couldn't allow it.

"I hope you will enjoy your travels. You must write to me occasionally to tell me where you are. Not too much though, I know you'll be busy."

She wouldn't think about what they would be busy doing. It was her father after all. And while she hadn't eaten much during the wedding breakfast, she had no wish to cast up the little bit she had managed.

"I've started my farewells with the person I'll miss most while we're away," her father said and kissed Gia's cheek. "You're sure you'll be all right, love?"

"Of course." She squared her shoulders and wiped away the last of her tears, showing a brave front. "I have plenty to keep me busy as well. Xandra is coming along nicely in her training, but still needs some work now that the races are over."

It was an exaggeration. In truth, Xandra took to everything easier than any horse she'd ever trained.

Owen often joked that her American blood made her more stubborn, but Xandra was quite pleasant.

"I will miss you most as well," Lydia said, brushing the remaining dampness from Gia's cheek with a sad smile.

"Thank you for trying to help me," Gia said. "I'm sorry I was such a mess."

"I'm sorry I attempted to contort you into something you're not. Someday, some man is going to realize how amazing you are, and he's going to sweep you off your feet. I hope we're back in time to see it." Lydia spoke as if this *sweeping* was imminent instead of a fairy tale.

Gia forced a smile and wished them a joyous honeymoon as they rode away. When they were gone and the lingering guests had left, Gia wandered to her room, noting the silence in the halls. She felt more alone than she ever had before.

She needed to act now. While her father and Lydia were away.

Gia would find a man who wanted to marry her, and they would be ready to wed as soon as her father and stepmother returned.

And Jeremy… he would remain forever her fondest memory.

CHAPTER TWENTY-SIX

WHILE LADY BIDDLE was a more watchful chaperone than Lydia, Gia appreciated the woman was willing to accompany her to the Beverley ball.

After all, how was Gia supposed to find a husband in time if she waited for her new stepmother to return home from her honeymoon so she could return to society?

When she'd arrived in London months ago, she'd been willing to do anything to get out of such an event, but now she willingly sought out her own chaperone so she could attend. How much she had changed in just a few months.

She groaned softly.

"Are you well, dear?" Lady Biddle asked.

"Oh, yes. I'm fine."

"Then don't make that noise. In fact, it would be best if you don't make any noises," the woman said with a stern frown.

"Of course. I'll remain silent the duration of the evening."

Gia's sarcasm was met by a lifted eyebrow and a hearty chuckle from the man standing behind her. Recognizing his laugh, she turned and smiled at the familiar dark-haired countenance of Lord Duncan.

"Miss Gia, might I have this dance?"

"Why, yes," Gia answered with a smile. Lord Duncan had been one of the only men she'd danced with capable of keeping his gaze on her face.

"How have you been? I've not seen you recently," she asked to start the conversation.

"Ah, so you've been looking for me?"

"Impertinent," she scolded playfully, causing him to smile.

"I had business at one of my estates and have only just returned to town. I just missed meeting with your father."

"You know my father?" Gia smiled.

"My father and yours were good friends long ago. I met Harold again at his club a few weeks ago before I left London. He told me about your horses and mentioned you'd recently received a new mare from America."

"Yes. A mustang. Her name is Xandra."

"Ah. Because of her adventures, I'd wager."

"Yes." Gia was fairly beaming at the man, so happy was she to have finally met a man who was interested in horses. Make that *another* man.

She still hadn't heard any word from Jeremy. Thinking of him, she found herself unwillingly comparing the two men. Lord Duncan lacked the rumbling brogue she was used to. He wasn't as tall or broad, though his dark looks were more like her own and suited him fine.

Lord Duncan didn't make her heart race or set her blood aflame. He was handsome enough. He just wasn't as handsome as Jeremy.

But Jeremy wasn't here. And even if he were, he wouldn't want to marry.

The question was, did Lord Duncan have the same aversion to marriage?

Over the weeks since Jeremy quit London, the men who had shown an interest had waned. She'd been glad of it, knowing they no more wished to offer marriage than Jeremy had. But when she'd held out her dance card to Lord Duncan with only two names scribbled on it, it made her cheeks warm.

She remembered how refreshing it had been to be in his company compared to the men who leered at her during their dances, or worse, the men who didn't bother to ask for a dance and suggested a walk through the gardens instead. Lord Duncan's humor and lack of interest in horticulture gave her hope.

Lord Duncan asked about the rest of her family. Since she had only her father, that conversation drifted off quickly. "Are you close with your family, then?"

"Yes. It's just my mother now that my sister married last year. I thought it would be easier this year not having to worry about finding a husband for my sister. But alas, my mother has turned her sights on me."

"She wishes to marry you off next?"

"Yes." He let out a breath. "I suppose it is time. I've held her off long enough."

"At least your mother did not feign a medical crisis to trick you into coming to London."

He tilted his head to study her.

"Truly?" He was smiling.

"Unfortunately, yes. Had I not been so concerned for my father's wellbeing, I might have noticed how atrocious his acting abilities were."

They shared another laugh and Gia felt a kinship start to form for the man leading her around the dance floor. He was perfectly polite. They had shared interests.

Perhaps this could be enough.

⇛⇚

AFTER A TIRING journey, Hale arrived home in time to change from his traveling clothes, bathe, and leave again for visiting hours. The last hour of his trip, he'd wished he had one of his horses so he could get to Gia faster.

He knew he'd missed her while he'd been away, but as he grew closer to London, his need for her continued to grow.

More than a few times, as he'd been overseeing the design for the expansion of his stables or upgrades for the castle, had Hale thought he should have proposed to Gia before he'd left. But he'd wanted to have his house in order so when he proposed and she said, yes—Dear God, let her say yes—they could marry immediately, and he could take her to her new home.

He knocked on the door at Tomison House, while hoping Lady Tomison would leave them alone so he might kiss Gia and tell her how he'd thought of her. Perhaps she'd sneak into his bed that night. He would need to speak to her father. Should he propose to her first or after speaking to Lord Waverly?

Luther greeted him with a look of surprise.

"Your Grace, it's been some time. Miss Gia is in the drawing room."

Hale gave a nod and headed in that direction, surprised that Gia wasn't painting in the gardens. It was a beautiful June day.

He strode into the room to find the most peculiar thing. Gia and her maid occupied two chairs by the windows and Gia was... embroidering.

When she looked up, she smiled, but not with the excitement he'd hoped for.

"Your Grace, you've returned. I hope you had a pleasant trip. I was worried."

She was more than worried. She was cross with him for leaving without an explanation. Or not sending a note to explain further, and she was justified in her anger. He'd only wanted it to be a surprise.

"I apologize. I should have sent—"

"No. I'm the one to apologize. Of course, you weren't required to tell me anything. It is surely none of my business."

He worried he'd somehow stumbled into a trap, but Gia continued to smile as she tugged a bright blue thread through the fabric in her lap.

"Whatever are you doing?" he finally asked when the curiosity became too much to bear.

She held up a jumbled mess of blue thread.

"It's a flower," she said with more than a hint of challenge in her eyes. If it was a flower, he was a goat.

"What kind, a forget-me-*knot*?" He chuckled at his pun as Gia frowned at her creation. Why did she not laugh? "It was a play on the name of the flower." A jest rather lost its sparkle when one had to explain it.

"Oh, yes, Your Grace." Gia tittered a laugh. *Tittered*. Gia never *tittered*. "It is rather a mess, isn't it? However, it is much better than my last attempt."

This was not the first time she'd sat in the drawing room while embroidering?

He glanced around the room. It looked to be the same as the one they'd shared for hours each day talking of horses and other things that interested them. Sharing laughter and occasionally, kisses.

But despite the familiarity he felt in the room, the woman seemed a complete stranger.

"Why are you embroidering rather than painting?" he asked, hoping the answer would give him a clue as to what was amiss.

She put the fabric down and looked at her maid.

"Bess, would you give us a moment alone?"

"Yes. I'll leave the door open." The maid curtseyed, which was not something Gia ever requested of her servant.

"Very good. Thank you."

He barely waited until the maid had gotten out of the room before blurting, "What the devil is going on?"

⤜⟫⟫⟫⟪⟪⟪⤛

GIA COULD SEE Jeremy's confusion, and wanted to tell him straight out what had transpired while he was away.

She hadn't been concerned about how this conversation would go before, but now that he was here, she found herself delaying.

She folded her hands in her lap, the way a countess should, and gestured to the seat in front of her.

"Please sit. Would you care for—"

"I don't want any bloody tea," he snapped before sitting and taking a breath. "Thank you, though." He waved a hand toward the windows. "It's a sunny day. Great light for painting and being outside."

"Yes, it is, Your Grace."

"And why are you calling me *Your Grace*? You call me Jeremy or Hale at the very least."

"It wouldn't be proper."

"Since when do you care about what is proper?" He looked around the room as if wondering if he'd wandered into the wrong house. So much had changed since he'd last been there.

"Since I am to be a countess," she said sharper than she'd planned. Apparently, it wasn't so easy to hide her irritation with him.

"What?"

"I'm to be married," she repeated, wishing the words made her heart race in excitement. The most she could say was that she no longer felt ill when sharing her news.

"*Married?* To whom?"

It should have bothered her more that he questioned her news as if it were preposterous.

"Lord Duncan."

Hale had said Lord Duncan was a respectable gentleman. It was one of the reasons she'd considered his offer. But now it seemed Hale despised the man.

"I need to sit down," he said.

"You are sitting, Your Grace."

"Aye." He rubbed his forehead. "I feel as if I've woken in a Dickens novel. I was only gone just shy of five weeks, and it's as if I've returned to some paradox."

"I know it is a surprise. But so much has happened since you left." She stopped herself from adding, *with no word*, because it was not her place.

"Please start at the beginning and explain so I can get my bearings."

"Yes, of course." She set aside the embroidery, glad to have a respite from the disaster she was making. "Shortly after you left, my father and Lydia were betrothed..." She went on to tell him they were going to have a child after securing his discretion.

"I am pleased for their happiness and sorry I missed the celebration, but this doesn't explain why *you* are betrothed," he said when she thought she'd explained enough. Obviously not.

"Don't you see, my father brought me to London to see me married so he could move on with his life. I didn't know how selfish I was being to resist his plans before. Once I realized I couldn't continue on as a burden for him and Lydia and eventually my younger brother or sister, I knew I needed to make the best of the Season and find a match."

"And Lord Duncan is that match? He's asked for your hand? And you've said yes."

"He hasn't asked for my hand yet. He is waiting for father to return to speak to him before he officially proposes, but he and I have come to an understanding."

"An understanding that includes embroidery and restricts laughter at incredibly witty puns?" he nearly shouted as he came out of his seat to pace about the room.

"It's time I put all of that aside so I can focus on being the countess he needs."

"All of that? Laughter and painting? *All of that* is the essence of who you are, Gia, and you're willing to give it all up so you will not be a burden to a father who loves you and would never think of you as such?"

He was speaking so quickly she had to concentrate to keep up.

"Whether he thinks me a burden or not isn't the issue. I can't continue on as I have. It's time to grow up."

"Do you love him?" The duke's motions were becoming

more frantic by the moment.

"My father? Yes. I mean, I'm still displeased by the way he manipulated me to—"

"No. Lord Duncan. Do you love him?"

"Well, no. But he is pleasant, and I've come to think of him as a friend."

"Have you and he…?"

Gia looked away and answered, though she wouldn't have had to.

"No. And we won't until the wedding night. I'll not lie and pretend to be chaste, but he didn't ask, so I don't think it matters to him."

She hoped that was the case. She thought perhaps the man simply *assumed* she was still a maiden and didn't think to question it.

Jeremy looked quite angry, so she decided to shift the conversation to the part he would enjoy.

"As a countess, I won't be able to train horses any longer, but I will be giving you Arabella as a gift. She is, after all, what brought you into my life and I will always think of you fondly."

"I come back to find the woman I hold in the highest regard has contorted her very existence into something she never wanted to be in an effort to do the very thing she never wanted to do, and ye think to appease me with a fucking *horse*?" His anger caused his Scottish lilt to be more pronounced. He took a deep breath, but it didn't seem to help calm him.

But no, the breath was just so he had more oxygen to continue yelling at her.

"Did ye consider once in this preposterous plan that I had offered for you already? If you wished to marry, you had only to speak to me about it and I would have renewed my offer."

"I did consider it. But you weren't here, and I didn't know when you would return. But even if you had been here, I knew you didn't really want to marry and I couldn't ask it of you."

"If you'll excuse me, I must return home." He turned for the door and didn't so much as look back at her as he stole from the house.

Tears flooded her eyes when she heard the front door open and close.

That hadn't gone as she'd expected at all.

She'd hoped that in the time he was gone she'd gotten over him. But when he left, it felt as if he'd taken a large part of her heart with him.

HALE WALKED ABOUT Mayfair unsure of where he was going or who he might have passed without so much as a greeting. He was angry and didn't know who he was angry at.

He wanted to be angry with Gia for abandoning him. For changing into someone he didn't even know anymore. But that wasn't fair. She wanted to marry. Despite her misguided reasons why, she wanted the very thing he'd told her he didn't want.

What did he expect her to do? She wasn't at fault. And hadn't he abandoned her first? Left to the country without a word. She didn't know he had changed his mind about the bloody business of marriage. That he'd wanted to marry her. His absence was only to ensure she would be happy as his wife.

He sought out the next person he could set his anger on.

"Lord Duncan," he muttered earning a squeak of dismay from a passing woman. He didn't know where the man lived, but Hale would search him out and confront him.

But what fault could he find with the earl? That he'd found Gia intriguing and beautiful enough to want to spend his life with her? Hale hardly knew the man, but he trusted Gia to see through any possible trick.

"Bloody Christ." He stopped rather abruptly in the path of two workmen who offered their own curses and walked around him.

If he couldn't be angry with Gia or Lord Duncan, that only left himself.

The list of his failings was egregious.

He should have told her he loved her before he'd left London.

He'd missed his chance.

CHAPTER TWENTY-SEVEN

AFTER SPENDING THE evening at home, thinking of how to win over Gia, with more whisky than was required, he'd groaned over his breakfast and cursed himself for his stupidity.

He'd not fallen to poor judgement like that since Julian, Kit and he were just out of Heriot's.

He was still nursing an aching head hours later when Hutchinson entered his study.

"A Lord Duncan to see you, Your Grace."

It wasn't often fate delivered the person you very needed at the moment you needed them, but here was the gentleman Hale required without having to call on the man himself.

"Please, send him in."

Hale only gave a moment's thought to his appearance. It didn't matter what Duncan thought of him. Only that Hale was able to entice Gia when and if the opportunity arose.

"Your Grace," the man stopped inside the room and bowed.

Hale offered a nod and gestured to the chair in front of his desk. "Please have a seat. Can I offer you something to drink?" Hale hoped the man would abstain because he didn't know if he could manage even the scent of drink at this point.

"No, thank you. I will be brief."

"Very well. How might I assist you?" Hale was impressed by how friendly he sounded when he felt quite the opposite.

He would wait to hear what the man wanted before making

his request that Lord Duncan find another marital prospect.

"There was a misunderstanding by Miss Gia."

"How so? I find Gia to be quite intelligent." Hale couldn't help but use her name in a casual way that made the earl wince. If points were to be awarded, surely Hale had scored a few already.

"I agree, she is usually very astute. However, I am to understand that she has bestowed a gift upon you. A horse. Arabella, in fact."

"Aye. She mentioned it to me yesterday when I visited upon my return to town." Let him know that she was his first priority after making himself presentable.

"In addition to the fact it is improper for an unmarried woman to offer gifts of such value to an unmarried gentleman, the horse, you see, was not Miss Gia's property to give away."

"You assume her father would not allow her to do what she wishes with her horses?" Hale asked, while leaning closer to rest his hands on his desk.

"Lord Waverly is not available at the moment as he is on his honeymoon. But I can assure you, before he left, he made it clear at his club that all the horses were to be part of Miss Gia's dowry."

"All of them? But the value of all of those horses would put her dowry in excess of five thousand pounds."

"Quite. I agree, it is rather exorbitant, but he knows his daughter is an oddity and was taken down from the shelf and dusted off for the Season." The man smiled. "Any man who offers for her, should be compensated fairly, don't you agree?"

Hale had felt raging, red anger in the past.

He had never realized there was something beyond that level of fury. Had never despised anyone or anything enough to elevate his wrath to this plane where bright stillness enveloped him.

Through sheer force of will he managed to stay in his seat rather than launch himself across the wide expanse of his desk and pummel this man to shreds.

"You are marrying her for her dowry?" He bit the words out.

"It will be no hardship to get an heir on her." He chuckled as if he could not see how closely he flirted with death. "But she's not for society, and I'm fine with her staying in the country with our children while I seek my entertainments elsewhere. We will both be quite content."

"Get out of my house." Rather than yell, the words came quietly. Hale seethed as his fingers pulled into fists. The thought of Gia giving this man anything let alone the honor of bearing him children was too much.

"Pardon?" the man finally noticed the tension. "Oh. Yes. I'm sure you have other things to attend to. If you could just refuse the gift when it arrives all will be put right."

"Get. Out."

He scurried toward the door and stopped only to offer a "Good day to you" before leaving.

"Your Grace?" Hutchinson was back before Hale had managed to curb his anger.

"Yes?" he said as calmly as he was able.

"I'm afraid Lord Duncan left before I could return his hat and cane."

"You may keep them, Hutch."

"Oh. Thank you, Your Grace." Hutchinson smiled and left the room.

Let the bastard make what he wanted of Hale gifting something that wasn't his to give.

Knowing he couldn't turn to a bottle again, he took his coat and hat, planning to go speak to Gia, before realizing he couldn't.

Except... She was not married yet. In fact, she wasn't even betrothed. Not officially. They only had an understanding. Perhaps it was time for her to understand how he felt about this.

Luther opened the door with a frown when Hale arrived at Tomison House.

Hale had just opened his mouth to ask what was amiss when he heard it.

Someone was playing the pianoforte.

Correction, someone was pounding on random keys in a sequence perfectly suited to make chills move up one's spine.

"Good God, what is that?" Hale asked with a wince.

"Miss Gia has given up on embroidery and moved to musical aspirations. I daresay, embroidery was much quieter." He pressed his lips together momentarily before adding. "Except maybe for the cursing."

Hale smiled and patted the butler on the shoulder.

"Let me put a stop to this before we're all harmed irrevocably."

"You are too kind, Your Grace."

Hale hurried to the music room—a room he'd never entered before—to find Gia frowning at the instrument as if it was at fault for her poor performance.

"I beg of you to please stop before my brains leak out of my ears," he said.

Despite his rudeness, Gia turned to him and smiled a smile that felt like it was only for him. And he wanted it to be.

"I do believe the pianoforte needs a good tuning," she said.

"I do believe the pianoforte needs a good pianist."

She blew out a puff of air.

"You are right. I'm miserable at it. I fear I am to be a dreadful countess."

"Then don't become a countess. Become a duchess instead."

"Pardon?" She squinted at him.

"Be *my* wife, Gia. You are already my dearest friend and my lover. The person I most want to see when I get up each morning and the person I desperately wish could stay in my bed each night. The person I can speak to about anything without worry, and whom I want to listen to and learn about in absurd detail. You are already everything else to me. Why not be my wife as well?"

He had hoped for a joyful yes, or maybe launching herself into his arms so they might share a kiss. What he hadn't expected when he'd finally gotten up the courage to tell the woman he loved how he truly felt about her was… nothing.

She simply blinked at him with her mouth hanging slightly open.

"Gia?" His only answer was more staring. After a moment, he reached out and gave her chin a slight push to shut her mouth.

"You wish to marry me?" She finally spoke, her voice barely a whisper.

"More than you can ever know."

GIA STARED AT the man who had come to sit beside her on the bench in the opposite direction as she was sitting. It made it easy to look into his face and study his expression as his words absorbed into her mind.

He was proposing marriage. But…

"But you said you did not wish to marry."

"I did not wish to marry for convenience. I did not wish to be wed to a stranger and live a cold life where my children would feel as I had. Like nothing more than an obligation to progress the line. We would not have a marriage like that, Gia."

He was right. Their marriage would be filled with laughter and all the things they had in common. And their nights would be filled with passion. She wouldn't need to leave him to return to her own bed. She would be welcome to stay with him even when the sun was fully up. But…

"But you do not like the country."

He smiled and brushed a stray piece of hair from her face.

"I realized when we were at Elmhurst that I actually do enjoy the country. It's living alone I despise. With you I would enjoy the country immensely. Especially knowing I would never be alone. I would have you and eventually our children to share the house with. There would be noise—though I pray not the noise I heard coming from this poor instrument when I arrived."

She laughed and gave him a small shove.

"I will never need to play the pianoforte or embroider or do any of those ladylike things?"

"Never. You can stroll about the estate in your buckskins. Or nothing if it pleases you."

She laughed again and leaned her head against his shoulder. "I feel like my every wish has come true."

"Then will you say *yes*, and marry me, Gia?"

"Yes. I would like nothing more."

He graced her with the smile she'd captured in her painting. Or had attempted to. She saw now her painting had not done him justice. He was beautiful and he was to be her husband.

Hers for the rest of their lives.

CHAPTER TWENTY-EIGHT

S HE'D SAID YES.

Gia had agreed to be his wife.

Hale leaned the few inches between them to kiss her. Silently thanking her for choosing him. Wordlessly promising all the happiness that would be theirs.

His arms wound around her waist and he pulled her closer still, eventually realizing he was moments from taking her right there in the music room. Not that anyone would dare come in and risk being even closer to the racket she'd exposed them to earlier.

With a grin, he pulled away from her.

"Please allow me to show you the proper way to utilize this instrument."

He stood and quietly closed the lid before sliding her from the bench and setting her up on the sturdy top. His hands deftly moved under her skirts and she gasped before winding her hands around his neck to pull him into a kiss.

He was barely able to separate himself from her long enough for her to reach between them and undo his breeches to free himself. He nearly laughed at the way she squirmed closer to the edge of the pianoforte to take him.

He didn't make her wait. He couldn't make himself wait. It had been too long since he'd been inside her.

She moaned in pleasure when he was seated deep in her.

"I've missed you, Jeremy."

His name on her lips had the effect it always did. A thrill of excitement rushed up his spine. She was the only one who would ever say his name like this.

She was the only one he'd ever be with like this. The thought was welcome instead of frightening. She was all he would ever need.

She was his. She had picked him.

This knowledge had him moving faster, deeper. His teeth caught the skin below her collarbone, marking her as his. She did the same thing on his shoulder, and he was grateful to be hers.

"Gia…"

"Yes," she answered the question he didn't have words for.

"Come with me." It was not an invitation, but an order and she relented, immediately bringing him with her into bliss as he released deep inside her.

This was right. This was how it should be.

Only after they had put their clothing back to rights and settled in the drawing room did Hale ask, "When will your father return?"

"A fortnight."

He nodded.

"I am of age to select my husband myself."

"I know. And I feel certain he will give us his blessing. But I do think it important for us to start our life in his good graces."

"Not that he deserves it after the dramatics he used to get me to London in the first place."

"I cannot be angry at him for it. After all it brought you to me."

"I guess I cannot either." She sighed, and looked at him with those dark eyes that melted his heart.

"We will be happy, Gia." It was the easiest promise he'd ever made.

"I know we will be."

For the rest of their lives.

Gia was staring out at the garden, enjoying her freedom from ladylike pursuits the next afternoon when Luther came into the drawing room to announce Lord Duncan had arrived.

It felt like years since she'd seen the man that she'd intended to marry.

Their conversation would not be pleasant, but it needed to be done. She respected him enough not to allow this to go on longer than necessary. She only hoped she would be able to keep from smiling for the duration of his visit, so it didn't seem she was absolutely gleeful while delivering the news.

While they were not formally betrothed, she owed him the respect of telling him they would never be.

"Please see him in," she said while she sat up straight. Lydia would be so proud.

"You look lovely today," Lord Duncan greeted her as he came into the room with Bess following closely behind, as was proper.

"It is a pleasant day," she offered in return since she wished the awkwardness that was certain to follow would be over with due haste.

"Have you heard word from your father and his bride?"

"Uh, yes."

"And when will they arrive to hear of our wonderful news?"

Gia bit her bottom lip and winced. This had to be the most uncomfortable thing she'd ever had to do.

But she was not a coward, and this needed to be done. She would endeavor to do it with the utmost care for his feelings.

"I'm afraid there has been a change of plans."

"They are not coming back to London? Perhaps we will have to move forward with our plan to marry without his blessing."

"That is not the change in plans. I'm afraid I am unable to marry you, my lord."

"Unable to marry me? Whyever for?"

"I don't know that we need to get into the why of it, since it doesn't change the fact that I cannot marry you." She repeated that last part a bit more sternly so he would pay special attention.

"Are you throwing me over?"

"I'd rather not word it like that, but as I've said, I cannot—"

"*Marry me*—yes, you've said as much a few times now. You'll forgive me if I persist on knowing *why* you can no longer marry me when you previously told me you would."

"If you will recall, I never actually said I would marry you, because you have not officially asked for my hand. Therefore, I'm not officially throwing you over, if you are determined to use that phrase." Things were turning quite official.

"We had an understanding."

"Yes, and an understanding is not the same as a betrothal, my lord. So, you see, no one has been thrown anywhere." She offered a bigger smile than the conversation warranted and held it tightly in place.

"Again, you've neglected to explain why our understanding is now void."

Giving up, she let out a breath. There was no sense avoiding the answer as the man would surely see the truth of it when banns were read on Sunday announcing her betrothal to Jeremy instead.

"Upon his return to London, the Duke of Roxburghe asked for my hand. As you are aware, he and I held a friendship before he went to the country. I assumed he was not interested in marriage but am happy to say I was wrong in my assumption."

The man laughed, a harsh sound that hinted at anger.

"I can assure you, Miss Gia, you were not wrong in your assumption at all. In fact, this is all my fault. You see, after I learned you planned to gift Arabella to the duke, I visited him to explain that the mare was part of the dowry promised by your father. What I neglected to realize was the level of deviousness the man would go to in order to get what he wanted. I should have allowed him the one horse rather than tempt him into marrying you to get all of them."

Gia suddenly felt cold in the warm room.

"I'm afraid I don't know anything about the horses being included as part of my dowry."

"As is common for the daughter who is to be married off. It is a matter for the men to discuss."

She didn't like his tone as if she were a silly girl who didn't understand the business dealings associated with marriage.

"My father told me my dowry was a modest sum."

"It had been, until right before he quit London. He let it be known at his club that all of the horses at his Surrey estate and the few you had with you here in town were to go with you when you married."

"But it makes no sense. Why would he offer such a thing? The value of those horses is astronomical."

"He has a new wife to provide for. One with expensive tastes as you well know." He held out his hand at the elaborate drawing room they were currently occupying. "He couldn't very well keep her in the way she is accustomed to while also supporting his spinster daughter. He had to spice up the pot."

"And my dowry is the reason you suggested marriage?" she asked, already knowing the answer.

"It surely was no deterrent." He glanced down at her chest in a way he had never done before. She felt a fool for believing he respected her.

She cleared her throat.

"Thank you for your visit today, my lord." She stood and gestured toward the open door, wanting him gone so she could breathe and think.

"If you think it's not the reason Roxburghe offered for you, ask yourself why he didn't offer before I told him of the dowry."

His parting words found purchase in her chest and burrowed deep.

So much for breathing.

"Miss, I'm certain he is mistaken, your father wouldn't have done this," Bess said immediately after Lord Duncan left the room.

Gia shook her head.

"Before he left, father told me not to count the Season over just yet. As if he had a plan. You know how desperate he was to have me married off. He even faked an illness to bring me to London. And he's not above using the horses in place of blunt when necessary."

"But His Grace cares for you, I'm sure of it."

"I'm sure of it too. But would he have wanted to marry me if not for…"

She knew the answer and Bess's silence confirmed she wasn't able to dispute the truth.

"My father has gone too far this time. If he is so desperate to get me out of the way, then I should go. Please pack my things. We leave within the hour."

"Where are we going?" she asked.

Gia didn't answer, mostly because she wasn't certain yet. She only knew she planned to get as far from London, manipulating fathers, and lying dukes as possible.

CHAPTER TWENTY-NINE

I F HALE HADN'T been so eager to see his betrothed upon entering her home, he might have asked Luther why the man looked so upset as Hale breezed through the foyer in his haste to get to the drawing room.

Finding it empty, he returned to the hall to find Luther had moved to the study to announce him.

Gia hardly ever spent time in the study and when Hale entered, he barely hid his disappointment at finding Lord Waverly sitting at the desk instead of his intended.

It was for the best though. Now that the man had returned, they had a bit of business to attend to.

"Welcome back. I was told you wouldn't return for a fortnight. I trust you had a lovely honeymoon." He greeted the man who would soon be his father-in-law.

"Thank you, we did. We came home immediately after we heard the news." The man didn't offer a smile and his words were stiff. Hale had assumed her father would approve the match, but perhaps he'd been mistaken.

"I apologize for not speaking to you before offering for her hand. Time was of the essence, and she is of age. We do not—"

Lord Waverly put up a hand to stop Hale's words.

"It's not that. I, of course, would have approved. I've thought for some time now that your friendship had blossomed into something more. Something that would get you through life's trials. But I knew you were not of a mind to marry. I'm glad to see that has changed."

"I see. But you do not seem pleased. And you said you *would have* approved."

"I'm afraid Gia is not here," he said while slumping in his chair and rubbing his forehead.

"Where is she?"

"We don't know."

"I'm sure wherever she is, she's safe. It's… It's all my fault. The bloody dowry was too much. And Lord Duncan apparently told her of the arrangement along with some other ideas as to why you had offered for her. Her letter was difficult to follow. Perhaps there is more in the one she left for you."

Hale was still processing the words as the man held out a sealed letter with Hale's name on it. Not Jeremy as she had taken to calling him, just Hale.

Your Grace,

I've decided we will not suit after all. I have left London.

As promised, I have ordered Owen to see that Arabella is delivered to you. I can think of no one else who has worked so tirelessly to get what they wanted. Any other horses you wish to acquire can be handled through my father.

I'm afraid you will have to purchase them straight out rather than get them in trade for taking someone so unsuitable to wife.

G

"I-I don't understand. She doesn't want to marry me?" That seemed the only fact Hale was able to focus on at the moment.

Another person had left him. Someone he'd grown to care for—bloody hell, he loved her. And she'd left him.

"I believe she does wish to marry you. The problem is, she thinks you only wished to marry her to obtain the bloody horses. That it was the only reason you asked for her hand." He tilted his head. "Is that true?"

"Nay. I want *her*. I thought she would want her horses. I would never make her give them up. I've been in Scotland at one of my homes making it ready so it had room for the horses. I just want her to be happy," he said quietly.

Finally, her father smiled, but Hale didn't understand why. Did the man take pleasure in seeing Hale suffer?

"You need to tell her how you feel so she knows the truth."

Hale nodded in agreement.

"Aye. I must see her." But Waverly had said he didn't know where his daughter was. "Where?"

"She's not at Elmhurst. I wrote to my other country estates and she's not at any of them. She didn't take Lydia's carriage, so I can't question the coachman. She doesn't wish to be found, and my daughter is quite clever."

Hale nodded again.

"Bess?" Surely her lady's maid would know everything.

"Bess went with her. I'm sorry. I am still looking."

"And you'll tell me when you find her? So I might go to her and explain..."

"Of course. She'll turn up."

Hale returned home and went to his study. Strange how his townhouse now felt as cold as the country homes where he'd spent his youth. He realized it wasn't the location of the homes that made them feel so bloody empty. It was the whispers that seemed to echo in the dark corners of the room.

"No one wants you."

He was on his seventh or tenth glass of whisky when Hutchinson announced Julian, Graham, and Kit.

"We were heading to the club and saw you had returned. Do you want to join us?" Julian asked.

"Nay." It was a small enough word, yet it didn't come out clearly.

"What's happened?" Kit came closer.

"Gia left. I don't know where she is. She thinks I only asked to marry her to get the horses."

Julian winced.

"I have to say, when I heard what was being offered, I almost thought to marry the chit myself," Kit joked, but cleared his throat when both Julian and Hale glared at him.

"It was a jest, I swear it," Kit said quickly when Hale took a step in his direction.

"You are in a bad way," Graham said while putting a restraining hand on Hale's chest. "Do you truly wish to marry her that badly?"

"Yes. I hadn't realized how much until she was gone."

"Isn't that the way of most things?" Julian mused.

"Now it's too late. Duncan told her I only wanted the dowry. She believed him. Why would she believe him? Why wouldn't she wait and ask me?" Hale wasn't certain if his friends understood anything he said since the words slurred together. But even in his drunken state, Hale thought he knew the answer to his own question.

Gia had left because she didn't trust in his love, because he hadn't told her he loved her.

"I dinna tell her. I was afraid she wouldn't love me back. I never wanted a cold marriage, an arrangement made for convenience."

"I can say this doesn't seem convenient at all," Kit joked again.

"You have to find her," Julian said as if no one had considered this already.

"No one knows where she is. I'm expected to wait here until someone hears from her." He waved his hand and only realized he was still holding his glass when whisky sloshed out onto his desk.

"How long do you think that might be, because if you keep waiting like this, you may not be fit to do anything about it when you find her," Kit pointed out.

"I should go looking for her. I won't stop until I've searched all of England."

"That sounds quite time consuming." Graham rubbed his chin. "Someone in the house has to know where she went. Her maid would have mentioned it to one of the other servants."

Hale shook his head. "Lord Waverly and his new wife questioned the servants already. He was certain they dinna know."

The fog of drunkenness kept him from forming an idea that hovered just outside his grasp. His friends must have helped him off to bed because Hale slept restlessly through the night still trying to piece together the puzzle.

The next morning, he thumped down the stairs to find them sitting in his breakfast room helping themselves to the sideboard.

"Good morning. How do you feel?" Kit asked, his voice too chipper.

"I feel as if the woman I love has run off and taken my heart with her. And I have no idea where she might be. I thought the rejection would be the worst part, but I find the worry that she could be in danger or need my help is nearly overwhelming."

"Now that you're in your right mind—or a bit closer at least—we wanted to offer our assistance. You said last night you planned to search all of England, but we will ensure you only have to search a third while we search the rest."

"You are good friends."

"We're aware." At another time, Hale might have called Kit out on his arrogance, but Hale felt he deserved to be smug. For the time being, at least.

Julian, Kit, and Graham had never left him.

"I still can't believe no one knows where she might have gone," Graham said as he stuffed another biscuit in his mouth.

The thought Hale had struggled to grasp hold of through the night came back to him with a snap.

"No one in the house knows. But I know who might." With that he left them to go find the information he needed.

The normal peace Hale felt when surrounded by the sweet smell of hay, leather, and horses did not come when he entered the stables this time.

He found Owen easily, brushing out one of the mares. The man greeted Hale with his normal frown and grunt.

"Where is she?" Hale asked, or rather demanded.

"Second stall on the left," Owen answered.

"No. Not Arabella. Where is Gia? I must see her."

His frown deepened. "I canna say." The words were deliberate. He didn't say he didn't *know*.

"But you know where she is. She asked you not to tell anyone. She wouldn't have left without telling you where she was going."

Owen shrugged. "She's given you what you wanted. Now, leave the lass in peace."

"You don't understand. I don't want the horses. I only want *her*." He paused.

He'd rather not tell the groom something Gia had not heard yet herself, but it was clear the man would not budge.

"I love her, Owen. Dowry or no, I just want her. Need her. She... She's my best friend." Hale put everything into those words. "Please help me find her. She's under a misapprehension that I only want the horses and she must know the truth. If she still doesn't want to marry me, I promise I will respect her decision, but she can't decide based on a misunderstanding."

Owen's face had not changed, and Hale wasn't sure if it was because he only owned the one expression.

"Are you saying you would refuse the dowry? The value of those horses is quite a large sum."

"Aye. Aye, I refuse the dowry. Please help me, man."

"I don't understand why you dinna say ye loved her so this doubt wouldn't ha kicked up such a fuss." He crossed his arms impassively.

"You're right. I should have told her. I got caught up in the moment and missed saying the most important thing. But you must have noticed how much I care about her." Hale stopped pacing to look the Scotsman in the eye. "You had to have seen how much she means to me. You know I don't give a bloody damn about any dowry."

Owen's mouth lifted on just the one side the smallest fraction. Even that tiny hint of a smile caused Hale to worry the man's face might splinter and crack.

"Aye. I did think you were true with her, but needed to hear you say it and watch ye answer before offering to help."

"Now you have the truth. Will you tell me where she is so I can go find the woman I love and tell her?"

"Waverly has a hunting box in Scotland. Right near the border. It's not rough since the lord spent more of his time there hosting house parties than hunting, but she knew her father wouldna expect her to go there because she'd never gone there before. The stable is quite small."

"She's in Scotland?"

"Aye."

"Thank you, Owen. Thank you."

With a slap on the man's back, Hale swept out of the stable and headed to his own mews to ready a carriage.

The last thing he wanted to do after weeks of traveling to and from Scotland was to set off for his homeland yet again, but he would journey to the ends of the Earth if it meant finding Gia and convincing her to marry him.

CHAPTER THIRTY

GIA FROWNED AT the blank canvas in front of her, then squinted at the beautiful valley spread out before her. Everything was lush and green. The stream cut deep curves into the land as it traced a path as old as time.

It would make the perfect landscape. If only she could decide on the proper paint color for the grass and whether she wanted to include the hills in the background or keep the focus on the twisted tree to the right.

She'd come to this spot nearly every day and had nothing to show for it but dried up paint and frustration.

The view was lovely but this wasn't what she yearned to paint.

The curves of the stream made her think of the curve of Jeremy's lips. The blue of the sky reminded her of his eyes crinkled in a smile so bright she couldn't help but join in.

Except he wasn't there to make her smile and she noticed she hadn't smiled much since arriving in Scotland. The manor house was lovely and the couple that tended it were kind enough, but so far this place didn't feel like home.

As was becoming their daily routine, Bess brought luncheon in a basket and spread out a blanket on the cool grass in the shade.

"I can't help but notice you've yet to paint anything."

"Thank you, Bess. It was kind of you to mention it." She

glared at her maid who only chuckled.

"I'd suggest you try to paint something you enjoy, but I know you already have a painting of the duke on the stand beside your bed, so you're not in need of another."

"Bess." Gia frowned. "How dare you snoop through my things."

"I didn't need to snoop. You left it out the first night we arrived." Bess twisted a piece of grass. "Maybe I was wrong. Perhaps you do need to paint another. I noticed the one you have was a bit wilted as if it had gotten wet."

They exchanged a look but neither of them spoke for some time. They shared their meal in silence and Gia wished her maid had brought her whisky to wash it down rather than just water.

"Did I make a mistake, Bess? Should I just have married him anyway despite the fact he only wanted to marry me for the horses?"

"Are you sure that is the reason he wanted to marry you?"

Gia opened her mouth to speak but Bess held up her hand to stop her.

"I know the timing of his proposal is suspect when you consider what Lord Duncan shared, but I saw the way he looked at you when you didn't notice. He did care for you something fierce. You'll not convince me otherwise."

"I suppose it seems silly to have run away from his offer after I'd planned to accept Lord Duncan despite not loving him. I could marry for convenience. I could marry someone I held only respect or friendship for. But I didn't think I could marry a man I loved, knowing he didn't love me. Wanting more from him than what he could give would have been too much."

"It's not silly. It makes good sense." Bess stood and gathered the basket, leaving the blanket since Gia was still sitting on it. "Unless you are wrong, and he did love you as much as you loved him."

Gia fell back on the blanket and looked up at the sunlight filtering through the trees. She studied the way the light breeze made the leaves twirl about above her.

She considered her life as Jeremy's wife. Even if he didn't love her, they were friends. She greatly enjoyed their physical relationship. He respected her as she did him. Shouldn't that be enough?

She recalled the conversation with her father before he left on his honeymoon. The many ways one might discover love. He'd said love could start out as friendship and she knew it to be true because that's how she'd fallen in love with Jeremy.

Was it possible he might learn to love her in the same way?

She would need to return to London and speak with him. But she would wait until tomorrow. Now that she had a plan, her earlier exhaustion caught up with her.

⇒⟫⟩⟨⟨⟸

HALE'S CARRIAGE WAS pulling into the lane just as Bess was emerging from a stand of trees carrying a basket. He barely waited for the coach to stop before jumping from the conveyance and calling to the maid.

"Your Grace," Bess said with a curtsey.

"Is Gia well?"

Bess pressed her lips together as if she wasn't sure how to answer him. Hale might have given her a shake if her lips hadn't pulled into a smile.

"Now that you are here, I think she will be quite well indeed. Unless you've not come here to tell her you love her and can't live without her."

He sniffed. "I have come to do just that."

Bess clapped her hands together.

"I am so happy."

"Where is she?"

"Follow this path to a meadow. She'll most likely be asleep. She's not been sleeping well."

"Thank you." He said this over his shoulder as he hurried for the path. All the words he'd planned to say when he arrived seemed to float away when he reached the meadow and found her lying on a blanket asleep.

An easel with a blank canvas sat close by. Had she been attempting to paint a landscape?

The light filtering through the tree above her moved across her face. She was so beautiful, but even more so now that he'd missed her and worried he might never see her again.

Taking advantage of the open space on the blanket, he lay down next to her to wait until she woke. Then he could tell her he loved her. And hoped she would still agree to be his wife.

⇉⇇

GIA WAS CHILLY. She didn't know why she had no covers and wasn't awake enough to open her eyes to find out, but she did manage to reach out in a small effort to find them. Instead, she found something even better.

A warm man. Jeremy.

She nestled closer until she was up against him and his arms came around her, protecting her and sharing his warmth.

She breathed in the scent of him. Leather warmed by the sun, spicy vanilla, and the slightest hint of hay. They had once joked that the smell of hay had sunk deep into their pores never to be washed away. It was not such a bad thing.

"Mmm... Jeremy," she said settling in closer. She felt his lips press against her forehead and again in her hair.

"Rest, love. I'll be here when you wake."

She answered with a sound of contentment. Jeremy would be there when she woke. He would always be there. Except...

A whisper of sadness trickled through her perfect dream with Jeremy.

She'd left him because she'd wanted more than he could give.

And she was going to go get him back. She needed him.

"I must go," she murmured.

"Where do you wish to go?" he asked, his voice so far away, yet she could feel his breath on her cheek.

"I must find him and tell him…"

"Will you tell him you wish to marry him?"

"Yes."

"And that you love him?"

"Yes." She felt the heaviness of sleep slip further away, as this odd conversation pulled her closer to awareness.

"Open your eyes, love, and let me tell you the same things."

She blinked and opened her eyes as he'd instructed and gasped when her gaze focused on him.

"You're here?"

"In the flesh."

She reached out to make sure and her palm rested softly against the prickly stubble on his jaw.

"Jeremy?"

"I came to Scotland to tell you I love you. I don't care about the horses or any dowry at all. I only wanted you to have them. All I want is you. Please marry me, Gia."

"Yes." She sat up to wrap her arms around him, just to be certain he was really there. "I love you, Jeremy. I was afraid you would never love me, but I realized earlier that it didn't matter, I still needed you. I was planning to leave for London tomorrow to find you."

"Well, I guess I've saved you the trip." He looked around the meadow and turned back to her with a beaming smile. "When I left England, it was so I could prepare one of my properties for us. I had wanted to make a home for us before I asked you to marry me. Had I asked first I fear we could have saved some pain. I'm sorry, love."

"We have a home in the country?"

"Aye. And it is not so far from here. Just a few hours north. With a huge stable for us to fill with horses and an enormous castle to fill with children."

"You forgot about a giant heart to fill with love." She smiled happier than she'd ever been.

"Do you know the best part about being in Scotland?"

She shook her head, not realizing he'd missed his homeland.

"In Scotland we can marry today if we wish it."

"I do," she said.

"I do, too."

EPILOGUE

Five years later…

"P APA, ARE YOU watching me?" Verona called.

"Of course, darling," Hale said with a smile.

"It looks like you are watching mama," his daughter rightfully accused him.

Hale looked across the paddock and grinned at the dark-haired beauty who had captured his attention from the first moment he'd seen her.

"My gaze might have wandered for a moment." His gaze had definitely wandered and for more than a moment. Gia knew how seeing her in those snug buckskins affected him. She cast him a naughty smile confirming his suspicion.

"Vee. Horsey." The new Earl of Wrycastle pointed at his sister upon her pony. At just over a year, Ethan said only a few words. But *papa* had been his first and Hale couldn't have been prouder.

In London, the Season was underway, but Hale had no interest in attending. He occasionally rode to town for important votes as was his duty as a peer, but he always longed to return home to the country.

As for finding his passion and his promise to his late friend, Ethan, he and Gia continued to raise, train, and race horses, but they came back home as soon as possible.

And when his children came running to see him and tell him everything he'd missed while he'd been away, he felt the love of family.

Sometimes he felt sympathy for his parents who never knew this kind of happiness.

It was strange how Hale had not once felt their home was too lonely, empty, or quiet.

Definitely never quiet now with two children running about and a new puppy he hadn't been able to say no to.

He loved his daughter and son, as well as the afternoons when the staff would take the children to the nursery so he could steal his wife away to have his wicked way with her. By the clearing next to the lake or any other part of the estate.

And yes, even occasionally in the hay of the stables.

The end.

About the Author

One very early morning, Allison B. Hanson woke up with a conversation going on in her head. It wasn't so much a dream as being forced awake by her imagination. Unable to go back to sleep, she gave in, went to the computer, and began writing. Years later it still hasn't stopped.

Allison lives near Hershey, Pennsylvania and writes Highlander Historical and Scottish Regencies.

Catch up with Allison on any of her social media platforms here:

Website:
allisonbhanson.wordpress.com

Facebook:
facebook.com/BlueRidgeRomance

Twitter:
@AllisonBHanson

Instagram:
@allisonbhanson

Goodreads:
goodreads.com/author/show/9860589

BookBub:
bookbub.com/authors/allison-b-hanson